NOWHERE

TO

RUN

A novel by

D. R. Evans

Inspired by a true story

© Copyright 2010 by D. R. Evans.

First Edition

ISBN: 978-1-936211-02-9

Author website: *www.sff.net/people/N7DR*

www.enginehousebooks.com

πεπεισμαι γαρ οτι ουτε θανατος ουτε ζωη ουτε αγγελοι ουτε αρχαι
ουτε ενεστωτα ουτε μελλοντα ουτε δυναμεις ουτε υψωμα ουτε βαθος
ουτε τις κτισις ετερα δυνησεται ημας χωρισαι απο της αγαπης του
θεου της εν χριστω ιησου τω κυριω ημων

Truly I have been persuaded that neither death nor life nor angels
nor rulers nor things now present nor things to come nor powers nor
things above nor things below; indeed, no created thing has the power
to separate us from the love of God in Jesus the Messiah, our Lord.

— Romans 8:38, 39
Translated by the author

WEDNESDAY

The Town of Replogle, Replogle County, Arkansas — 7:00 p.m.

The doorbell rang.

George Ellsworth — the Reverend Doctor George Matthew Ellsworth to give him his full dignity — lifted his bookmark from the arm of his chair and closed his book around it. He looked at his wife, Mary, who had raised her eyes from her own book at the sound of the bell, and gave her as much of a smile as he could muster.

Mary returned his smile, the encouragement on her face contrasting with the resignation on his. Neither of them spoke. Feeling much older than his thirty nine years, the pastor got out of his comfortable chair. She returned her attention to her book.

He paused in front of the front door, gathered himself, then opened the door. A man of about fifty stood on the porch, sheltering from the rain.

Ellsworth greeted him: "Good evening, Tom. Come on in while I get my coat."

"Good evening, pastor. How are you?"

Tom Murdoch was heavily constructed, like one of the houses his company built, and he had a deep and powerful voice that matched his bulk. A small shower of drops fell from his coat as he crossed the threshold.

For a moment, the minister considered replying with the truth. Instead, the meaningless words "Fine, and how about you?" escaped his lips before the revolutionary thought had time to gel.

"Fine," Tom replied. "But I sure hope the weather changes soon. We've just started a house over on Tenth Street; you know, on the vacant lot next to the Schultz's" — Ellsworth nodded vaguely while he found his coat in the closet — "and there's not a lot we can do while it's raining like this."

Tom glanced into the living room and greeted Mary cheerily. She smiled, said "Hi!" then continued reading.

A thought occurred to George as he donned his coat.

"Do they have Bibles?"

"No, but I brought some from Pastor Ives' church. New Internationals. That OK?"

"Yes. Sure. Fine. Bye, honey." This last was to Mary, who replied vaguely, "Bye, hon. See you sometime," without looking up from her book.

"Any idea what time we'll be back?" George asked the builder.

"Oh, not very late. Around nine, I should think."

"We'll be back around nine," the pastor relayed the information to his wife.

"OK. See you later." Mary was still reading. Ellsworth was not convinced she had heard him.

The two men went outside. Sheltering on the porch, the rain seemed heavier to George than it had been earlier, although perhaps that was merely a trick of the light. The bulb above their heads lit a hundred ephemeral glistening splinters of rain. Drops pattered on the grass, on the gravel of the driveway, on the wooden shakes of the roof, on the leaves of the encroaching trees.

George Ellsworth paused for a moment to breathe deeply of the cool air. It was rare to have a full day of rain at this time of year, and the moist coolness of the evening was something to be savored and appreciated.

Tom dashed toward his Dodge Caravan. He nimbly dodged a puddle and opened the door. More sedately, the pastor followed. His foot landed in an unseen puddle, and water entered through the small hole in the side of his shoe, soaking his foot.

George climbed in. Even though he had been exposed to the rain for no more than twenty seconds, water had somehow managed to dribble down his neck. As he pulled the door closed, his shirt stuck to his skin.

The vehicle started first time and Tom pulled cautiously forward, following the tight curve of the semicircular driveway. As he moved out on to the street, the wipers thumped steadily.

George glanced back at the house as they drove away. He wished that, just once, he could spend an evening at home doing nothing more spiritual than reading or — perish the thought — watching television. He caught himself wondering, not for the first time, if he was really cut out for this job.

He forced himself to concentrate on the task ahead.

"So, Tom, what exactly have I let myself in for?"

He tried to say it lightheartedly, but only half succeeded.

"Well, it's nothing much really. The guards let us have a room to ourselves. I have a stack of Bibles and hymn books back there" — Tom gestured toward the rear of the vehicle — "and we'll put them on the chairs before we start. Officially, we begin at half after.

"There won't be much of a turnout, probably somewhere between six and twelve. I'm never sure how many are there because the service means something to them and how many come just to relieve the boredom. Anyway, we'll start by singing a hymn or two, probably a few verses of *How Great Thou Art* and *Amazing Grace* — nearly everyone knows them — then I'll introduce you and you can give your talk. If you talk for fifteen minutes or so, that'll be perfect.

"Then we'll have a brief time for prayer — I'll lead that if you like. I always tell them they can pray out loud if they want, but nobody ever does. Then the benediction at the end. Oh, be careful about that. A few months ago one of the pastors started with 'Go out into the world' and then realized what he'd said. It was rather embarrassing. Afterwards, we usually hang around for a few minutes in case anyone wants to know more about the Lord. Then we pack up and come home. We should be finished easily inside of an hour."

George nodded; it was more or less what he had expected. He mentally thanked Tom for warning him about the benediction; he didn't want the inmates to think him a complete fool.

They turned on to Main Street after slowing perfunctorily at the stop sign. There was no other traffic in sight; the steady rain was keeping everyone at home.

"What's your text going to be?" Tom asked as he accelerated away from the corner.

"I thought that the start of Ecclesiastes, maybe beginning at verse four, would be appropriate. I didn't want something too obvious. I expect they get bored with hearing the same passages."

Tom considered for a moment, then said: "That's part of the 'vanity of vanities' litany, isn't it? 'A generation goes, and a generation comes, yet the earth stands firm for ever,' something like that?"

George was impressed. He was not at all sure he could have quoted the text as accurately as Tom if he had not spent most of yesterday working on the evening's homily.

Tom continued, "That's certainly one they won't have heard before."

4

Tom slowed for a light and turned right. George felt the rear wheels skid a few inches as the vehicle turned the corner. The surface of the road was slick from the combination of rain and oil. Tom drove the rest of the way more carefully.

They arrived at 7:18 by the clock in the dash. There were plenty of spaces in the parking lot of the Replogle County Justice Center, which was a small complex of buildings that combined police department, fire station, courthouse and jail. Tom halted and killed the engine. Within moments, rain covered the windshield.

"Go on inside; I'll get the books out the trunk and meet you in a minute," Tom said.

He opened his door and got out.

George did likewise. Even though Tom had told him to go inside, some vague feeling of guilt kept him from doing so — it somehow seemed wrong that he should be dry inside while Tom was out here getting wet.

He looked up at the building and wondered how it must feel to have one's freedom curtailed by society. He knew nothing about the people inside. He could not even begin to guess what made them tick.

The rear door slammed and Tom appeared carrying a box of books. George hurried to the building and held the door open. Tom passed through, the hymn books and Bibles mostly unscathed by their few seconds' exposure to the rain.

Seated beside a table in the lobby was a police officer with a prominent holster. The officer put down the book he had been reading.

"Good evening," Tom greeted the guard jovially. "We're here for an evangelistic meeting at the jail."

The guard consulted a clipboard. "Names?"

"Tom Murdoch and the Reverend George Ellsworth."

The guard passed the clipboard across the table. "Sign in, please. The time is 7:22. You know the way?"

"Yes, thank you," said the builder, and he confidently led the pastor into a concrete labyrinth of hallways.

The room that had been set aside for them was a vacant box with unadorned concrete walls. A single doorway opened at the rear, and five rows of canvas and metal chairs faced the front where two chairs looked back at the bleak, empty rows.

A cheerless place to try to save men's souls, thought George as he helped Tom put a book on each chair, alternating Bibles with hymn books.

The first inmate entered just as they were finishing. George tried hard not to stare as he evaluated the man, trying to comprehend an entire alien species from a single specimen.

The inmate appeared to be in his mid fifties. He was dressed in gray workclothes that were a size too small for his lanky frame. Strands of gray hair fell forward over a long, thin, sallow, hollow-cheeked face. The man needed a shave: the gray beginnings of a beard were obvious in the harsh light from the overhead fluorescent tubes. The man stepped forward, an anxious look on his face. He nodded towards them, seemed to consider tugging a nonexistent forelock, then thought better of it. Tom moved to greet him.

"Good evening. Ken, isn't it? Glad you could make it."

"I seen you here before. You going to be the preacher tonight?" the man asked, hanging back from shaking the hand that Tom had extended in greeting.

"No, I'm just helping. This is pastor George; he'll be giving the message tonight."

George held out his own hand to be shaken, and the gray man promptly switched his attention to the pastor. His handshake was oddly insubstantial.

"I believe in God."

Ken made the statement with a strange belligerence, as if he was accusing the pastor of unbelief. George felt embarrassed and wished himself far away.

"I believe in God," the man repeated, sounding less sure of himself this time.

Then he withdrew his hand and turned away, scanning the chairs. He walked to the far end of the third row, moved the book on that chair to an adjacent seat, sat down, and stared blankly at the visitors.

Another inmate entered the room, followed within seconds by two more, and George realized that the gray clothing was a kind of uniform.

He greeted the three newcomers, making an effort to be friendly. He was surprised by something that seemed to be missing. He had expected that there would be something common to the faces of all these men: some hollowness, or a hunted look, or simply an admission of defeat. All of these were easy to read in the face of the first inmate, but the same could not be said for the others who were entering the room. Certainly some of them appeared that way, but others looked lively and intelligent. A couple of men entered the room laughing gaily, but they smothered their laughter when they saw that the preacher was already present.

By 7:30 there were ten inmates present. Only Ken had taken any interest in the books on the chairs. Ken was now leaning forward in his seat, a Bible open on his knees, his fingers tracing the lines, lips moving slowly to form the words as he read. An unnatural calm had descended over the others as they stared expectantly toward the front of the room, waiting for something to happen.

George wondered what the inmates thought of these monthly meetings. Were they simply an entertaining break in the deadly monotony that must pervade life inside the walls of the jail, or was there something more? Were some of these men really interested in being saved? He tried hard not to judge, but it was impossible not to think that these men, with perhaps the exception of Ken, were here simply because it was something to do on a Wednesday evening.

Tom stood to begin the meeting.

He welcomed the men and introduced George. There was a studied informality to his manner, the builder referring both to himself and his pastor by their first names. He greeted a couple of the men by name. Then he led the group in a short prayer. George bowed his head and closed his eyes. As Tom was drawing to a close, he looked up. He was surprised to find that all the prisoners' heads were lowered. He felt a soupçon of guilt: perhaps he had misjudged them.

"Now let's sing a hymn before we hear from pastor George," continued Tom. "Hoiw about number 25, *How Great Thou Art?*"

The men rose noisily to their feet, scraping their chairs on the linoleum floor, and slowly they flicked pages until, one by one, they found the hymn. Tom began to sing with gusto, leading the men *a capella*. George joined in loudly. The prisoners sang with more or less interest. The result didn't sound much like a hymn of praise.

As they struggled to the end of the last verse, George's concentration was briefly broken by the arrival of another inmate. The newcomer looked as if he had wandered into the room by mistake. His gray clothing was crumpled; the expression on his face was vacant and unreadable. From his chin sprouted a wispy red beard. His thinning auburn hair was long and uncombed and hung down the side of his head in unwashed strands.

The man slowly scanned the room with wide, open eyes that fronted a brain that seemed not to be functioning very well. His eyes met George's. George smiled, but the man simply stared at him as if he had not seen the gesture of friendliness. The man took a step forward, then sat in the chair closest to the door, as if he wanted to be sure he could escape should the need arise. He continued to stare at George. The pastor looked away.

"Amen," the group sang in a long, weighty discord.

The prisoners seated themselves noisily, and Tom indicated to George that the floor was his.

Afterwards, George had no recollection of his homily, but at the time he spent the entire fifteen minutes listening to himself speak while watching the blank looks on the prisoners' faces and repeating to himself: *I'm not reaching these men. I'm speaking my language, not theirs. What can I do to make them hear me?* Somehow, he reached the final point of his sermon; but by then his heart was no longer in it, and he knew that his homily was a failure.

Tom stood and introduced the final hymn of the evening. George made a vow to himself that he would never do this again. He turned to hymn number 163. His eyes lighted on the title, and he returned the book to the chair. This was one hymn he knew by heart.

Tom began to lead the singing; this time several of the prisoners joined in enthusiastically.

"Amazing Grace, how sweet the sound that saved a wretch like me," they began. As they gathered confidence, harmonies began to emerge.

George found his attention wandering as a stream of thoughts flashed through his head, brought to mind by the appropriateness of the words. These men understood that they were wretches. They knew how worthless they were because society had told them so. Not for them the illusion of basic goodness that plagued so many people and kept them from the Truth. These prisoners, in their very wretchedness, had one advantage over ordinary people: they could not be deluded into the common heresy that people were good and had no need of a Savior. George found himself thinking, *Yet God's grace is so boundless that it reaches down even to these people and can lift them up in glory.*

8

He stopped singing and let the words wash over him. Surprisingly, for he was not an emotional man, he felt his eyes beginning to water.

They sang, "I once was lost..." and the minister thought: *Yes, that's right. They really were lost. They had no one to turn to for help and their sins caught up with them. But now they've been found. God has come to them where they are and He offers them all an opportunity to leave their mistakes behind them, for ever. If only they'll listen and accept Him.*

He looked at the men. Several of them, like him, had lowered their hymnals. Singing the words from memory, their faces echoed a joy and radiance that made it impossible not to believe that there was hope for them: even here in jail they might still be saved.

Every man in the room was singing, save only two. One was the pastor himself, too emotional to trust his voice; the other was the man who had entered late, who was standing at the rear of the room, staring vacantly towards the front. The man had not opened the hymnal on the chair beside him. He was separated by several empty chairs from the other prisoners.

In the world but not of the world — the unlikely phrase came unbidden to the pastor's mind, and he felt a sudden yearning to help the man who could not bring himself even to sit with the other inmates.

Reluctantly, George dragged his eyes from the man and prepared to sing the last verse. He closed his eyes and raised his hands, losing himself in his praise of the One who offers hope, not just to these men, but to all mankind.

The hymn drew to its climactic close; then there was a long silence. George lowered his hands and found himself delivering a prayer that God's grace should descend on each and every man in the room, for every one of them, himself and Tom included, desperately needed it. All were wretches in God's sight, and only the blood of Jesus could lift them from a state of wretchedness to one of glory.

He paused to take a breath and, in the momentary hiatus, his prayer was taken up by another.

The voice came from near the doorway. George opened his eyes and looked at the strange man with the vacant look, but it was not he who was praying. Another man had silently entered the room. He must have come in while George was praying. George could not see the newcomer clearly; the lighting in that corner seemed suddenly wanting: perhaps one of the lights had fused. The newcomer was standing directly behind the man with the vacant face; one hand was lifted to God, the other was on the head of the man before him.

The man's prayer drew to a close. George lifted his hands and said, "And now, receive a benediction." He paused for a moment, remembering Tom's admonition and realizing anew how inappropriate were the usual words that he would normally have used. As he paused, trying to think of the right words to say, the room suddenly seemed to darken.

A beam of light, warm and yellow, quite unlike the harsh glare of the fluorescent lights, illuminated a single corner of the room, resting on one man — a man who now stood alone: the latecomer who had so recently prayed over him was nowhere to be seen.

George began his benediction, but his mind was not on the words. He was aware only of a command that echoed around and around inside his head: *Pray for him, pray for him, pray for him.*

And then, suddenly, it was all over: the lighting returned to normal; men lifted their heads; the man in the corner looked up and glanced vacantly at George. Before George could make a move towards him, the man turned and left the room.

"Thank you; thank you, pastor," someone was saying.

George pulled his eyes from the doorway to see Ken making his way to the front, calling out his thanks. The others were drifting away. No one else spoke to him or Tom. There was just Ken, repeatedly thanking him for his message.

George asked Ken, "Did you see that man in the back, sitting by himself?"

"Williamson? The one with the red beard?"

"Yes, that's the one."

"Oh, don't waste your time on him. He's vicious, he is. He's only here for a few days; they ran short of room at the Pen. He held up a clerk at gunpoint. He just came tonight for the fun of it, like most of them. They don't believe in God like I do."

"Williamson, you say?"

"Yeah. David Williamson. But don't bother about him. He don't believe in God. I believe in God."

"Yes, no, right.... Well, thank you for coming."

Ken turned to Tom, "The regular pastor; will he be back next time?"

"Yes. He's away on vacation this month."

"Good. I like him. He believes in God too."

And with that Ken, who was the last remaining inmate in the room, strode quickly out the doorway.

"Good job, pastor," Tom said to George as he began to gather the books.

"You..., er..., you didn't happen to know the person who gave that prayer, did you?" George asked.

"Prayer? What prayer?"

"That one just before the benediction."

Tom stopped picking up the books and looked curiously at his pastor.

"Before the benediction? Sorry. I don't remember anyone praying except you." He paused for a moment. "But your prayer was a good one. Very appropriate I thought."

But George was no longer listening; his thoughts were elsewhere.

The McGuire House, Southwestern Replogle County — 8:30 p.m.

Alan McGuire looked at the other members of the church small group and said, "It's our daughter Pam. I think we need some advice. And certainly prayer."

Bob Hunter, who was leading the group this week, said, "Pam? I'm sure it's nothing serious. She's a wonderful girl. But what's the matter? Of course we'd all be glad to help in any way we can."

Alan looked at his wife Louise for support. She nodded. "Go ahead, honey."

"I'm not sure where to start," said Alan. He thought for a moment. "Last Saturday, I guess."

Pam McGuire was just past her eighteenth birthday. A senior in the local high school, she had accepted a place at university to start that fall. Not many blacks from Replogle County aspired to university, and her parents were quietly proud of their daughter.

But now they were worried.

"You know she's been seeing Craig Lang for some time now?" Alan said.

Bob Hunter nodded. "Yes; it's pretty obvious from the way they look at each other in church when Craig's home from college. How long's it been now? Six months?"

"A year. It started last summer."

"I didn't realize it was that long. But Craig's a good boy. Isn't he?"

Louise McGuire said, "Yes. At least, we've never been given reason to think otherwise."

"So what's the problem? He's a good boy from a good family."

Everyone in the room knew that the Langs were white. And if Craig and Pam were now what was known locally as "an item", that could cause trouble. Not everyone was as open-minded about such things as they should be.

"It's not Craig that's the problem," Alan said. "But let me just tell you the situation. Maybe we're worrying about nothing important.

"Pam has a midnight curfew. She's very good about honoring that. As far as I know, she's broken it only once, a couple of months ago. She seemed very upset one night when she came home around one o'clock. I think they'd had an argument or something, but they seemed to recover, and since then she's been careful to be home on time.

"On Saturday, though, she came home very early."

Alan looked at Louise.

"About ten thirty, it was," said Louise.

"Normally she doesn't get home from a date until about eleven thirty," continued Alan. "We heard her come in. She shouted 'Good night' and then went straight up to her room.

"On Sunday she seemed OK. She and Craig sat together as usual in church, but there was definitely something different. They seemed a bit distant with each other — or, at least, Pam seemed a bit distant with Craig. But when we asked her about it, she said it was nothing important."

Louise said, "She spent most of the day in her room, which is very unlike her. I went up to talk to her, but she insisted that nothing was wrong. But I'm almost sure she'd been crying.

"It was the same on Monday. She spent the day in her room. She said she wasn't feeling well, but I think that was just so's I wouldn't worry.

"But she seemed better yesterday. She went shopping over at Greenminster Mall. I wanted to go with her, to kind of make an outing of it. But she said she wanted to be by herself. I didn't want to start an argument so I let her go alone. At least she looked happier than she had for the past couple of days, so I figured that whatever was the matter must have sorted itself out."

She stopped talking. When she continued, it was with an obvious effort.

"Nothing prepared me for today...." She looked like she was going to cry, but she blinked back the tears and said, "She's never treated me that way before. Never."

"What happened?" asked Rachel Horner.

"I was doing the laundry like I usually do on Wednesday. It was about nine thirty this morning. Pam came downstairs and it was obvious she'd been crying. I asked her what was the matter and she just walked past me like I hadn't said a word.

"My purse was on the counter in the kitchen, and she just went right up to it and opened it. I couldn't believe my eyes. She opened my purse and took out my car keys.

"She said she was going out, and I said, 'Oh no you're not, young lady. You don't just take my keys and go out without explaining yourself.'

"But she just ignored me. She went out to the car. By the time I'd recovered and run to the back door, she'd already started the engine. I shouted at her to stop, but she just spun the car around, kicking up gravel, and then she was gone. I can't imagine what's gotten into her."

Alan took up the story.

"Louise called me at the office and I came straight home. We spent most of the day trying to find her, but no one had seen her. Then, just before you all arrived for small group, I got a call from Craig to say that she'd shown up at his place and told him they needed to go out someplace they could talk.

"I asked him if he knew what was going on, but he said he didn't have time to talk because she was waiting for him in the car.

"So that's the situation. He's with her now, somewhere. Goodness only knows what she wanted to talk to him about. Or what time she'll be home tonight."

"If she comes home tonight," interjected Louise.

"Anyway, we need your prayers and advice, if you have any," concluded Alan.

A heavy silence hung in the air, broken only by the rhythmic, deep ticking of the long case clock in one corner of the room and the random heavy plops as water dripped from the trees on to the roof of the sun room that abutted the McGuires' living room.

Eventually, Bob Hunter cleared his throat and began to offer his opinion.

Near Replogle — 5:04 p.m.

Pam was amazed to discover that she had put nearly two hundred miles on her mother's car. She looked at her watch. It was just after five. How long had she been driving? Nearly eight hours? Something like that. She vaguely remembered stopping three times: once for gas, and twice at small parklike rest areas that offered the peace and seclusion she needed. Vacant because of the unceasing rain, the rest areas gave her a chance to think constructively about the monstrous problem that lay before her.

But the problem was too big, and each time she drove on after only a few minutes. She drove aimlessly, keeping to the narrow roads that wound around the hills.

Somewhere around three o'clock, some part of her mind told her that eventually she was going to have to go home. She turned the car around and began to follow a twisting path back towards Replogle.

She stopped one last time, at a small park about six miles from home. For some time she contented herself with looking out through the rain-covered windshield at the virid grass. Then, ignoring the fact that she had no coat, she got out of the car and began to walk desultorily along the footpath that led away from the parking lot. She came to a trash can and stopped for a moment, her eyes resting unseeingly on a Coke can that had missed the receptacle and lodged in a rhododendron bush. She walked on.

She had no idea how long she walked; by the time she returned to the car, she was soaked. She got back into the car and looked blankly out through the windshield. Then she sighed heavily and started the car.

She arrived at Craig's house just before five thirty. She stopped the car in the driveway and looked at the house, considering Craig, his circumstances, his family. How would he react when he heard her devastating news? She was, she admitted, terrified of what his reaction might be. Would he be willing to marry her? But then, that question assumed that she wanted to marry him, and that was something of which she was no longer sure....

She took one final deep breath, then opened the car door and dashed through the rain to the front door. Craig himself answered the doorbell. Behind him, hovering in the hallway, Pam could see Craig's mother.

"Please; I have to talk to you," Pam said.

"Where've you been? Everyone's been worried about you. And you're soaking wet. Come on in and get dry."

"No. We need to talk. It's important."

Craig opened his mouth to argue, but Pam interrupted. "Really. We have to talk."

"OK. Let me get my coat. Wait for me in the car. I'll just be a minute."

She returned to the car; a minute later he appeared, running through the rain, an anxious look on his face as he dropped into the seat beside her. She started the car.

"Where are we going?" he asked.

"Who cares? Anywhere we can be alone."

She pressed the accelerator, and the car shot out into the road and disappeared around the corner.

Nowhere to Run

THURSDAY

Replogle County Justice Center — 10:00 a.m.

"Come on. Time to say goodbye."

David Williamson ignored the guard's sarcasm and fixed him with his habitual vacant stare.

Williamson was one of those prisoners whom the guards referred to as "two cans short of a six-pack" — often within Williamson's hearing. He had been an inmate of the Replogle County Jail for almost eight weeks, pending the availability of space in the crowded state prison in Ferguson. In all that time he had given no indication that he fully understood where he was or what had brought him to the jail. His conversation, such as it was, was limited to short sentences delivered in a vapid monotone that left the guards with the impression that his thoughts, if he had any, were somewhere else entirely.

"You ready?" the guard asked.

Williamson nodded vaguely and slowly lifted himself off the hard mattress. He was wearing a striped black and white loose-fitting two-piece outfit straight out of the pages of an old children's comic.

"Two of you going, I hear," the guard said as he followed Williamson down the corridor, passing the closed doors with thick plastic windows that enabled those in the hallway to look into the cells.

By rights, the guard should have handcuffed his prisoner; but, despite the reason for Williamson's incarceration, he had exhibited no tendency to violence and the guard had decided that to handcuff this particular inmate would be a waste of his time.

Williamson grunted something which might have meant "Yes" or "No" or "I don't know."

Discouraged by this response, the guard made no further attempts at conversation and in silence the two men made their way to the conference room, one shuffling in his transportation garb, the other three paces behind, his mouth a grim line and his hand never far from his holster.

The conference room was empty. They sat on opposite sides of the table, waiting.

A minute or so later, a secretary walked in and handed the guard a thin sheaf of papers.

"This is the paperwork for prisoners Williamson and McLaughlin," she said. "Give it to the deputies when they arrive. They'll give it to the folks at Ferguson."

"OK, I'll pass it all on. Thanks."

The secretary glanced at Williamson. He was staring vacantly at her. She quickly turned away and left the room.

Silence descended once more, to be broken a couple of minutes later as two uniformed sheriff's deputies entered. They were followed by two more men, one dressed in the same black-and-white garb as David Williamson, the other obviously his guard. The new prisoner was wearing handcuffs.

The formalities of the hand-over were completed in less than thirty seconds. The handcuffs on the second prisoner were unlocked and removed, and the two guards left the room, leaving the prisoners alone with the deputies. One of the deputies faced the two convicts, who were standing side-by-side against the wall.

"Either of you all ever been moved before?" The officer's name was Baker, according to the flash above his breast pocket.

A grunt and a shake of the head from Williamson.

"Yes," from the other.

Being transferred from one prison to another was hardly a new experience for Duke McLaughlin. At five feet eight inches, he was the shortest man in the room. He was also undoubtedly the most dangerous. His dark, lank, unwashed hair was falling forward, hiding his high brow and accentuating the belligerence with which he regarded the world. McLaughlin looked contemptuously at the police officers, then turned and regarded the other inmate.

David Williamson looked blankly into McLaughlin's dark, almost-black eyes. McLaughlin stared back at him with undisguised hostility.

Williamson barely knew McLaughlin, but he had seen him often enough around the jail to know that the stubble on his chin and the combative expression on his face were both permanent features of the man's visage. McLaughlin's term was ten years. He had finally been captured after a string of armed robberies and had been sentenced to the maximum term "on account of being a dangerous habitual criminal" as the judge described him. One look at Duke McLaughlin was enough to know that here was someone who was going to spend most of his life sequestered from society.

"You Williamson?" Baker asked.

Williamson nodded.

"And you're McLaughlin?"

The reply was unprintable.

The police officer shrugged.

"OK; here's the drill. The prison is about a hundred and twenty miles away. Deputy Palmer and I are responsible for you from now until the moment we hand you over to the authorities there. In a minute, you will both be handcuffed. The cuffs won't come off for any reason until we hand you over. Once the two of you are cuffed, we will leave this building together.

"In the parking lot is a car modified for transporting prisoners. You will both sit in back. A steel grill will separate you from where Deputy Palmer and I will be sitting in front. There will be absolutely no talking by either of you while we are *en route*. Any questions?"

Williamson shook his head. McLaughlin gave no indication of having heard.

The officer stepped in front of McLaughlin and looked down into the prisoner's face.

"You. Prisoner McLaughlin. Any questions?"

For a moment, Williamson thought that McLaughlin was going to spit in the deputy's face. But if he had been considering it, McLaughlin obviously thought better of it. His eyes locked on the policeman's and he shook his head by all of a quarter of an inch.

"Good." The officer took two steps backward. "Well, let's put the cuffs on them."

Deputy Palmer stepped forward and the two of them quickly handcuffed the prisoners.

Deputy Palmer led them out the room. They trooped in single file down a long corridor, Palmer in front, Baker in the rear, the prisoners sandwiched between them. They turned a corner, passed a desk at which a receptionist sat, and continued past an armed guard and thence outside. For the second consecutive day, heavy rain was falling.

There was a single vehicle parked near the center of the wire-fenced enclosure in which they found themselves. It was a police car emblazoned with the state seal and the words "State Trooper — To Protect And To Serve" on the front doors.

"To the car," Palmer said.

"Which route should we take?" Deputy Baker asked his colleague as they approached the car. "The highway is shorter, but if we stick to the back roads we can probably make this last all day."

"The back roads then, don't you think?"

"You! What d'you think you're staring at? The car's unlocked; you and McLaughlin get in back, put your belts on, then we'll lock you in and we'll be on our way."

Hampered by their handcuffs, the two convicts opened the rear doors of the vehicle and slid on to the rear seat. Williamson, after several seconds of struggling, finally succeeded in snapping closed the seatbelt. The task was made more difficult by the fact that even in the short time he had been outside, his hands had become slippery with the rain.

McLaughlin sat immobile, making no attempt to fasten his belt.

Deputy Palmer sighed and said to McLaughlin, "Look, if you don't give us any trouble, we won't give you any. There's really no point in making this difficult. Do you understand me?"

McLaughlin looked at the officer, seemed once more to consider the possibility of spitting, then silently turned and reached for the seatbelt. He buckled himself in.

Palmer said, "Good," slammed the door, then turned a key in the lock. He walked around the vehicle and went through the same motions on Williamson's side.

Baker slid into the driver's seat and lifted the handset of the car radio. As Palmer got in beside him, Deputy Baker told the dispatcher that they had taken charge of the prisoners and were about to leave the compound. He turned the key in the ignition. The car purred with a deep-voiced authority, betraying the fact that the engine was rather different from the one a customer would see if he were to lift the hood of a similar car at a dealership.

"Here we go then, one big happy family," Baker said.

He pressed an unobtrusive button in the dash, and a gate in the tall perimeter fence slid open. He eased the car through the narrow gateway, then pressed the button again. The gate slid closed behind them. As the car turned out of the parking lot, neither of the officers made any movement to strap himself in.

David Williamson looked out the car window. There was nothing noteworthy about their surroundings. He could have been in any one

21

of half a dozen counties in the area. Hardwood trees grew in a dense forest, hiding everything except the complex of buildings they were now leaving.

The car halted at a junction. The town of Replogle was signed to the left, half a mile away. The car pulled forward and turned right. There was no sign to indicate which towns lay in this direction. Deputy Baker turned on the windshield wipers, and a repetitive *thwack, thwack* was superimposed on the low throb of the car's engine.

The roads were narrow, winding and steep. Williamson looked at the speedometer through the close-meshed steel grill that separated the prisoners from the officers in front. Thirty miles per hour was about as fast as they could go on these roads in this weather.

He wondered how long it would take them to reach the prison. A hundred and twenty miles. Probably they would get there sometime early in the afternoon. And then what? His eyes resumed their blank stare and his thoughts turned inward.

Apart from the mechanical sounds of the vehicle, the patter of rain on the roof, and the high-pitched swish of water hitting the underside of the car, they travelled onward in silence.

They drove in this manner for thirty two minutes, in which time they covered a little more than fifteen miles and encountered one other vehicle: a sedan with out-of-state plates going in the opposite direction.

They reached the top of a high ridge and Deputy Baker slowed the car almost to walking pace to make a tight turn to the left. Ahead of them opened up a long, straight hill at the bottom of which was a sharp turn to the right.

"Let's have some fun," said Deputy Baker, the first words anyone had spoken since they had left the compound.

With no warning, the car suddenly accelerated down the hill. Williamson leaned forward against the acceleration and looked through the grill. Deputy Baker's hands were clenched whitely on the wheel, and he was concentrating tensely as he gauged the distance to the turn at the bottom of the hill. Next to him, Deputy Palmer flicked his eyes nervously between the road ahead and his colleague in the driver's seat.

The car roared down the hill, gathering speed.

Williamson watched the speedometer. Fifty. Fifty five. Sixty. He looked away, staring at the onrushing turn ahead.

His right foot moved forward, pressing an imaginary brake pedal. Officer Palmer's foot did the same thing a fraction of a second later.

Then, at last, Deputy Baker's foot moved away from the accelerator and hovered over the brake pedal. His foot stamped down. And the tires skidded on the wet road.

Williamson threw himself down on the seat, curling up tightly. McLaughlin, who until that moment had looked as if he were completely ignoring everything that was happening, had anticipated him and was already tucked up tightly in a fetal position, his handcuffed hands over his head, pressing his head down tightly against his knees.

The slide continued... it seemed like forever. The car swerved hard to the right, and then the vehicle began to rotate counterclockwise.

Afterwards, Williamson remembered the crash as being oddly silent, although in fact the sound of the car sliding into the tree must have been enough to shatter the peace for a considerable distance. But as Williamson later recalled the sequence of events, it seemed that one moment the car was sliding and pivoting slowly, and the next there was a sudden, powerful deceleration which whipped his entire body sideways against the seatbelt while the front of the car was smashed by what seemed like an enormous mallet.

And then there was nothing.

Ever so slowly, David Williamson lifted his head.

A sound erupted close to his ear. He turned at the sudden incongruous noise. It was a moment before he was sure of what he was seeing and hearing. Duke McLaughlin was laughing!

McLaughlin laughed for at least twenty seconds before he realized that Williamson was looking at him. His dark eyes shone as he shouted, "The idiots! What unbelievable effing idiots." A trickle of tears escaped each eye as he continued to laugh, shaking his head, repeating his assessment of the officers' intelligence with a remarkable variety of uncomplimentary epithets.

David looked away and tried to take stock of their situation.

The car was no longer on the road; the closest part of the car to the road, the left rear fender, was perhaps five feet from the blacktop. It was obvious what had happened. Deputy Baker had lost control as he had tried to take the sharp bend at the bottom of the hill, and even though he had been braking hard, they had had too much momentum and too little traction on the wet surface.

So they had skidded off the road and climbed a short bank, and then the front of the car had wrapped itself around the massive trunk of a tall tree that seemed completely undamaged by the incident.

The car had hit the tree a few inches forward of the front seat. Deputy Baker had been thrown forward on to the steering wheel at the same time that the column was being sheared sideways by the sudden intrusion of the tree into the rear of the car's engine compartment. What remained of Deputy Baker's head was not a pretty sight — not that much could be seen through the blood. The angle of his neck was enough to make it obvious that the deputy was dead.

Williamson heard a moan, barely audible through McLaughlin's laughter. It came from Deputy Palmer. The deputy had been flung through the windshield and he was now draped over the crumpled right half of the hood.

Palmer moaned again. Blood covered most of his face. Williamson watched as Palmer tried to lift an arm to brush the blood from his eyes. The arm stopped half-way to its destination and fell to the hood as Palmer screamed in agony.

A motion at Williamson's side attracted his attention. Duke McLaughlin, no longer laughing, was unclipping his seatbelt.

McLaughlin unbuckled himself and then maneuvered so that he was on his back on the seat, his head and shoulders resting against the legs of his fellow convict.

"Brace yourself," said McLaughlin.

McLaughlin thrust his feet forward, shattering the cracked glass of the locked door on his side of the car. He kicked several times, knocking away the sharp edges of the destroyed window.

McLaughlin poked his cuffed hands and then his head outside. Then he scrambled out the hole where the window had been, landing with a heavy roll on the grass. He stood up and peered inside the car.

"Come on, man. We'll never get another chance like this."

Slowly, the full reality of the situation dawned on David Williamson: Duke McLaughlin intended to escape and was inviting David to join him.

"What are you waiting for? Let's get moving."

McLaughlin was almost shouting at him.

Without stopping to weigh the consequences, Williamson unbuckled himself and shuffled across the seat to where McLaughlin had been sitting and then held up his cuffed hands. McLaughlin grabbed the cuffs and pulled while Williamson pushed against the car seat. He fell headfirst on to the grass beside the car. Momentarily dazed, he shook his head and then, with McLaughlin's help, he got to his feet.

McLaughlin moved to the driver's window. Apparently oblivious to Baker's mutilation, McLaughlin scrabbled at the man's waist and, after a few moments, jangled the officer's key ring aloft.

"Come here," he said. "Give me your cuffs."

Williamson wordlessly held out his hands. There were five likely-looking keys on the ring. The fourth opened the cuffs. McLaughlin passed the ring to Williamson, who quickly unlocked McLaughlin's cuffs.

McLaughlin raised his hands into the air and let out a cry of triumph. Then he knelt at Baker's body and retrieved the deputy's gun. He handed it to Williamson.

Williamson looked down at it.

The car, and McLaughlin, and the forest, and the events of the past few minutes all ceased to exist.

He could see instead the clerk of the convenience store looking with horror, first at the gun, then at him. "Money, I need money." He could hear himself saying the words, then adding plaintively, "It's not for me."

McLaughlin was talking to him, saying something that Williamson had not taken in.

"Huh?" Williamson said.

"I said: you keep that gun, I'll get the other one."

Williamson watched vacantly as McLaughlin walked around the front of the car to where Deputy Palmer was still lying sprawled across the hood, his blood mixing with the steady rain. He was still alive, but the only sound he was making now was a painful grunt that accompanied every shallow breath.

Suddenly, a scream shattered the silence.

McLaughlin had grasped the deputy and manhandled him on to his back in order to reach his weapon more easily. Palmer's eyes were screwed shut in agony. McLaughlin leaned across and without so much as a glance at the man's face removed the pistol from the holster.

He held the weapon in his hands, turning it around, as if admiring its functional beauty.

Palmer's eyes opened.

"No...," the word escaped Palmer's lips as half gurgle, half entreaty.

Palmer's eyes were fixed on the pistol in McLaughlin's hands. He opened his mouth to say more, but the effort and pain were too much. He closed his mouth and shook his head slightly, his eyes pleading with McLaughlin not to use the gun.

Williamson watched with horror as McLaughlin lifted the pistol and eyed along it directly at the police officer's heart.

"No!" Williamson cried. "You can't do that."

McLaughlin turned toward Williamson; the expression on his face was unreadable.

"I can do whatever I effing well want," he said flatly.

"If he hadn't made you wear your belt, you'd probably be dead now," Williamson said.

McLaughlin raised one eyebrow slightly, considering this statement.

He looked back at the deputy, then at Williamson once more. He shrugged and slowly lowered the pistol. Then he leaned forward and spat directly in the policeman's eye.

"Thank you," McLaughlin said.

Then he placed the safety catch on and pushed the pistol into the waistband of his striped pants.

"We'll need some clothes," he said. "Take whatever you can salvage from the other one, if there's anything that isn't covered with blood. At least his shoes should be OK if they fit."

He grabbed Palmer and manhandled him across the hood and dragged him down on to the ground. After a single long, horrendous scream, Palmer fell silent. He was unconscious long before McLaughlin had maneuvered his pants, socks and shoes off his legs and feet.

Williamson watched for several seconds and then, swallowing several times and distancing his mind from the task he was performing, he set about doing the same with the blood-drenched corpse of what had been Deputy Baker.

Ten minutes later, the two appraised one another. Neither of them was an attractive sight. Williamson was dressed in the dead man's pants and socks and Palmer's shoes. He still wore his black and white top, and there were several all-too-obvious dark stains in the navy of his pants. McLaughlin was wearing Palmer's socks and pants — which, although unstained, were clearly too large for him — as well as Palmer's blood-stained shirt. The dead officer's shirt was stained beyond hope, and his shoes lay discarded on the wet ground, too large for either of the convicts.

Palmer had lain unconscious throughout the time it had taken the men to change their clothes. Now he began to regain consciousness and a quiet groan escaped his lips.

"Shhh!" hissed McLaughlin as Williamson opened his mouth to say something.

McLaughlin cocked his head, listening. In a moment, Williamson heard it too. Not far away, a vehicle was coming their way.

"Quick!" McLaughlin said, and he dashed across the road with Williamson hard at his heels.

They ran into the forest and then dropped to the ground, looking back past the trees at the scene they had left. Ten seconds later, a car came to a halt not far from the wreck of the police car. A pair of middle-aged men got out and walked hesitantly toward the wreck. They stopped beside it. Then one of the men turned, retched, and threw up on the grass.

Northern Replogle County — 11:15 a.m.

"Good God!"

The words escaped Fred Price's lips before he could stop them. A religious man, he mentally asked forgiveness for his breaking of the third commandment even as he continued: "It's a police car. It's been in some sort of accident."

Fred slowed the car to a standstill a short distance from the police car, then got out. His brother John followed.

From here, the wreck did not look too bad. At first, neither of the brothers noticed the men, stripped of their clothing, who lay motionless on the verge, near the front of the car.

Cautiously, the brothers approached the vehicle.

"Looks like they skidded off the road," John offered.

They halted for a moment, looking. Then they saw the bodies.

Fred broke into a run. "You look at the other one," he called.

He knelt by the side of the closest body, trying to make sense of the fact that the man was in his underclothes. He held a hand against the man's chest and felt a shallow movement.

"Sweet Jesus!" he exclaimed. This time he forgot to ask for forgiveness. "This one's alive. But only just!"

He stood up to see his brother wiping his mouth with a handkerchief.

"Sorry. Couldn't help it," John said, swallowing to prevent a recurrence. "You should see the state this one's in."

He gestured towards the man on the ground near the driver's door, while steadfastly keeping his eyes averted from the sight that had caused him to lose his breakfast.

Fred stepped around the car, looked at the body, and then immediately turned away. He told himself that this was no worse than things he had seen in Vietnam, and forced himself to look once more. Like the man on the passenger side of the vehicle, this man had been stripped to his underclothes, except that he still wore a shirt that, despite the blood, identified him as a police officer.

What was left of the officer's face stared up at the sky, although there were no eyes through which he could have seen, just as there was no true nose through which he could have breathed, and no mouth through which he could have spoken. The only identifiable feature on the front of the man's head was a fleshy appendage that once had been a nose, dangling at one side of what had once been a face. Rainwater mixed freely with the blood that covered all, but it barely diluted the scarlet, sticky liquid. There was no need to check whether this man was breathing.

"Ugh!" The sound escaped Fred's throat involuntarily and he turned away. "Nothing we can do for this one. But the other's one's alive, just barely. I'm sure we can't move him, though. One of us needs to go for help and the other one should stay here."

"I'm not staying," said his younger brother. "Not with that," he gestured towards the man whose face had been ripped from his skull.

"All right. You drive and I'll stay. Don't be long, though."

John nodded. "I'll be as quick as I can."

John began to walk towards their car. He had just reached it when a horrible thought struck him. He turned and called to his brother: "Wait a minute. You can't stay."

"Why not?"

As soon as the question was out of his mouth, Fred knew the answer. "They've been stripped. Someone else has been here."

Fred nodded and began to walk quickly back towards their car.

Another thought struck John.

"Do they still have their guns?"

Fred returned to the man who was lying close to the passenger door. "This one doesn't," he said.

He placed his mouth close to the man's ear. "Listen. I don't know if you can hear me. We're going to have to go away and get help. We'll be as quick as we can. I'm sorry. There's nothing we can do. You need medical attention, and neither of us is trained for that sort of thing. I'm really sorry. We'll be back as soon as possible. Do you understand?"

There was no response.

Fred Price got to his feet and jogged back to the car. "There's got to be a house not too far away," he said.

The car doors slammed and in seconds the brothers were on their way.

Replogle — 12:30 p.m.

George Ellsworth eyed his lunch desultorily. It was not that it was unappetizing — the tuna salad sandwich, with its red tomatoes, white onions, green romaine lettuce, and brown whole wheat bread looked great. But he was simply in no mood for eating.

He had arrived home last night confused and at least partly in shock. The drive home with Tom Murdoch had been silent and introspective. Only once had he spoken to the builder, to ask whether Tom had noticed anyone standing close to the inmate at the rear of the room.

The builder's answer was the one that the pastor had feared.

"No, he's a loner all right, that one, and the other prisoners seem to stay clear of him just as much as he stays away from them. I don't know much about him. I don't think anyone does, really.

"One of the guards told me there was a rumor he was once a model citizen, but then something went wrong and he turned against society and took to the streets. Eventually, he got a gun from somewhere and was caught holding up a convenience store over in Mulberry County.

He's in for five years, but he's being held here temporarily until there's room for him at the prison over in Ferguson. He came to our meeting last month, but he just sat over in the corner like he did tonight. I've never seen him talk to anyone. I expect he'll have been transferred by next month. That's about all I know."

"So you didn't see anyone else talking to him or even standing close to him during the meeting?"

"No." Tom's voice held a query in it, and he looked at his pastor as if wondering whether something was the matter.

But George Ellsworth kept his own counsel. If he was going crazy, there was no need for anyone else to know.

When they reached his house, George said goodbye to the builder without inviting him in.

Mary was already in bed, her nose still buried in her romance novel. After exchanging meaningless pleasantries, George went back downstairs. He needed to be alone. Uncharacteristically, he poured himself a glass of Christmas whiskey, then sat heavily in his chair and ruminated long and hard on what had happened at the jail.

He went to bed an hour and a half later, still unsure what to make of it all. He didn't *feel* crazy. But how else to explain what he had seen? Visions weren't for the likes of him. And in any case, no matter what anyone claimed, they didn't really happen any more. Not really.

He slept poorly, and his moodiness continued through the next morning.

Thursday was the day he reserved for working on his sermon. Until last night, he had been planning to speak on the sanctity of marriage and the desperate need for families to stay together while secular society became ever more corrupt and depraved. But now he discovered that the subject no longer held any interest. He found himself scouring his Bible, looking for clues that might help him understand what had really happened last night.

The possibility of visions and the reality of such beings as angels were not things he had ever really thought about much. He had no difficulty believing in miracles — after all, what was prayer but a request for God to intervene in the affairs of man? And were not all such interventions miracles? But modern-day visions were something else entirely. At best the idea smacked of Catholicism. At worst it

30

seemed like some kind of witchcraft. God in the late twentieth century behaved rationally; the days of dreams and visions were long gone.

Yet how else to understand the presence of a man whom no one else had seen or heard? He could not deny the evidence of his senses, no matter how much he wanted to.

He remembered it clearly: the powerful prayer that had started when he paused for a breath during his own prayer; and the shadowed figure speaking the prayer while resting his hand on the solitary prisoner near the door.

Perhaps the oddest thing was that there had seemed nothing supernatural about it at the time — the only odd thing was that the speaker had somehow managed to enter the room unnoticed. But there was nothing to indicate this was somehow God's doing. There were, he supposed, those strange changes in the lighting in that corner of the room, but that might easily have been just his eyes playing tricks... or simply his imagination.

He remembered the urgent unspoken command he had heard inside his head, telling him to pray for the man — what was his name, Williamson? — but this phenomenon, while hardly common, was not completely outside his experience. Perhaps three or four times in the past twenty years such a command had popped urgently into his head. Whether anything had ever come of those prayers, he had no way of knowing. Until now, he had doubted it.

So he grappled all morning with the events of the evening before. Part of him wanted to believe that he had imagined the whole thing. But he knew that that was simply not true. Perhaps the voice in his head was imaginary, but he had seen and heard the man praying over Williamson. That was as ineluctable fact.

At last it was time for lunch, and now he was sitting at the kitchen table, gazing at the colorful sandwich his wife had prepared.

"Honey, what's the matter? You've been very quiet since last night. You haven't said much about the meeting. How did it go?"

George looked at his wife. Now there was something, or someone, to be thankful for. His wife was all that a pastor could ask for. She supported him unquestioningly in public, holding him up as a pillar of strength even though she knew all his weaknesses, all his moments of doubt, his frustrations, his frequent confusion. But would she understand something like this? He looked at her, wondering if perhaps this would be asking too much.

She stretched out her hand and touched his arm.

"Come on, honey. What is it? You can share anything with me, you know. That's what wives are for."

She was right, of course.

"You'll laugh," he said. "Either that or you'll think I'm crazy."

Neither of these possibilities was remotely likely, but his words might at least serve to prepare her for the extraordinariness of what he was about to say.

"Don't be silly, hon. I'd never do that."

"Well... it's about last night...."

He proceeded to tell her everything: the solitary, vacant-eyed man near the door; the powerful, emphatic prayer offered by the shadowy stranger who had lain his hand on the loner while he prayed; the inner voice commanding him to pray for this man; the apparent darkening of the room and the shaft of light that had lit the man like a spotlight from heaven. Finally, most reluctantly of all, he explained how none of this had been visible or audible to Tom Murdoch.

"So what do you make of it?" he concluded. "Am I going crazy?"

He looked at Mary, whose brow was furrowed in thought. For a long time there was silence, broken only by the sound of the refrigerator suddenly turning on.

Eventually, she said quietly, "You've been in your study all morning. You haven't heard the news, have you?"

"What news?"

"It was on the radio while I was making lunch. They broke into the program with a news flash to say that there's been an accident on County Road 64 up in the northern part of the county. Apparently a police car came off the road. There's been at least one fatality. The car was carrying two prisoners who were being moved from Replogle jail to the prison in Ferguson. Both the prisoners are missing, and so far there's no word on whether they might be injured."

There was a heavy silence which lasted some fifteen seconds before George Ellsworth finally spoke.

"You don't think...? Do you...?"

"The radio didn't give any names. Do you know the name of the man you were supposed to pray for?"

He nodded. "Yes. Williamson. And he was being held in Replogle jail only temporarily, until there was space for him in Ferguson."

"Perhaps you'd better call the sheriff's department or the jail and see if they'll tell you anything."

He nodded again. He went to the phone and flipped through the blue pages of the telephone book where the government numbers were listed, then dialled the number of the county jail.

He put the telephone down two minutes later, but Mary had overheard enough to know what he was going to say.

"It was him, wasn't it?"

"Yes. Him and another man whose name I didn't recognize," — he looked down at the pad on which he had taken notes — "Darren McLaughlin, usually known as 'Duke.' They were both in for the same thing, attempted robbery with violence, but McLaughlin had a much longer sentence because apparently he's a repeat offender while it was Williamson's first offense.

"The warden said that he doesn't know much more than what's been on the radio, although he appreciated my concern. He did say that there were two police officers in the car, and one of them is dead and the other isn't expected to live. The injured officer just arrived at Replogle hospital, but they're going to fly in a chopper from Dixon as soon as they think it's safe to move him. Neither of the convicts have been found. And one last thing...."

"Yes?"

"Some of the policemen's clothing had been removed, and so had both of their guns."

It took a moment for this to sink in. When it did, an "oh" escaped Mary's lips. She visibly gathered herself, then spoke again.

"Then it's clear what we have to do, isn't it? We'd better get on our knees and pray."

Replogle — 2:00 p.m.

Pam McGuire was terrified.

It had all seemed so simple last night when Craig had explained it to her.

"Look," he had said, his arm around her shoulder, squeezing gently to assure her that he loved her even after she had blurted it all out between sobs, "this happened to someone at school, and it's really not that hard. The problems are all psychological, not physical. These days it's safe and easy. All you have to do is to accept the facts and do what has to be done."

"But Craig, it's wrong; we both know that."

"Yes, you're right. Obviously it *is* wrong. But which is worse: to bring an unwanted child into the world and to ruin two lives in the process? Or to agree to a simple procedure that will solve the problem for ever? We shouldn't have done it; I admit that. We both got carried away, and I suppose this is the price we must pay, and we won't make the same mistake again, but really, when you think about it, we have no option, do we? It's the only answer."

She had been in no mood to argue. She was too relieved that someone else was willing to do her thinking for her, to make the decision that she had been too weak to make, even though it was the obvious one. She had nearly asked him if he would marry her if she kept the baby, but her resolve was not strong enough, and she was too afraid of what his answer might be. Much simpler to do as he suggested and put the whole mess behind her.

But that was last night, and now that she was actually taking the first steps, what had seemed so simple then appeared impossible now.

She wished desperately that Craig was with her in the waiting room, but last night when she had suggested it, he had refused, saying that while he was certainly willing to support her, he didn't think it either necessary or wise that he accompany her. Last night, when she had been incapable of rational thought, when the visit to the doctor still lay in the future, it had not been hard to accept Craig's argument; but now, as her anxiety turned by gradations to terror, she knew that she should have insisted.

Her stomach churned. She looked at the clock, then at the scattered magazines on the table before her, then back at the clock because the time had failed to register the first time.

Five minutes past two. The doctor was already late; the appointment was for two o'clock. How would he react when she told him the real purpose of her visit? "Queasiness," was all she had told the receptionist.

And was it a mistake coming to her usual doctor, who was, after all, a friend of the family? She could have gone to some anonymous doctor in Faraday. Why hadn't she thought of that earlier? It was not too late; she could still get up and leave....

"Pam?" The nurse had appeared from nowhere and was smiling sweetly at her. "We're ready for you now."

Pam's mind went blank. She got up and followed the nurse toward the examining rooms.

"And how are you today? Feeling a bit under the weather?"

Pam was surprised that it was not obvious how she was feeling; her lightheadedness was making itself known with every step she took. She was half walking, half floating across the carpet.

"Yes," she mumbled.

"Sit on the examining table, please," the nurse said as they reached the examining room. "Lift up your sleeve so I can take your blood pressure. Now, what's the matter? You say you're feeling queasy and nauseous? How long has that been going on?"

The nurse was trying to be interested in her, but Pam knew that she wasn't really listening to the answers as she pumped the bulb: she was simply making polite conversation until the doctor arrived. Pam felt the cuff tighten on her arm. She wished that the nurse would simply shut up, but through a haze Pam tried to give coherent, if not particularly truthful, answers.

At last the ordeal was over. The doctor came in just as the nurse stood to leave.

"Ah, good afternoon, Pam." Dr. Hunter took a seat next to the examination table on which Pam was seated. "Now, what seems to be the problem? The information sheet is rather vague, I'm afraid." The nurse closed the door as she left.

Dr. Hunter was middle-aged, with hair that was gray but thick. He had a kindly face, and as he looked at her he was smiling. It was only slowly that the smile turned first to a look of enquiry and then to something rather more businesslike.

Even now it was not too late. How much confidence did Pam have in this friend of her father's? Would he honor his professional vow of confidentiality? The bile in her stomach seemed suddenly acid. Perhaps she should leave and instead go to someone else while she still had the chance. Another few seconds and the chance would be gone. She vacillated, and, as she did so, the doctor looked at her with increasing concern.

Then he leaned back in his chair, visibly relaxing, his body language communicating that he was not a threat.

He said, "You can tell me, you know. I won't tell anyone else. Anything you say is strictly between the two of us unless you want it otherwise."

He knows, she thought. *Somehow, God only knows how, he knows.*

And with that realization, it all began to pour out in an uncontrollable flood of words and tears.

"Oh, Dr. Hunter. I should have known better, I know I should. I didn't think that anything would happen if we just did it once. I don't know what came over me. But... but... I don't know. Oh, doctor, I don't know what to do. My parents would kill me if they knew, and... and... we've talked it over, and we've decided that the best thing really, for all our sakes is... is to have... have...."

She couldn't say the word.

For nearly half a minute the room was filled with the sound of her sobs.

She wiped the tears from her eyes and sat up straight. "I want an abortion," she said, enunciating the words slowly and carefully, as if to prove to herself that she could say them.

The doctor offered her a tissue. "Here. Take this."

For several seconds, he said nothing, waiting for her to regain control. At last, in a relaxed, affable voice, as if they were discussing nothing more important than the weather, he began to talk softly.

"First of all, you must understand that even if I wanted to tell anyone about this, I couldn't. It would be neither ethical nor moral nor legal for me to do so. There are strict laws about what information a doctor may divulge to third parties in a case like this. You are old enough that for me to tell anyone, even your parents, would be against the law. Secondly, please try not to be upset if I ask you a couple of simple questions. I'm afraid that I must ask them; all right? I'm not judging you, Pam, you do understand that, don't you?"

Pam nodded, not trusting herself to speak. She twisted the tissue in her hands, then compressed it tightly into a sodden ball.

"All right. Thank you. Now, how certain are you that you're pregnant? How do you know?"

"I took a test. I've missed my last two periods, and this past couple of weeks I've been feeling nauseous in the mornings. I haven't actually been sick, but I've definitely felt queasy for an hour or so after getting up."

"All right. You took a test. Now, what kind of test?"

"One of those they sell down at the drugstore. I bought it over in Greenminster Mall; I was afraid Mom would find out if I bought it in Replogle or Faraday."

"What kind was it?"

"EPT, they called it. I guess it stands for 'Early Pregnancy Test' or something."

"You followed the instructions exactly?"

"Yes. I did it yesterday morning. I put my urine in the bottle thing and looked about an hour later and sure enough, there was this brown circle."

"OK. I just wanted to be sure before we went any further."

"Should I take another one then?"

There was no real hope in her voice.

"These home tests aren't wrong very often, but perhaps in a case like this it might be best to be sure. Don't worry about the cost. We'll just do it here when we've finished talking. You can call me later and I'll let you know the result. But since you've had other symptoms.... When did you last have a period? And how regular are you?"

"Like clockwork, usually, every twenty eight days, beginning on Wednesdays. I've missed the last two. I should have had one last week."

The doctor was scrawling indecipherable notations on his notepad.

"All right. Now, do I understand you right: you had intercourse only once recently?"

"Only once. Yes. That's right."

"And when was that?"

"June the first."

"I see. So that would be, let's see" — he looked at a table-top calendar and did some calculations in his head — "fifteen days before your first missed period."

"I guess so."

"All right. Well, that certainly looks like it fits."

The doctor lowered his pen, straightened his back and looked Pam McGuire in the eye.

"There's no use crying about it, Pam. You aren't the first to come here in this condition, both physically and emotionally, and I can assure you that you won't be the last. Now, the question is: where do we go from here, isn't it?"

Pam looked down at the sodden, partially shredded ball in her hands and nodded.

Dr. Hunter continued, "I'll tell you right now, Pam, that I don't perform abortions. If it were legal for me to give you ethical advice instead of just medical advice, I'd tell you not to, no matter how bleak things look. But I'm not allowed to tell you that, so I won't.

"There are other doctors who do perform abortions, not here in Replogle, but there's one over in Faraday and a couple in Greenminster, and you should have no trouble finding one if that's really what you think needs to be done. I'll give you the name of one if you insist on it."

He took a breath as if to begin again, seemed to think better of it, took another breath, and continued in a perceptibly softer tone.

"Pam... I hope you don't mind. I'm not going to lecture you or anything, but I would like to say something, if that's all right?"

Pam made a noise somewhere between a grunt and a squeak.

"OK. Thank you. I notice that you haven't said who the father is. Don't worry, I don't want to know unless you want to tell me. And of course it's your body, not his; but how much have you talked this over with him? Is this really your decision or is it his?"

"Ours. We've talked about it. We both think it's for the best."

"Any chance he'll marry you? If that's what you want."

"Yes, I think so. We do want to get married. But not yet. I haven't even started college yet. I need to get my degree before we marry and have children. And anyway, our parents...." Her voice trailed away. Elaboration was unnecessary.

"All right, I understand. Can you wait here a minute? I want to get something for you."

Silently, looking at the floor, she nodded.

The doctor left Pam to her thoughts for a couple of minutes. She poked at the sodden tissue. When he returned, he was carrying

38

something small, black and rectangular. He held it out to her. It was a videotape. There was no label.

"Please, Pam. I'll give you the name of a doctor in Faraday before you leave, but I'd be grateful if you'd take this tape as well. I'm not telling you to watch it, but I am asking you to do so, as a friend of the family. It's not preachy. In fact, it takes no moral stand at all. But it does tell you some facts you might not know. And I'm sure that a clever girl like you, about to go to college, would rather marshal all her facts before making an irrevocable decision, wouldn't she?"

She nodded. "I guess so. Thank you," she added automatically as she he handed her the tape.

The doctor tore a page off his notebook and wrote down a name and a telephone number. "If you decide to go ahead, Dr. Carpenter will take good care of you. Now, if you'll wait a moment, I'll send the nurse in and we'll give you another test."

An hour later, Bob Hunter sat at the desk in his office and heaved a deep sigh. For a long while, he looked at the telephone. It would be simple to call Pam's father.

After pondering this for more than a minute, he instead did something much more effective: he closed his eyes in prayer.

Between Dixon and Replogle — 2:27 p.m.

"You're patched through now."

"Thank you. Flight for Life? This is St. Luke's hospital in Replogle."

"Good afternoon. This is Dixon General Hospital Flight For Life One."

"I'm sorry, FFL 1. We won't be needing your services. The patient is deceased."

"Flight for Life One. We copy that our services are no longer required. Returning to Dixon. Thank you. And we're sorry. Good afternoon."

"Thank you. Good afternoon."

Southern Hill County — 3:10 p.m.

"Well, at least the rain is letting up."

David Williamson looked up at the sky, which was at last beginning to clear.

His companion nodded.

"If there's anything worse than being on the run, it's being on the run and *wet*."

"You done this before?"

"Dreamed about it, but never had the chance until now."

The two men were sitting under a tall oak tree near the top of a hill. There was a small clearing in front of them, permitting them to look across the valley to miles of rolling hills blanketed in bosky hardwoods. At a guess, they could see perhaps twenty miles, to a distant lake that glistened brightly as the mid-afternoon sun peeked through the breaking clouds.

It was hard to judge how far they had travelled. According to the watches they had taken from the deputies, the wreck had occurred about four hours ago. In that time they had scaled and descended three hills. Now, atop the fourth, they had halted for a rest and were looking back in the direction they had come. Since leaving the scene of the crash they had seen not a single sign of humanity, not even a building or a road.

They sat against the oak tree, halfway to exhaustion, their clothes sopping from the light rain that was at last diminishing.

"So what now? Any ideas?" Williamson asked.

"Nope."

"Think they think we killed the policemen?"

McLaughlin shrugged. "Dunno."

"We could get the chair for that, you know."

"Does it matter? They'll lock me away forever now if they ever catch us anyway." McLaughlin paused for a moment. "But not you, though. They'd increase your sentence to ten years or so; but this isn't your final chance like it is for me. Maybe you should give yourself up."

Instead of responding to this idea, Williamson asked, "Is that why you were going to kill that officer back there? Because there's nothing else for you to lose?"

McLaughlin shrugged.

"Dunno. That was part of it, I s'pose. Maybe I was just sick and tired of the pigs throwing their weight around all the time. I wanted, just once, to get my own back. It was the feeling of having the pig in my power, I think, after he'd been pushing us around back at the jail. It seemed like a waste not to give him a taste of his own medicine. That make sense to you?"

"Yeah, I guess so."

"Well, explain it to me sometime, 'cause I'm not sure it does to me."

The two fell silent once again.

At length, Williamson asked another question.

"Would you have shot him? Really? If I hadn't been there to stop you, I mean."

"What? Oh, the pig... yeah, I guess I would've shot him. He's probably dead by now anyway. He didn't look to be in too good shape to me."

"No.... Say, what do you think our chances are?"

"Dunno. I was just thinking about that. You know your way around here?"

"No."

"Neither do I. I'm from the city. All this nature gives me the creeps. I didn't know places like this still existed."

"Oh, yes, they do. I used to live somewhere like this when I was a kid. A hundred miles or so north of here."

"Yeah? What happened?"

"You don't want to know."

"BC, huh?"

"What?"

"BC: Before Crime."

"Oh, yes; I suppose so. I was just a kid."

"Well, maybe it'll be helpful having a guy like you with me — someone who knows his way around the woods, I mean. Is it safe to drink the water in the streams around here?"

"Yes, I should think so. Even if it isn't, we probably have more pressing things to worry about."

"Well, I guess time's getting on. Let's get going and see if we can't put another five miles between us and that car before nightfall. Then we'll rest for a few hours and try moving on again before it gets light."

41

"Where are we heading for?"

"Anywhere they ain't looking for us," Duke said simply.

Wearily, they stood. With a last look across the clearing at the land they had already traversed, they plunged once more into the tightly packed forest.

Northern Replogle County — 3:15 p.m.

"Boss?"

Bradley Armitage, fifty five years old, in his eighteenth consecutive year as the elected sheriff of Replogle County, and known to almost the entire population of the county as "Boss," looked up from his clipboard.

Official vehicles were parked all around the sheriff as he reviewed the disposition of his deputies. The road was sealed off in both directions, half a mile away to his right, and three quarters of a mile behind him. Diverted traffic was being sent on a circuitous three-mile detour around the accident. Police cars were stationed at both roadblocks, ensuring that only those with legitimate business were granted access to the site of the accident.

Ignoring the call, Brad Armitage, the word SHERIFF emblazoned across the back of his luminous yellow anorak, looked up at the sky. The overcast gray of the low cloudbase was finally beginning to lift. The rain, which until an hour ago had been falling steadily, was now no more than a light drizzle, and the weather gave every indication that it was going to conform to the forecast and would keep improving, at least until nightfall.

A walkie talkie clipped to his belt squawked as the voice repeated, "Boss? Sir?"

He turned to the person who had called him: a tall, rangy man in his early thirties, his hair immaculately coiffed even in the drizzle, and carrying a microphone as he walked towards the sheriff. Trailing behind was a television news cameraman with a minicam. Armitage gestured for the pair to wait while he lifted the walkie talkie.

"Armitage here. Go."

42

"Hello, Boss." The speaker was shouting to be heard over a loud, roaring background. "We're airborne. Should be over you in about seven minutes. How's the weather looking?"

"Still low cloud, but its getting better by the minute. We should be able to cover quite a bit of ground before it gets dark. Give me a call when you're overhead."

"OK, Boss. Out."

Clipping the walkie talkie back on his belt, the sheriff ambled over to the reporter and his cameraman. The reporter held out his hand in greeting.

"Todd Livingstone, Channel 7 news." The cameraman hung back behind the reporter and said nothing.

Livingstone's introduction was unnecessary; the sheriff had recognized immediately the man who was responsible for Channel 7's "Replogle County Bureau" from his almost-nightly reporting of the county's happenings for the big-city channel. Teams from the other channels were doubtless making their way as quickly as they could to this remote spot, but it would be some time before the first of them arrived, giving Channel 7 a short-lived opportunity for a scoop.

"I want to thank you for agreeing to talk to our viewers, sheriff. Is there anything you want to ask before we begin, or are you ready to go live?"

"I'm ready."

The sheriff's face assumed a grim expression, to impress the viewers with the somber reality of what had happened here.

The reporter stood close to the sheriff, angling himself so that the camera could focus on both of them simultaneously. An almost-invisible earpiece trailed a wire down into one of the reporter's pockets.

"Ready?" Livingstone asked the cameraman.

The cameraman nodded.

"Five seconds," the reporter said, pressing the earpiece more tightly into his ear so that he could hear the promptings of the anchorman back in the studio.

They waited the five seconds. A small red LED came to life on the front of the minicam.

"Hello, Ernie," said Livingstone, his voice suddenly somber. "I'm out here live at the site of the crash with Replogle County sheriff Brad

Armitage. Sheriff Armitage, could you please describe in own own words exactly what happened here this morning?"

"Thank you. Yes. Two prisoners were being taken from the county jail in Replogle to the Ferguson prison in the vehicle you see behind me."

The cameraman swung his camera and refocused on the wreck of the police car, which was still wrapped around a tall oak tree. He zoomed in for a close-up of the crumpled vehicle while the sheriff continued.

"The initial report came from two civilians who were driving by shortly after eleven this morning. They reported a wrecked police car; one of the two officers in the vehicle was dead, one badly injured. Naturally, we got here as quickly as possible and found the car exactly as you see it now."

"And the officers?"

"As we had been informed, one officer was dead, the other was severely injured."

"You mentioned that the car had been transporting prisoners."

"Yes."

"What about them? Has there been any sign of them?"

The camera swung back and focused on the sheriff, whose expression studiously tightened.

"No," he said, "and the officers had clearly been manhandled after the accident. They were both found on the ground near the car, in locations that it would have been impossible for them to reach without assistance."

"And I believe that at least some of their clothing had been taken?"

"Yes. One officer, the one who was still alive, had been stripped of his shirt, pants and socks. The other still had his shirt. We believe that it was too badly stained to be of any use to the prisoners. One pair of shoes was found discarded about ten feet away in the woods. Both the officers' wristwatches had been removed."

"And the officers' weapons?"

"They have yet to be found. Our information is that the bodies as we found them were in exactly the same condition as when they were discovered by the civilians shortly after eleven this morning."

"Sheriff Armitage, turning to the accident itself for a moment, is there any speculation as to what might have caused it?"

"Plenty of speculation, but not enough facts as yet. I think it would be premature to talk about that."

"But is it possible that the two prisoners were somehow instrumental in causing the accident?"

"It's possible. But I must emphasize that at this point that's just speculation, and it's certainly too soon to talk about it."

"All right. Now, these two prisoners, you say there hasn't been any sign of them?"

"Not yet."

"Is there any indication that they might be injured?"

"So far we have no evidence one way or the other. They certainly can't be injured as badly as the deputies, otherwise they could never have left the scene. Also, we found the handcuffs they would have been wearing unlocked and discarded on the ground near one of the officers' key rings."

"So they might be completely unhampered?"

"We think that's likely, yes."

"All right. Obviously, these prisoners are armed and should not be approached by civilians?"

"Correct. The two men" — at this point, two grainy black and white photographs were flashed on to viewers' screens — "were both serving time for armed robbery. One was a first-time offender, one was what we might call a habitual criminal. I must stress" — the sheriff turned full face to the camera, and the photographs were replaced by the image of his face filling the viewers' screens — "that on no account should any member of the public attempt to apprehend or even to approach these men. They are to be considered armed and extremely dangerous. We have every reason to believe that they won't hesitate to use the weapons we think they're carrying. If any member of the public believes they have information about the whereabouts of these men, do not approach them. Call the police."

The camera zoomed out once more, and the reporter, responding to an instruction in his ear, drew the interview to a close. "Sheriff Armitage, thank you for your time." He looked up at the sky as a sudden loud chopping noise filled the air. "It looks like the chopper has arrived to help look for the prisoners. Once again, to those watching — and we can't stress this enough — if you see either of these two men, do not under any circumstances approach them. Call the nearest police station and stay away from them. This is Todd Livingstone, reporting for Channel 7 News As It Happens, in Replogle County."

The light on the camera held steady for perhaps three seconds, then winked out. The reporter turned to thank the sheriff, but the latter had already moved several steps away and was talking into his walkie talkie.

"What does the pilot think of the weather?" the sheriff asked the radio.

He held the device tightly against his ear to hear the reply over the sound of the blades cutting through the air only a few hundred feet above his head.

"He says he's seen better, but he's willing to give it a shot. Which direction do you want us to try first, Boss?"

"South. That's the direction where we found the shoes. It's nothing much, and may even be a blind, but it's as good a direction as any. Go out about ten miles, they couldn't have gotten any farther than that yet, I don't think. It's not easy terrain."

"OK. We'll be in touch."

"Boss!" The shout came from a uniformed officer fifty feet away, walking towards the sheriff with a civilian in tow.

The sheriff clipped the walkie talkie to his belt and waited for the pair to arrive within comfortable talking distance. The sound of the helicopter's engine rose to a new volume and then diminished as the copter flew south at a height barely sufficient to avoid the trees growing atop the hills.

"This is Professor Cagney, the crash expert."

For a moment, Armitage wondered what the officer was talking about. Then he remembered.

James Cagney, named most unfortunately after a famous actor of his parents' day, was as unlike his namesake as could be imagined: he was quiet and self deprecating, thoughtful and slow-moving.

This James Cagney had once been a professor of rheology at a public university in another state. He resigned his position after he became wealthy from a patented invention that was now routinely incorporated in automobile engines. Professor Cagney had relocated to Replogle and, after a couple of years of indolence, had opened a one-man consulting agency specializing in accident reconstruction.

46

Over the years, he had become a well-known figure in courtrooms in the surrounding counties, where it was his custom to sit insouciantly in the witness box and give quiet, polished explanations of how an underground gasoline storage tank had leaked, how a propane tank thought to be empty must in fact have contained enough flammable liquid to cause the subsequent explosion, or how the vehicle which the driver testified was doing no more than forty five miles per hour must, by virtue of the tell-tale skid marks, have been travelling at a minimum of seventy miles per hour moments before the accident.

It was a fact accepted by all the local attorneys (as well as the various law-enforcement agencies) that once James Cagney appeared in the witness stand for the opposition in a jury trial, one might as well cut one's losses and go home, for Cagney was implacable in cross examination and adept at explaining the evidence quietly, slowly and above all comprehensibly to the jury.

It was because of Cagney's expertise that Boss Armitage had summoned him to the scene. Cagney approached, dressed in his habitual jeans and with a padded anorak partly unzipped to reveal a checked shirt. There was an affable smile on the expert's face as he held out a hand in greeting.

"Good afternoon, Mr. Armitage. I've been listening to the news on the radio. Sounds like a nasty affair."

"It is. We're hoping you could help us with a problem."

"At your service as always, Mr. Armitage. What's the problem?"

"We want to know how fast the police car was travelling as it came down the hill. You've probably noticed the skid marks already."

Cagney nodded. "And no doubt the road was considerably wetter this morning than it is now."

"Exactly. The skid marks don't look very long, just extending this short distance in front of the tree."

The sheriff pointed to a series of parallel marks on the road stretching away from the car.

"But you're worried about aquaplaning?"

"Yes. That wouldn't leave a mark, would it?"

"No, it wouldn't. Any idea exactly how much rain fell out here in the past day or two?"

"No. Does it matter?"

"Yes. At least it will if you want my testimony to stand up in court. I'll measure these tracks, of course, and look for more tracks up the hill to match with these; but we'll need to know for sure whether aquaplaning occurred.

"For now, privately, I'm willing to work on the assumption that aquaplaning took place, but I want you to know up front that I will eventually need to be satisfied about the amount of rain that fell here. I'll also want to do some experiments with this piece of road in various states of wetness before I can testify with any certainty about what happened here this morning."

The sheriff wasn't particularly interested in all these details. He interrupted the expert.

"Sure; I understand. For now just go ahead with your measurements and calculations. We'll worry about proving it later, if and when it becomes necessary; OK?"

"All right. Thank you."

With a nod to the sheriff, James Cagney turned and retreated in the direction of the roadblock.

The McGuire House — 5:15 p.m.

Alan McGuire arrived home as usual at a quarter past five. His wife's car stood on the concrete pad outside the garage, and he construed this as a good sign: it meant that at least Pam had not driven away who-knew-where again. For the thousandth time in the past twenty four hours, he wondered what was wrong with the child.

He reluctantly corrected himself. She was no longer a child. She was eighteen, a young woman with a mind of her own and, it seemed, problems that were so private that she would not willingly share them with her parents.

He looked at the house. It was a testament to his worldly success; but Alan knew that material wealth has little to do with personal peace, and right now he would have given his last possession to be at peace with his daughter. Wearily, he got out of the car and walked toward the back door.

Louise was setting the table for supper. "How's Pam?" he asked quietly.

There was no sign of their daughter.

"She's in her room. She went out early this afternoon and came back about an hour and a half later. She went straight up to her room and I haven't seen her since."

"Do you think I should go up and try to talk to her?"

"I don't think it would do any good. The Lord only knows what's got into that girl, because I certainly don't. Anyway, supper will be ready in about five minutes; why don't you just go up and tell her?"

"OK," he said, and disappeared, returning a minute later with their daughter in tow.

"Pam was listening to the news reports on the radio," Alan said. "Did you hear?"

"No. What's happened?"

"Tell her, Pam."

"They say a couple of convicts escaped this morning. They were being taken from Replogle jail to Ferguson. There was an accident and both the policemen in the car were killed. The prisoners escaped before anyone found the wreck. They took the policemen's guns and some of their clothes. It sounds like the accident wasn't too far away, maybe twenty five miles, up in the northern part of the county. The police are searching, but they haven't found any sign of them yet."

"Mercy! Well, I hope they don't get this far."

"Shouldn't think so," said Alan. "Twenty five miles is a good long walk, and in any case there's nothing much for them in this direction. My guess is that they'll be making for Greenminster; that's the closest town of any size. Now, how's that meal coming along? Need any help?"

They chatted about the news over dinner, and Alan and Louise were both quietly pleased to see that their daughter seemed to be taking a more active interest in things.

"Would you like to come to church with us this evening, dear? It's prayer meeting night," said her mother when they got up from the table.

Pam shook her head. "No. I think I'll just stay home, if that's all right. Maybe I'll watch some television, take a bath, wash my hair. I'll probably go to bed early."

"All right, dear. Well, I expect we'll be home around nine thirty. We do love you, honey. You do know that, don't you?"

"Yes, Mom. Don't worry about me. I'm sure I'll be fine. I'm just a bit moody, that's all."

Her parents left at a quarter past seven. From her bedroom window, Pam watched them go. She waited five minutes to be sure they hadn't forgotten anything, then she retrieved the doctor's videotape from the drawer of her bedside table. Clutching it tightly and wearing a determined expression she went downstairs to the television in the living room.

The tape lasted about twenty minutes. Just as Dr. Hunter had promised, it contained not a single word of preaching. It had no need: the pictures on the screen and the terse, factual commentary made their point more powerfully than any sermon.

The tape showed a long series of ultrasound pictures of a baby in the womb, growing almost imperceptibly over the course of twenty minutes from a barely discernible blob of tissue until it became a healthy baby boy only hours from birth. What little narrative there was was calm and unemotional. For minutes at a time there was no narrative at all as the pictures alone told the story of the baby's development — which they did with almost palpable force.

Three minutes into the video was a sequence showing the fetus between seven and nine weeks after conception — the age of the baby growing inside Pam's body. A few seconds was enough to change her mind forever, no matter what the consequences.

She realized now that the thing inside her was not simply the blob of inanimate tissue that she had imagined it to be: some kind of growth that could be excised just as one might surgically remove a cyst or tumor. The jerky black and white pictures on the screen abolished that comfortable fantasy for ever.

She watched the video through to its conclusion, although her mind was already made up. The only color pictures came at the end of the video, taken moments after the baby's birth. Its cries filled the hospital birthing room while the mother smiled and exhaustedly reached out for the newborn infant. The picture froze as she clasped the baby to her breast, then it faded slowly away.

A caption appeared: "The End...." The words dissolved, to be replaced by new ones: "...and the Beginning."

The words stayed on the screen for several seconds before dissolving to blackness. The baby's cries died away to nothing, and the tape ended. Pam's sobs filled the room.

Eventually, she found the strength to pray.

Lord, thank You for this video. And give me the strength to hold to my decision and to be a good mother to my child. Oh! Lord! Please, please, let it be healthy, and show me how to love it properly.

She opened her tear-filled eyes, turned off the television and ejected the tape.

Friday

Hill County — 2 a.m.

The last of the clouds dissipated in the warm night air as the fugitives slept. The men had collapsed, exhausted and hungry, at around ten in the evening, when the darkness made it difficult to find a path through the close-packed trees without making a noise. They stopped at the bottom of a hill near a brook at which they slaked their thirst before falling asleep on the leaf-padded ground.

While they slept, the last of the clouds dispersed and the summer stars shone forth bright and steady in the still air.

David Williamson wondered what had woken him. For perhaps thirty seconds he did not move, wondering if there had been a noise and, if so, whether it was natural or manmade. Would the authorities be out searching for them at night? He didn't think so, but there was no way to be certain.

The occasional frog sounded a forlorn and solitary cry into the darkness of the night, but there were no other sounds.

Some small animal began to snuffle around nearby. Perhaps it was this animal — a raccoon? a skunk? — that had wakened him.

He tried to roll over on the loamy earth. His muscles knotted painfully and he almost cried out at a sudden spasm in his side. He rubbed his muscles for a while, looking up through the branches at the brilliant stars overhead. There was no sign of a moon. He wondered if it would rise later. It would not be easy to move in the dark; they would need some moonlight if they were to go much farther before dawn.

He wondered how far they had come. They had been moving almost continuously for perhaps ten hours. The terrain did not make for rapid progress, though. Perhaps they had made as much as four miles per hour. By this reckoning, then, they might already be forty miles from the scene of the accident. Maybe thirty miles was more likely.

The calculation cheered him. He doubted that the police were looking for them this far away. Late in the afternoon they had seen the dot of a helicopter hovering miles away to the south. It had turned and moved farther away, its sound too distant to be heard, but they had shared a fear that it would turn north and come seeking them, methodically tracking overhead, searching every inch of ground for evidence of the fugitives. The canopy of greenery was not quite complete, and they could not be certain of remaining unseen if a helicopter flew overhead.

But their fears had not been realized. They had seen no other sign of the helicopter and, as darkness fell, they had relaxed in the knowledge that they were now probably safe, at least until the morning.

He tried to figure out what day of the week it was. Friday, he eventually decided. If they could get through the next day, maybe the search would be less intense over the weekend.

He tried to move again. Using the trunk a tree for support, he got to his feet. He rubbed and stretched to restore his circulation, then walked out into a small clearing.

Duke McLaughlin slumbered on, occasionally emitting a half-formed grunt of a snore. Williamson listened intently. His movements, quiet though they were, must have frightened the snuffling creature, for he could no longer hear it. The occasional sound of a frog still carried on the still air. The brook, not far away, was nearly silent. Sporadic fireflies flashed momentarily around him, then were swallowed by the shadowed darkness of the night. No movement of the wind disturbed the leaf-covered branches of the trees. They stood silently, creating a sieved canopy everywhere but over the small clearing in which he was standing. The night sky shone with a majestic splendor.

He contemplated the panoply of stars.

The last time he had seen them this brightly must have been... when? On that trip to Wyoming... which was... how long ago? Seven? No, eight years ago now. The realization of how many years had passed since that vacation gripped him with a physical chill. He shivered despite the sultry warmth of the night.

Eight years ago.

Late July it had been, just as it was now. Perhaps tonight was the very anniversary of that evening when he had woken Derek and Danielle to show them the stars. He remembered offering to take Alice outside as well, and the muffled grunt from the depths of her sleeping bag. He and the children had dressed in warm clothes by the light of a flashlight, and then gone outside to see the glorious majesty of the night sky as it was meant to be seen, undiluted by the aura of artificial lighting that accompanied civilization wherever it reached.

He remembered walking with the children to the shore of a lake. The air had been biting cold even though it was midsummer: a chill wind had drifted silently across the water and lazily through their parkas.

They had not stayed outside for long. Perhaps only five minutes, although the memory had been etched into his brain as if they had stood there for years. He had pointed out the summer constellations and the planets — which planets had been visible? He tried to remember. Jupiter and Mars, he thought. He found it oddly annoying that he could not be certain — and the bejewelled dusty haze of the Milky Way.

Danielle, he remembered, had stood next to him, her arm around his leg for warmth and protection against imagined terrors of the night. Derek he had held in his arms, but even so it had been Derek who had complained first of the cold. Derek could not have been more than five years old. Danielle must have been seven, nearly eight. If they were still alive that would make them, what? — he found the calculation suddenly difficult — thirteen and fifteen, nearly sixteen.

Sixteen.

He tried to remember himself at that age. Without thinking, he turned to face the north, toward the place where, not too far from this very spot, he had grown up.

Sixteen.

At that age, his parents had still been alive, before the twin terrors of heart attack and cancer had claimed them, his beseeching prayers falling on the deaf ears of a powerless god who, most emphatically, deserved only a small "g".

But at sixteen, all that had lain unsuspected in the future. At sixteen he was still at Arborville High School, and unsure how he measured up academically to others of his own age.

He knew that his future most likely lay in college, even though he had no chance of any kind of an athletic scholarship. Perhaps if he had grown up in a northern state things would have been different, for he had lately — was that right? Yes, he had just turned fifteen when the discovery had come — he had lately developed a surprising talent for hockey, but such a talent was looked at with condescending amusement in warm southern states. Skating ability was an interesting anomaly, but hardly a passport to college.

But academically he had been without peer. At sixteen he was just beginning to realize that while even the most intelligent of his classmates was beginning to struggle with math and the sciences, he was sailing through the work almost without effort.

And so it had continued for the next several years. College on a full academic scholarship had replaced Arborville High School. Unlike many of the freshmen, he had known exactly what he wanted to study. He began the prerequisites for his chosen field of astronomy at the start of his first semester and had completed them before the first year was out. He graduated in four years, and would have done so even earlier if his life had not been unbalanced, first by his father's fatal heart attack, and then, less than six months later, by the news that his mother had only a few months to live before the cancer that riddled her body would claim her.

He had taken a semester off to be with his mother in her last days. Until the day before her death his mother had been lucid, and she had been especially determined that the deaths of both his parents in such a short space of time should not cause David to waver in his faith.

Guiltily, David had lived the only lie of his adult life in those last few days, for his faith was already reduced to a dessicated shadow. The death of his father had killed it; only its remains clung to him like a marcescent leaf hanging on a deciduous tree as winter advanced, awaiting only a breath of wind to cause its fall. His mother's death provided that breath, and his faith fell away, leaving only a cicatrice in his memory, a scar that soon became unmourned and unnoticed as he returned to college and tried to pull his life together.

Alice had entered his life the following semester. They met for the first time at the ice arena one Saturday afternoon.

David was by now a senior, in his final year and making up for the lost semester so that he would graduate on schedule. He had little time (and no inclination) to do much except study. But twice a week he worked out for ninety minutes at the ice rink, where he punished his body with sprints, sudden stops, quirky changes in direction and, occasionally, painfully hard falls.

As he worked out that afternoon it would have been impossible not to notice the newcomer, a fresh-faced girl wearing a red sweater and tight jeans that looked as if they had been molded to her contours, practicing figures in one corner.

The ice was relatively empty, no doubt because of the football game that was taking place across campus. David counted fifteen other skaters. Seven of these were male, every one of whom was clearly distracted by the co-ed practicing in the corner.

David had no particular feelings about the woman other than that she was undoubtedly a very pleasant addition to the landscape. He barely noticed that she was also a talented figure skater.

She left the ice early, but returned five minutes later having exchanged her figure skates for hockey skates. She stepped on to the ice and blasted down the rink dribbling an imaginary puck with an assurance and at a speed that made it obvious that this was something she had done many times before.

He watched as she closed on the barrier at the far end of the rink at full speed, and for a dreadful, horrifying moment, David was certain that she had made a mistake and was going to collide with the barrier; but at the last instant, she leaned over so far that she seemed almost horizontal and without breaking stride followed the curve of the rink in a series of powerful crossovers.

He applauded her; she looked across the ice and threw him a smile he would never forget.

She joined David, and they skated and chatted together for the last ten minutes of the session.

Two years later, a year into David's doctorate, they married.

It was Alice who brought him back to God. She had no explanation for the early deaths of his parents, but in his new-found happiness he found a warmth and comfort that allowed him to forgive God for what He had done. His faith was renewed, and he entered into the happiest years of his life.

After obtaining his doctorate, David was appointed to a tenure-track position at the State University of Virginia as an assistant professor of astronomy in the physics department. While in Virginia, his daughter Danielle was born.

While Danielle was still a toddler, he accepted a promotion to become an associate professor at the University of Trenton in Trenton, Mississippi. They moved. Alice was by now pregnant with Derek, and, pleased with the low cost of living in Mississippi, they decided that David's small inheritance, combined with the money he received from the university, would allow Alice to stay at home with the children during their formative years.

In Trenton, they began to put down real roots. They found a small church pastored by a man who truly loved every member of his congregation. Their son, Derek, was born. They bought their first house.

Life had been perfect.

Even at the time, some niggling part of him had told him that it was all too good to last, but in his darkest nightmares he could not have credited the sheer malevolence of the way in which it would all end. Poor school grades by the children; the kids getting in with a "bad lot"; even such a terrifying prospect as his wife turning to alcohol (or a lover) in her boredom now that the children were in school: all these were prospects that his imagination had conjured for him, and all were plausible ways in which his happiness might be shattered.

But the years passed and nothing happened.

Danielle and Derek both excelled in school. Danielle was moved into the Talented and Gifted program as soon as she was eligible, and Derek gave every indication that he would follow as soon as he was old enough. Although Alice had given up skating with the move to Trenton, she now satisfied a long-held ambition by beginning to write a mystery novel set in the world of professional figure skating.

Life was as close to perfect as David Williamson could imagine.

The car crash had killed all three of them.

"They died immediately," the coroner had said. "They never knew what hit them. They felt no pain, no awareness that anything was happening at all."

The man, David decided, was probably lying.

He had left home that morning just as he had done a thousand times before, never giving a moment's thought to the possibility that he was seeing the face of his beloved wife for the last time as she kissed him goodbye, that this was the last time he would fight to extract kisses from the children as they rushed around trying to find everything they needed for school.

He paid no attention to these things, they were so commonplace. Afterwards, he tried to remember the details, but it was impossible. Even such simple memories as what clothes they were wearing escaped him. It had been a morning just like all the others, absolutely nothing memorable about it at all. Except that it was the *last* morning.

The police had strongly advised him not to look at the bodies. They were, as the police physician delicately put it, "greatly disfigured."

There was no question of him needing to identify them. The car was his wife's; they had been hit only quarter of a mile from school; his wife's purse and the children's backpacks had escaped the crash virtually undamaged; Alice and Danielle's teeth matched their dental records.

There were several eyewitnesses and, in the manner of eyewitnesses everywhere, their stories differed in detail, but the important points were agreed by everyone.

Alice had been driving the children to school (some said she was breaking the speed limit, others not; David doubted it; they were not running late, and Alice rarely exceeded the limit even when she was in a hurry). Roughly a quarter of a mile from the gates, she approached the "school zone" signs.

A large truck laden with wood from a builders' merchant began to accelerate away from the school zone. The car and the truck were almost passing one another when a dog, a large mastiff, bounded into the road in front of Alice.

Perhaps, the police officer had said, things would have been different if the dog had been a small breed, but the natural reaction when confronted with a sudden large animal in one's path is to try to avoid it. This was exactly what Alice had tried to do. The car had swerved to the left, the screech of tires clearly remembered by several of the witnesses. The car had slammed into the front of the accelerating truck.

And so David's life had ended.

The deaths of his parents had embittered him deeply toward God, and it was only the love and patience of his wife that had healed that wound. Now, with the sudden death of his wife and children because of the irresponsible behavior of a single individual who had slipped her dog off its leash — "How could I have known he was going to do that? He's never done anything like it before. He must have seen something. Maybe the children were encouraging him." — his spiritual and emotional resources were crushed by the mælstrom that overwhelmed him.

This time, instead of moving away from God, he moved away from everything.

For the first week or so, he seemed little altered except for the distracted air that seemed to envelop him and his thoughts. People who tried to talk to him would discover that he was not listening, and seemed unaware even of their presence.

Then, about ten days after the accident, he failed to show up for work. He also failed to appear the next day, and the day afterward.

The department head tried to call David, but the phone went unanswered. Worried, he advised the faculty dean of David's absence. Dean Prothero waited one more day before he too tried to call David at home. He received the disturbing news that the number had been disconnected.

Concerned for the mental state of one of the most highly regarded members of Trenton's faculty, Dean Prothero drove the five miles to David's house.

David lived in a nondescript middle class neighborhood of well-built semi-custom homes. The neighborhood had been built some thirty years earlier, giving time for the trees to grow and the first visible signs of decay to appear in those houses that had not been maintained.

The Williamson home was partially obscured by tall hickories, but it was clear that the house was carefully looked after: it had received a coat of paint sometime in the not-very-distant past, and there were no obvious signs of neglect, except that the grass was a shade too long and here and there weeds were making tentative appearances in an otherwise immaculate flower bed.

The dean walked up the path and rang the doorbell.

For a while, he thought no one was at home, and he was just beginning to wonder what he might do next when, after the third ring and just as he was on the point of turning away, the door opened.

The man who opened the door stank, quite literally. He seemed not to have changed his clothes in several days. The odor that escaped the house through the doorway suggested that the windows were closed and had been in that state for some time. The man's clothes hung on him like a tatterdemalion; wispy red hairs on his chest were exposed by the unfastened buttons of his shirt, and his rumpled pants gave every impression of having been slept in not once but several times. The man sported several days' growth of beard; his eyes seemed simultaneously both vacant and hunted.

Obviously, this specter had to be David Williamson, although the dean arrived at that conclusion solely because there was no one else it could be, not because any aspect of the man now before him brought the associate professor to mind.

David gazed blankly at the dean.

"Professor Williamson?" the dean said.

The professor did not respond.

"May I come in, please?"

This at least elicited a reaction. Williamson moved slightly, blocking the doorway as if he was afraid that the dean intended to force his way inside.

"Do I know you?" Williamson slowly asked, with the distracted air of someone whose thoughts were far away.

"I'm Dean Prothero, from the Faculty of Science at the university."

"I resign."

Williamson took a step backward, preparing to closing the door.

"No, wait," the dean interjected. "Please, let's talk."

Williamson shook his head slightly, no more than an inch.

"Go away," he said. He repeated, "I resign."

The dean put out his hand to stop the door from closing, but Williamson simply leaned heavily against the door and forced it closed. Dean Prothero heard the sound of a dead bolt being thrown.

He tried the doorbell several times, but there was no response.

That was the last contact David Williamson had with the university. Indeed, it was the last known contact he had with anybody for a long, long time.

The weeds grew up around the house and the mail remained uncollected in the mailbox until it overflowed and the post office stopped delivering to the address. Bills, then reminders, then threatening letters remained unanswered until, eventually, the bank that held the mortgage obtained a warrant and, some six months after the visit from Dean Prothero, the lock was forced and an officer of the First State Bank of Trenton, Mississippi entered the house accompanied by a police officer and a doctor.

They were expecting the worst — perhaps a body hanging limply from a light fixture, or an inert, fetid form draped over the bed with an empty pill bottle nearby. But instead they found nothing, nothing at all to indicate the whereabouts of David Williamson. They scoured the house from top to bottom, but the only signs of life were the cockroaches in the kitchen and the mold on the food in the refrigerator.

David Williamson had vanished.

Williamson himself, of course, knew nothing of this, just as he knew nothing of the attempts that were made to trace him and, finally, the admission of defeat by all those involved. His house was sold without his knowledge, and the proceeds, after the creditors' liens were taken care of, were placed into his savings account at the First State Bank.

Exactly what had happened after the visit of Dean Prothero was vague even in Williamson's own mind. Indeed, everything that happened after the first shocked sight of the crumpled metal shell that had been Alice's car was vague.

He stayed in the house for a while. Then, one night with a cloudy sky lit by a bright, full moon, he walked out of his home wearing a winter overcoat with $125.69 in cash in one pocket — all the money he could find in the house.

For some reason, he had carefully locked the door behind him, as if he was merely stepping out on an errand and intended to return before long. But he had no such intention. Indeed, he had no intentions of any kind. He had kept the key of the house with him for some time, wearing it on a loop of string around his neck, until one day it had been torn from him in a fight outside a bar somewhere. He was not sure what state the bar was in. Louisiana? Arkansas? He could not even remember what the fight had been about. Booze, he supposed. Not that it mattered.

Nothing mattered.

Replogle — 2:30 a.m.

After lunch, too distracted to make a start on his sermon, George Ellsworth retired to his office, but only to stare unseeingly at the paper on which he had scribbled a few notes. In the kitchen, Mary kept the radio on in case there was more news about the escaped prisoners, and in the study the muffled sound from the radio precluded any chance to concentrate.

Twice Mary came to tell him of developments. The third time, she informed him that Channel 7 was breaking into the afternoon game shows with news from their reporter, Todd Livingstone, at the scene of the wreck. That was the last straw, and the pastor gave up all hope of producing anything worthwhile. He joined his wife in the living room and stayed there until suppertime, dividing his time among doodling on his notepad, looking up apocalyptic verses in his battered Bible, and watching the unfolding news.

By the time that the early evening news came on just before supper, both the police and the local television channels had made progress. The early, blurred pictures of the two convicts had been replaced by recent color photographs. They served only to confirm that one of the men was the man whom George Ellsworth had seen on Wednesday evening. The man who had stood at the rear of the meeting in the jail now stared at him vacantly from the screen. The hollow stare, the rings around the eyes, the thin hair plastered over his scalp, the long, thin face, the protruding cheekbones, the thin, wispy red beard: he recognized them all. The voice-over briefly recited several facts about David Williamson and his crime. The voice spent longer on the other man, Duke McLaughlin, who was evidently a hardened criminal and deemed the more dangerous of the two, although the reporters repeatedly stressed that members of the public were not to approach either man. As yet, there was still no trace of them.

After supper, there was the weekly prayer meeting at the church. Amidst the mundane — the prayers for healing; for jobs; for cars that would not start; for the church; for himself — the pastor almost managed to forget about the fugitives until Tom Murdoch suggested that the group should pray for the men.

The builder led a prayer that the men's hearts would be moved by the Lord, that the fugitives would realize that just as it was impossible to keep running from the enforcers of man-made law, it was impossible to run from the Lord.

George Ellsworth mouthed an "Amen," but his heart was not in it. He felt like he was just going through the motions. He was uncomfortably sure that God wanted something more from him than a mere echoing of the builder's words.

After the prayer meeting the pastor came home and watched the local news before turning in for the night. The only new information was that it was now believed that the police car had been speeding, possibly travelling as fast as seventy miles per hour in the few seconds

64

before the crash. It was conjectured that because of the slick surface of
the road, the driver had been unable to turn in time to meet the sharp
bend at the bottom of the incline. The station weatherwoman explained
in detail a computer-generated animation that prettily demonstrated
the physics of aquaplaning; but no one advanced any explanation for
why the car might have been traveling at such an unsafe speed.

Ellsworth went to bed and tried to sleep. Four hours later, he
dragged himself despairingly from his bed. He padded out of the room
and closed the door quietly. After stopping in the kitchen to pour
himself a glass of orange juice, he made his way to his study.

He slumped in his chair with his head in his hands, and spoke out
loud to the God whom he supposed was in the room with him — even
though he felt just as alone as always.

"All right. I know when I'm beaten. You want me to help this
man Williamson. But what do I pray? What do You want me to do?
I don't know anything about him except that he held up a store at
gunpoint."

God remained stubbornly silent.

Wearily, Ellsworth pulled his Bible across the desk and flipped it
open to a page in the New Testament. His eyes landed on Luke 15:20:

> While he was still a long way off, his father saw him and
> was moved with pity. He ran to the boy, clasped him in his
> arms, and kissed him tenderly.

And at last he knew how he must pray.

Hill County — 2:35 a.m.

David Williamson looked up at the stars.

They were his friends. *The summer sky...,* he thought. *There's Vega;
there's the Andromeda galaxy.* He mentally named the constellations
and the stars as he scanned the heavens.

There, barely visible over an adolescent hickory, was the King of
Planets himself. Jupiter shone forth, identifiable not by the steadiness
of his glare — for tonight all the lights in the sky shone steadily — but
rather by his yellow-white color and, most of all, by his position, for

the planet hung in the sky in the middle of the constellation of Aries, where no star had any right to be.

Williamson gazed at the luminous dot. When he was a boy — how long ago that seemed — it was distant and mysterious, a place of infinite possibilities. In the intervening years, spacecraft had flown past the planet, rudely stripping it of its mystery, replacing it instead with simple, mundane questions: were the bright patches on the dark side auroras or lightning or enormous fires burning in the atmosphere? just how complicated was the planet's enormous magnetic field? was the Great Red Spot an inescapable consequence of atmospheric dynamics? This, he supposed, was the price of progress. But it was a pity nevertheless. Some things should remain mysteries.

He tore his mind forcefully from the distant planet. Jupiter belonged to his old life and a different time — a time when he had believed that life had a purpose, when the way electrons moved in a gigantic magnetic field four hundred million miles away had seemed important.

A noise startled him.

Duke McLaughlin groaned and slowly clambered to his feet. Duke shambled unsteadily across the clearing towards David.

"Hear something?" Duke asked.

"Not really. Just couldn't sleep."

"Well, maybe we should try to put on a few more miles, although if the moon doesn't come up it's going to be hard work trying to get through this stuff." He vaguely indicated the hardwood forest around them.

"All right. Let's get going then."

Without another glance at the sky, David Williamson turned and walked into the forest.

Central Hill County — 8:10 a.m.

The sound of a sharp *crack!* rent the air and shocked the convicts awake. Both of them knew instantly that they had not imagined the sound: echoes of the report came reverberating back from the surrounding hills.

David's memories of the night before flooded back.

They had tried to press on, but had given up after a couple of hours, having travelled no more than three or four miles in the darkness. The moon had not risen, and although the light of Jupiter and the stars had been enough to convert everything from blackness into a spectrum of silvery grays, it was still too difficult to spot the paths through the trees. Progress was slow and noisy. After a while, Duke had called a halt and the two of them had stretched out to take several more hours' sleep, with the intent of moving on when it was light.

They must have been more tired than they had thought. It was now full daylight, although a glance at Deputy Baker's wristwatch told David that it was still early. His stomach told him that whatever the watch said, it was time for food.

A second report came.

Now that they were awake and alert, there could be no mistaking the sound.

"Gunshot!" Duke exclaimed as the echoes came back from the hills.

They scrambled to their feet and looked around, trying to locate the source.

A third shot. Surrounded by trees, it was hard to be sure of anything, but one thing was certain: the shots were coming from not far away: the sharp, distinct crack of each report was unmuffled by distance.

Duke nodded and pointed through the trees, down the hill. David nodded in agreement.

Moving slowly, the two began to thread their way downhill.

They found what they were looking for at the bottom of the hill. A ruined stone cottage stood in a grassy meadow. Looking out from behind the trees at the edge of the meadow they could see a figure standing with its back to them. The figure had a gun in its hand, and was aiming at a target in the shape of a man held up by an invisible support between two tall stacks of old tires.

A shot rang out, followed almost immediately by a tinny *clang*. Smoke eddied from the gun. The shooter's arms had been jerked by the recoil; slowly, he straightened his arm and took aim once more along the gun sight. Another shot came, followed by the same sequence of a tinny clang and smoke.

The figure lowered his arms and walked slowly towards the target.

The shooter was a man in his late thirties or early forties, wearing jeans and a long-sleeved flannel shirt. His hair was dark, with a badger's stripe of gray visible in a flash near the crown. A pair of ear protectors were clamped over his head.

Not far away David saw a beat-up, rust-spotted, olive-green Buick parked on a dirt road that ended a few feet short of the ruined house.

The man reached the target, inspected it, then turned to retrace his steps, fiddling with the gun as he did so.

The fugitives withdrew further into the protection of the trees, although the man seemed to be fully occupied with the pistol. As he came closer, David could see that the man was placing a new magazine in the weapon.

A movement at the fringe of his vision caught David's eye. Turning, he saw that Duke had removed his pistol from his belt and flicked off the safety catch.

In answer to his querying look Duke said, "That car would be useful, and so would his clothes."

A shot rang out. The man had resumed his target practice.

"There were nine shots last time," Duke said. "We'll wait until he's emptied the magazine. No point in taking chances."

They waited, counting slowly. The shots came steadily, about twenty seconds apart. When the man had fired his seventh shot, Duke began to move cautiously forward. By the time the eighth shot came, he was standing no more than ten feet behind the man.

David edged forward and watched, holding his breath. Suddenly, he knew that something was wrong. The man had inclined his head slightly and seemed to have lost interest in his target practice. He seemed to be looking at the ground where... a shadow! Duke's shadow darkened the grass, unmistakable.

Before Williamson could shout a warning, the man with the pistol span around and in a split second adjusted his aim so that his gun pointed directly at Duke's heart.

The man looked at Duke for what seemed an age. His eyes flickered over Duke's clothes, rested momentarily on the gun partly raised by his side, and then returned to his face.

"Drop the gun, or I'll shoot," the man said.

He lifted one hand and removed the ear protectors, letting them fall to the ground.

The man's words hung in the air, waiting for some sort of a response, but for several seconds nothing happened.

When he finally spoke, Duke's voice held both contempt and confidence.

"I think that's extremely unlikely. Could you really shoot a human being? I doubt it. And in any case, you have only one bullet left and there's two of us."

"Wha..." the man began, and David took his cue, stepping out into the light.

As the man's eyes flickered towards him, there was just enough time for him to register that he had made a mistake.

A shot exploded.

The report momentarily stunned David. By the time he recovered, three seconds had elapsed and the situation before him had changed dramatically. The man whose target practice they had disturbed was clutching his right shoulder, from which a red stain was spreading into the flannel of his shirt. His gun was already on the ground, and Duke was standing next to him, the barrel of his gun pressing against the man's stomach.

"Pick up the gun, David," Duke said.

Automatically, David obeyed. He lifted the gun from where it had fallen. It looked remarkably similar to the ones that he and McLaughlin were carrying. He tugged his gun from his belt and compared the weapons. They were identical.

"You killed two cops. I suppose now you're going to kill a third."

The man spoke with no fear in his voice, merely an unmistakable antagonism. He continued, "My name is Bill Brewer. I'm a sheriff's deputy, and I was just getting in some practice before going on duty later this morning."

David interrupted: "What do you mean: 'You killed two cops'? We haven't killed anybody."

"Be quiet!" Duke warned him.

Brewer ignored them both.

"You're the two escaped prisoners, I'd recognize you from the clothing you took from those cops even if I hadn't seen your photos so many times yesterday that I'm sick of them. You killed two cops when you escaped, as you well know. I suppose you think your chance to kill another one makes this your lucky day."

David looked first at Brewer and then at Duke.

"But we didn't kill those cops...."

"Yeah," said Duke, "like they'll take our word for it. Sure, they're going to admit that a crazy cop was driving too fast and slammed his car into a tree without any help from us. Sure, they'll believe we walked away unscathed from a crash that killed two cops. Sure, they'll be understanding when we tell them we're just two guys who happened to grasp an opportunity when it was presented."

He spat emphatically on the ground, then turned towards the off-duty policeman.

"OK, Brewer. There's good news and there's bad news. The good news is that we're going to treat you just like we treated the other cops. Which means, like Williamson here says, that we're just going to walk away from you after we've stripped you of anything we want. The bad news is that we're taking your car."

Brewer looked at him without speaking, his face hard and suspicious.

Duke raised an arm and pushed against Brewer's shoulder where it was still bleeding. Brewer staggered and cried out in pain.

"Understand?"

Brewer nodded. "Yeah, I get it," he grunted.

He clutched his shoulder where McLaughlin had shoved it.

"All right. That's better, pig. Now, lie down on the grass. Your shirt is no good to us, but we'll take your pants, shoes and socks."

It took but two minutes to relieve Deputy Brewer of the items, along with his billfold. The shoes fit McLaughlin; the other items they carried to the policeman's car.

From the place where he was lying on the grass, Brewer watched them nervously. The wound on his shoulder hurt but it had stopped bleeding, and it was clear to him now that, unpleasant though the next few hours were likely to be, he was going to live through them. He breathed a silent prayer of thanks.

The fugitives returned for one last look.

"OK, Brewer," Duke said, waving the gun, "tell us where we are, what roads are around here, and where the nearest towns are."

"How do you know you can trust me to tell the truth?" Brewer asked.

"Because we just spared your life. You owe us. And because we have your billfold. We know where you live. You have a family?"

70

Brewer nodded.

"That's how I know you won't lie."

Brewer explained the geography of the area. The closest house was nearly two miles away. The dirt track on which the car stood meandered for nearly half a mile through the forest before joining County Road 12.

If they turned right on County Road 12, they would reach, after about two miles, the hamlet of Georgestown, which had about a dozen houses. On the far side of Georgestown the road joined State Highway 43, which led to the town of Greenminster, about fifteen miles away.

If they turned left when they reached County Road 12, they would soon pass a commercial antenna installation on a hill to their right, but although there were huts for the transmitters, no one lived there. A bit farther on, scattered houses were hidden in the trees some distance back from the road. These houses continued at sporadic intervals until the road reached Parlerville, maybe three miles past the transmitters.

Parlerville was similar to Georgestown, except that it was even smaller. County Road 12 continued in this way for perhaps another twenty miles, passing though villages every few miles, with occasional turnoffs, until it finally reached Possum, a real, honest-to-goodness town counting a supermarket and a liquor store among its amenities.

The two convicts absorbed the information silently. When Brewer had concluded, McLaughlin waved his pistol in the policeman's face.

"I'll give you one warning: if you've lied at all, we won't rest till we've found you."

Without waiting for a response, he turned away and led Williamson to the car.

McLaughlin took the driver's seat. As Williamson slipped the seat belt over his shoulder, he asked McLaughlin, "Are we just going to leave him here?"

"Sure, why not? It's only a couple of miles' walk to civilization. He's not going to die from that wound. An hour from now, he'll have alerted every cop in the state. I was tempted to slow him down forever but, I don't know... killing a cop in cold blood... I guess maybe you were right yesterday: that's going too far. We'll just try to get as far away as possible before he gets to a phone."

He started the car and they began to bounce down the track.

David inspected the car. It was perhaps a decade old, and every year showed. The olive-green body was covered in dents, and rust was evident in several places. Inside, the car was a disorganized mélange of rural junk. On the rear seat and in the space behind the front seats were stuffed fishing tackle, a paddle for a canoe, and assorted coils of rope and wire. The front part of the car was relatively clear of such rubbish, although a layer of dust and grime seemed to cover everything except the driver's seat. The plastic of the dash was sun-cracked, and there was a deep craze in one corner of the windshield. As they bounced down the track, the needle of the tachometer flickered crazily between 500 and 4,000 rpm, although the engine was running smoothly enough.

Underneath the center of the dash, below the usual radio and cassette player, a small black police-band transceiver winked into life. McLaughlin turned up the volume. No sound came from the radio.

"Busted," he said in disgust.

Williamson leaned over and depressed a switch on the side of the microphone. As he released the switch there was a short burst of static from the radio, then silence.

"No, it's working. It's FM. It's just the squelch circuit."

McLaughlin looked at him speculatively. Williamson was explaining the radio, but McLaughlin wasn't listening: he was too busy coming to terms with the realization that since yesterday the vacant gaze with which Williamson habitually looked out at the world was gone, and in its place was something completely unexpected: animated intelligence.

It was obvious that Williamson knew exactly what he was talking about, although it was just so much gobbledegook to McLaughlin.

"Squelch," Williamson was saying, "is a common feature in little FM transceivers like this. It means that the radio stays silent until someone comes on the channel to speak. There's no background hiss to distract you."

As if to confirm his words, the radio suddenly squawked into life.

"Boss just arrived at the scene."

"10-4."

There was a quarter-second burst of background noise, then the radio fell silent once again.

"How come you know about radios?" McLaughlin asked, still trying to come to terms with a suddenly-intelligent David Williamson.

72

Williamson paused for a moment, then said, "I have a Ph.D. in astronomy. My particular area of expertise is radio astronomy."

McLaughlin let loose a four-letter expletive, followed by a roar of laughter.

"A Ph.D. in radio astronomy? And all this time we thought you was effing retarded. You serious? A Ph.D? Don't that mean you're like a doctor or something?"

"'Fraid so. Yes, it does."

McLaughlin chuckled loudly and shook his head, swearing softly to himself. He was still laughing two minutes later when they reached the road.

The McGuire House — 10:30 a.m.

Louise McGuire looked up at the old-style clock with its large, easy-to-see white hands and numerals against a red plastic face. Ten thirty. Not too early to take a break for midmorning coffee. She gave the dough one final squeeze, then lifted the pliant, heavy ball and dropped it into a large china bowl. She moved to the kitchen sink, fastidiously scrubbed her hands free of dough, wetted a towel, and draped it over the bowl on the counter, where it basked in the warmth of the sun.

The catharsis of kneading over, the anxious bile once more rose in her stomach.

Louise wondered what was still worrying Pam. Her initial theory that Pam wanted to marry Craig and was anxious about receiving her parents' approval was no longer tenable, for Louise had made it clear that their approval could be taken for granted. Now she was wondering if the two had had an argument, perhaps even one fatal to their relationship, for, apart from that one inexplicable occasion when Pam had met with Craig on Wednesday, the two had been unusually uncommunicative with one another for several days now.

Pam was upstairs in her bedroom, where she had been all morning.

Ever since she had been a small girl, Pam's method of dealing with problems had been to retire to her room, close the door and simply stare out the window until either a solution presented itself or physical needs forced her to move. Louise was sure that that was where Pam was now: leaning against the wide windowsill, staring outside, her thoughts far away. But what was she worried about?

Louise made coffee and drank it thoughtfully. She decided that enough was enough: it was time for Pam to share whatever was bothering her.

With a heavy sigh, Louise lifted herself from the chair and made her way upstairs.

She stopped outside Pam's door and knocked lightly.

Pam called, "Come in."

The room was as tidy as always: bed made, dirty clothes in the hamper next to the closet, books on the shelves, except for the Bible on the bedside table. Pam was leaning on the windowsill. She turned to look at her mother as she entered the room.

Louise closed the door, symbolically cutting them off from the rest of the world. She looked at Pam. Her daughter's eyes were red and looked tired.

Louise sat on the bed and patted the duvet. "Come here, Pam. There's something I want to say."

Pam joined her mother on the bed. She looked down at the carpet, not meeting her mother's eyes.

"Come on, honey. I don't know what the matter is, but you can't go on like this. If you won't tell me, I hope you've at least shared your troubles with the Lord."

Pam shook her head.

"Please don't be silly, Pam. You can't keep it bottled up. Don't you know that your father and I love you unconditionally? There's nothing you could possibly do, no kind of trouble you could be in, that could stop us from loving you. If there's anything we can do to help, please tell me."

She waited, but there was no discernible reaction from her daughter.

She continued, "And if you don't trust us, then please trust the Lord. You know that He understands. You remember the shepherd's psalm, don't you? 'Yeah, though I walk through the Valley of the Shadow of Death, Thou art with me.' If He'll be with you even when death comes for you, surely you know He can be trusted to carry you through whatever it is that's troubling you now."

She put her arm around her daughter's shoulder, and something inside Pam collapsed.

Still looking at the ground, she blurted, "Mom, I'm pregnant."

She thrust her bare arm forward. It took a moment for Louise to understand what her daughter meant by the gesture. Then she realized: the thin golden chastity chain that Alan had given her when she was eleven was no longer around her wrist.

The air in the room seemed suddenly heavy. There was a long silence.

Inside Louise McGuire's head, a silent prayer flew heavenward: *Lord, do I tell her?*

With her right arm still around her daughter's shoulder, she gave Pam's knee a light squeeze with her left hand.

When Louise spoke, there was no trace of condemnation in her voice. There was not even an "Are you sure?" Instead, Pam's mother said quietly, "Come on, honey, it's not the end of the world, although I expect you think it is right now. Come downstairs with me. I'll make some coffee, and then I think you need to hear some family history."

Pam had thought that she was prepared for anything: speechless horror; judgmental silence; an uncomprehending, "Oh, Pam! How could you?"; even — although considerably less likely — "You stay right here. I'm going to call your father and then you're going to tell him everything," or perhaps even "Pam! Don't you know anything about birth control?" — any of these might have been a reasonable response to the bombshell she had just dropped.

Instead of these there was something she had never anticipated: a strange air of unconcern, as if she had confessed to burning the toast instead of indulging in sexual intercourse outside the sacred bounds of marriage, with this most tragic of consequences. She had betrayed her parents' trust, and ruined her life in the process. How could her mother not understand that?

She felt her mother draw away, but it was not in condemnation, it was simply to lift herself from the bed. Louise walked to the door and as Pam's eyes followed her, she thought that her mother was the most collected and serene person she had ever seen. Pam wondered if perhaps her mother had misheard or somehow failed to understand her confession.

"Mom, did you hear me? I'm pregnant."

"Yes, dear, and sitting here mooning over the fact for hours and days on end won't change a thing. So come along downstairs and, like I said, let me tell you some family history. You need to hear it."

Pam followed her mother downstairs, too astonished to think clearly.

Eight minutes later, the sense of unreality still had not lifted. Pam was seated on the sofa in the living room, a mug of coffee on the table in front of her. Her mother settled in a chair on the opposite side of the table.

Louise said, "Well, Pam. I don't really know how to begin. Over the years, I guess we've never spoken much about the family. How much do you know?"

The question puzzled Pam. What was her mother about to tell her? That Pam was adopted? Or that Alan McGuire was not her father? Neither of these seemed at all likely; but neither, she supposed, was completely impossible. Of one thing she was sure: her father and her mother had been married for several years before she was born, so there was no questioning her legitimacy. Not that her evangelical parents could ever have had a child out of wedlock. Not like her.

"What do you mean?" she asked before she could carry that thought any further.

"Well, dear, you must have wondered some about our family history. After all, you're eighteen now, yet we've never told you very much."

This was true, although she had assumed until recently that all families were like her own, that the past was something that families never really discussed. She remembered how surprised she had been when Craig had seemed fully informed about the details of the lives of a bevy of aunts, uncles, cousins and grandparents, and how he had been surprised in turn that she knew so little even about her parents.

She shrugged. "I don't know. I've never really thought about it very much."

"Well, dear. I'm going to tell you how I met your father."

"OK," Pam nodded, still puzzled.

And Louise McGuire began her story.

Louise McGuire, bastion of the church, sometime campaigner against the twin devils of alcohol and cosmetics, loving wife of Alan and mother of Pamela, had been born under very different circumstances. She was born Louise Brown in 1947 in Parsimony, Mississippi, the fifth of seven children — the two youngest of whom died in infancy — and the only daughter of the brood.

Her father Gideon worked long days on a nearby farm and was rarely seen in the four-room, tin-roof, wooden shack that served as the family home. Her father was a figure of whom she had few detailed memories, remembering instead a miasmic montage of events that probably occurred over a span of a dozen or more years but which had somehow melded in her mind. She never saw her father during the week. He left the house before she was awake and returned long after she was in bed.

She remembered times when she had still been awake when he came home, or perhaps it was simply that he had woken her with his uncaring noises. She recollected shouting, and the sound of things being thrown, although rarely breaking — they were too poor to afford china, which in any case would have lasted only the briefest of intervals under her father's (and, later, her brothers') tantrums. They ate off wooden plates, using rusted "stainless steel" implements, which were sturdy and could (and did) survive many smashings against walls and floors with little visible damage.

Associated with these memories was the sound of her mother sobbing or, even worse, noises that she only later understood as her father having his way with her mother.

Even at weekends her father was rarely home, preferring to spend his time in the company of other men who worked on the farm, all living more or less the same squalid life as his own, spending what little money they had on hard liquor to while away the boredom between paydays.

Like her four brothers, she began to attend the local public school at the age of six. Unlike them, she learned later that she had made an immediate positive impression on her teachers. Years later, one of the teachers told her that they had known from the beginning that she was "salvable" — "that means we knew we could make something of you, honey," the teacher explained.

Looking back on it, she now knew that her mother must have protected her from the worst excesses of her father and brothers in those early years. She remembered her mother shouting at the boys to be quiet so Louise could concentrate on her homework. It never crossed her mind to wonder why her brothers never seemed to have any homework; even less did she notice that they never asked Mom any questions related to schoolwork.

After all, they were boys, and they already knew what they were going to do when they grew up: they would work on the farm like their father and his father before him. The only exception was Daniel, the youngest of her siblings, who had told her his great secret when she was nine and he was eleven: one day he was going to run away and earn his fortune in one of the cities up north.

"That's where rich people are", he said simply, "and I want to be rich."

When she was eleven she transferred to junior high with no noticeable change in her life except that, at about the same time, her body underwent a series of frightening changes. Her horror was barely assuaged by her mother's off-hand comment that she was "not to worry because it's just your body getting rid of its bad blood." Try as she might, she found no way to stop the intermittent bleeding. Whatever she did, it seemed like whenever she thought she was better, the bleeding would start again.

Eventually, by some sort of osmosis, she learned the truth, or at least enough of it that she ceased to be concerned about the monthly flows.

By now, her three eldest brothers had left school. Two had married girls already obviously pregnant by some process that Louise did not fully understand. The third, William, was "courting" as her mother called it; in due course he left their house to live with a girl only a year older than Louise herself.

William and Theresa did not bother with the formality of a wedding. He simply walked into the house one day and announced that Theresa was leaving school and that he had found somewhere they could afford to live, which turned out to be a two-room, filthy shack on the outskirts of Parsimony.

William's departure left only Louise and Daniel at home with their rarely present father and their mother, who was by now an ancient woman of forty five with little strength left for fighting.

Daniel stayed on at school much longer than any of his brothers. They had all ended their formal education sometime between their thirteenth and fourteenth birthdays, eager to put the wasted learning behind them and to begin earning money on the farm.

Louise had just turned fifteen and Daniel, fast approaching his seventeenth birthday, was still at school, still sharing with her in snatched moments of privacy his dream of riches, when Louise arrived home one day to find their mother motionless on the floor of the tiny kitchen, already cold.

What followed was a nightmare that Louise's protective mechanisms would not allow her to remember with any clarity.

A short time after her mother's death — Louise was unclear how long after; sometimes she thought as little as a week, other times it seemed like it might have been as long as three months — her father walked into the house one Saturday with a pretty young woman on his arm. He must have been about fifty; the woman who accompanied him was much less than half that. He looked belligerently at Louise and Daniel, who were whiling away the afternoon playing cards, as if he was surprised to find them there.

"This is Marcie Perkins," he said, and Louise suddenly recognized the woman. Marcie had left school four or five years earlier; Louise did not know what she had done in the intervening years. She did know that Marcie couldn't be more than nineteen.

"She's coming to live here," her father continued. "Me and Marcie plan on being married if it works out."

Another pause, and then with no word of warning or apology, he continued, "You all will have to move out. A man can't support his family forever, especially if'n he gets hisself a new wife. I don't reckon to see either of you here past next week. That seems fair, don't it?"

The question was addressed to Marcie, who simply leaned more heavily on her man's arm, smiled deeply into his eyes, and said, "Yes, honey, whatever you say." She gave him a full kiss on the mouth.

Louise's father turned to his children and said, "Now, gitton out o' here, you two. Marcie and me want to be alone together. Ain't that right?" Again, the question was directed at Marcie, who giggled, then dropped her hand and caressed the front of Gideon's pants, which began to show an unmistakable bulge.

Speechless with rage and frustration, Louise stormed out the house. Daniel followed moments later. They stood for a moment on the patch of scrubby ground in front of the only home either of them had ever known. They looked at each other, then Daniel looked back towards the house and made an obscene gesture.

He turned toward Louise and said, "That's it. I'm gone."

And without another word, he stalked away down the street in the direction of the railroad station.

At the time, Louise could not believe that Daniel meant what he had said. After all, although Daniel had been threatening to leave for nearly as long as she could remember, he had made no preparations to do so at this particular moment.

He was dressed lightly, as befitted the early fall weather, and all his possessions, such as they were, were inside the house. He had no money, certainly no bank account (and in any case the local bank was closed on Saturday afternoons), nothing to prepare him in any way for the long journey he had always said he was going to make. But the sight of him stalking away down the street was the very last time that Louise saw Daniel.

She heard from him twice in the succeeding years, in letters that somehow, through a tortuous serious of redirections, eventually found her. The first came from New York, the second from Los Angeles. In both of them, Daniel asserted that he expected to "make some real money very soon." Shortly after the second letter, she received a communication from the Los Angeles Police Department saying that Daniel Joshua Brown, of no fixed abode, had been shot and fatally wounded in an incident believed to be related to a drug transaction.

But all that lay in the future. On this particular Saturday afternoon in 1962, thrown out of her home and with no place to go, she wandered the streets of Parsimony attracting the attention of the stray dogs and of the men loitering at their numerous gathering places. Several of the men made lewd suggestions that she tried to ignore; each time, the blood rushed to her face and she was thankful (for one of the few times in her life) that her embarrassment was hidden by the color of her skin.

She went home that evening as darkness fell and found the door to what had been her parents' room closed. Muffled sounds came from the far side. There was no sign of Daniel.

She began to cook a meager supper for herself, but she was interrupted after a few minutes by her father, dishevelled, his clothes hastily buttoned, telling her that, "since you'm cooking, you can cook for the three of us. Like I said, Marcie's staying here from now on."

Turning around to return to the bedroom — in which Louise could just see Marcie, naked, sitting up in bed with an unreadable expression on her face — her father glanced back towards the stove and reminded his daughter: "Don't you forget I want you out of here by this time next week. And Dan'l too."

He stalked back into the bedroom and closed the door. His look of greedy expectation was one that Louise could never forget.

The week passed with infinite slowness at the time, but it was all a vague blur now. Her only clear recollection was of an event that occurred on Monday evening.

Louise was watching the television, trying to ignore the sounds that were coming from the bedroom. Even though it was barely eight thirty, her father had been home since seven, an event unheard of in the entire fifteen years of her life. As he staggered in, it was obvious that he was already awash in alcohol.

Louise had been dreading this first weekday evening, wondering how she would be able to ignore the gloating presence of Marcie, but there was no cause for her to have worried. Her father took one drunken look around the room; his eyes settled first on Louise, then moved on as if she were no more than some piece of trash that had been left on the floor, and alighted on his newfound bedmate. His face widened in a grin.

"Ah! Marcie! Bed!" he ordered.

Marcie smiled and obediently rose and walked to the bedroom. Gideon pinched her bottom as she passed. It was a hard pinch, and it must have hurt, but Marcie simply turned and said, "You ol' brute; can't wait, can you?"

"Nah, and neither can you."

Louise's father closed the door behind them.

Louise returned her attention to the television, ignoring the muffled sounds from behind the closed door.

Around half past eight there was a sharp knock on the front door. Louise could not remember the last time anyone had come visiting after dark. She moved uncertainly to open the door.

On the threshold was her teacher, Mrs. Saville.

For a moment, embarrassment for her squalid home swept over Louise; she remained mute, standing with the door open and Mrs. Saville on the doorstep.

81

"Louise, is your father home?" the teacher finally asked.

"Well, er...."

There was a thump from the bedroom.

"That him?"

"Yes, Mrs. Saville. But he's not alone."

"I didn't think he would be, Louise. No matter. There's something that has to be said to that man, and no one else is going to say it and so I'm agoin' to say it now. Louise, do I have your leave to come in?"

Louise stood aside, and her teacher swept past, without stopping for a moment to survey the poverty of Louise's life: the ancient, cracked linoleum with dirt buried deeply in the cracks; walls covered with old, thin paint that was now blotchy and uneven; a rickety table and chair in one corner; chairs and a sofa, none of them with matching coverings, all stained and dirty; no books anywhere; and in one corner the television, its volume now turned down, showing a commercial for underarm deodorant in which athletic young white people were smilingly completing a tennis game without a sign of wetness anywhere on their perfect bodies.

Mrs. Saville passed all this without so much as a glance. She strode to the bedroom door and thumped loudly, then called through the door, "Mister Brown, this is Lavinia Saville, your daughter's teacher, and I'm goin' to stand here and count to five, then I'm a comin' in, so if there's anything in there you don't want me to see, you'd better be hiding it away immediate like. One. Two. Three."

There was the sound of movement and swearing.

"Four. Five."

She turned the handle and went in.

Louise was standing several feet behind her teacher and her view was instantly cut off by the closing of the door. She had only the briefest glimpse of her father pulling on his pants and Marcie still in bed, a yellowed sheet pulled up for the sake of modesty.

Mrs. Saville's voice carried easily through the door.

"Marcie Perkins, there's no need to hide your body from me. And let me tell you that if you was my daughter, you'd be sent home and tanned 'til your hide was so raw you couldn't sit for a week; I don't care how old you are."

Louise heard the beginning of a feeble response from Marcie, but Marcie was steamrollered as Mrs. Saville turned her attention to the real object of her visit.

"Mister Brown, I am ashamed of you, even more so because you don't have the decency to be ashamed of yourself. Yes. Well might you stand there and look at me like that. I declare, this is probably the first time anyone has stood up to you, isn't it? Well, let me tell you, Mr. Brown, I've come here for one reason and one reason only, and that's to try to save your daughter.

"You're obviously either too stupid or too self-centered to know it, but that daughter of yours is something special. If she was a white girl in the Northeast, she'd be thinking of going to Radcliffe or some other of them fancy women's colleges. She's clever, that one is, and she has a real chance of pulling herself out of this dirty, stinking life that you and Marcie and everyone else in this rat-hole of a town seems to regard as normal."

There was the sound of movement.

"Now, just you wait there a minute, I ain't finished with you yet."

But now her father's ire was up. "Oh yes you are, you great black witch. Ain't no woman telling me what to do in my own house. You got two seconds to get outta here otherwise I'm a gonna throw you out and I won't be none too gentle about'n it either."

"Mister...."

Whatever Mrs. Saville was going to say was curtailed by the sharp sound of a powerful slap.

"Get out, or there'll be plenty more."

The door opened and Louise was horrified to see Mrs. Saville, her left eye inflamed, tears roiling down her cheeks, stumble out of the room.

"And stay out," her father yelled.

The teacher made her way past Louise apparently without seeing her. She opened the front door, walked out, and slammed the door behind her.

"And you. Did you put her up to that?" her father shouted at Louise.

She was too terrified to answer.

Her father shook his head. "Naw. You're too stupid. She thought it up all by herself. Well, much good it did her. Or you, either. Remember, out of here by Saturday or I throw you out. Got it?"

Louise nodded dumbly.

"Right. Now, go to bed."

Her father turned and slammed the bedroom door behind him.

Mrs. Saville, for all her bravery, was not up to the task of extending the battle with Gideon Brown. She said nothing to Louise about the encounter all week, and so on Saturday Louise walked to the railroad station and purchased a one-way ticket to the city of Riverbend. It took most of her savings.

The train arrived and Louise boarded with her entire earthly possessions bundled limply into a half-filled cardboard suitcase. The train left Parsimony station on time. Louise closed her eyes and let the tears dribble down her cheeks.

The first week in Riverbend was a nightmare. Louise had no idea what she intended to do there, but with her youthful naïveté, spurred on perhaps by her brother Daniel's propaganda about the wealth to be found in cities, she had assumed that it would be easy to make a living.

For four days she walked the streets, enquiring in hotels and stores if there was any work.

Her money, little enough on Saturday, by Tuesday was nearly gone.

She figured that if she went without food all day, she would be able to afford one more night at the run-down hotel in which she was staying, but by Wednesday night she would be destitute. The tears in her soul, if not in her eyes, were clearly visible to anyone who cared to look as she slowly descended the stone steps of the Grand Hotel after yet another rebuff.

At first, she did not notice the woman watching her. Louise was too absorbed, trying to decide what to do next. There were only a few places left to try, and she realized that the simple truth was that no one wanted her.

She walked a few paces down Gulf Street but then something made her stop. She was certain she was being watched.

The woman was leaning against the façade of the Grand. She was black, in her mid twenties, wore heavy make-up, and eyed Louise closely, as if appraising her. When the woman realized that Louise had spotted her, she stepped forward and approached.

"Want a smoke?" she offered.

"No thanks, I don't smoke"

"Smart girl; I like that," the woman said.

From her voluminous handbag, she pulled a cigarette: a short, stubby thing with brown weed straggling untidily from a loose wrap of yellowed paper. She lit the cigarette and dragged deeply of the pallid smoke while she eyed Louise with a look that made the latter feel uncomfortably like a carton of fruit being scrutinized by a prospective purchaser.

"Looking for a job, were you?" The woman jerked her head toward the entrance of the hotel.

"Yeah."

"They didn't have one, though?"

"No."

"Got any training? Anything you're good at?"

"No, not really."

"Been looking long?"

"A few days."

"Not from the 'round here though, are you, honey?"

"No. I'm from Parsimony. It's a small town on the railroad maybe thirty five miles away."

The woman shook her head. "Sorry, honey. Don't know it." Then, apparently changing the subject, she asked, "So, what're you doing around here then, looking for work? Didn't run away from home or nothing, did you, honey?"

"My pa threw me out."

Louise said it without any particular rancor: it was hardly an uncommon story.

"Sorry to hear that. You all right for money? Or do you need somewhere to stay? You look like a nice girl; you can stay with me for a while if you like, just until you find a job and somewhere else to live."

Louise could hardly believe her luck.

"Can I? Would you really let me stay with you?"

"Of course. It's a tough world, and we girls've got to stick together, don't we?"

And thus Louise began the slow descent into the life of a prostitute.

When she met Cleo she was three months past her fifteenth birthday. She was also a virgin. By her sixteenth birthday, she had lain with more than a hundred men. By her seventeenth, she had long ago lost both count and interest in the matter.

She lived in a rundown tenement building, sharing it with a dozen women between the ages of fourteen and forty engaged in the same profession.

Madame DeLemerest owned the building. Madame was a jolly, hearty soul in her mid fifties. No one could say that she was heartless or uncaring, or even that most of her girls were unhappy. Madame DeLemerest went to great pains to look after her assets. She ensured that they had ready access to competent medical care. Unlike the case in some other houses, none of Madame's girls had ever suffered more than the expected difficulties after an abortion. Conception was regarded lightly by Madame DeLemerest: it was simply a hazard of the profession, and any girl finding herself pregnant was offered the chance to leave her employment (if they wanted to keep the child) or, following a stern lecture, a free abortion (if they did not).

Louise discovered that the life of a prostitute suited her: it was not at all an unpleasant way to earn a living. Once she had overcome her initial inhibitions and her fear of what her customers might ask of her, she realized that even after paying off Madame, she was still earning a tidy income for what was essentially trivial work.

Not everyone in the house had it so easy. Louise was fortunate that she was young and slim and, if not exactly beautiful, at least passably attractive. Other women, those twenty five or older, or who had had numerous abortions, had a much harder time of it and held a considerably more sour outlook on life.

But Louise prospered. She discovered that she had the money to buy, and the time to read, the books she had always wanted but which had been denied her back in the hovel in Parsimony. And so, in a somewhat unorthodox manner, she continued her education as best as circumstances allowed.

There seemed little point in studying academic subjects, but she loved to read the great stories of literature. She devoured the classical works of the English language, both old and modern, and bought a thick dictionary that she kept hidden in the closet during working hours but which sat at her side most days as she sought to improve her vocabulary and her understanding of the world around her, and the wider world far beyond her own experience.

And so things continued until the spring of her eighteenth year.

She was wakened one morning when her door was flung open at eleven o'clock and one of the other girls, a half-breed Cherokee called Maria, ran into the room and shook her sharply to make sure she was awake.

"Louise, we gotta get out of here, fast. Madame has been killed and word is that Johnny Ternot is heading this way."

Maria hurried on down the passageway to tell the other girls.

Johnny Ternot was well known among the girls — all too well known by those who had worked for him before defecting to Madame DeLemerest.

He ran a supposedly high-class house on the other side of town. In fact, it was nothing more than a slaving brothel with little interest in cleanliness, propriety, honesty or any other of the virtues that characterized Madame DeLemerest's operation.

Rumors had been rife ever since Louise had arrived in Riverbend that the simmering state of near-warfare between Johnny Ternot and Madame DeLemerest would one day erupt into real bullets, and although none of the girls expected it to happen on any given day, they all were sure that the current situation could not last forever and that one day it would all change. Apparently, that day had now arrived.

Barely stopping to think, Louise got up and dressed, which took exactly ninety seconds. Another two minutes was spent packing her suitcase — still the battered cardboard affair she had carried into town some three years before. Forty five more seconds, and she had prised open a loose floorboard and removed her money, which totalled $572 at last count.

Maria stuck her head in the doorway again just as Louise stood up with the money in her hand. Maria must have seen the money, but she ignored it.

"Hurry, Louise. We gotta go."

Louise stuffed the money into the pocket of her jeans, rammed a handkerchief on top to provide a degree of insurance against loss, glanced one last time around the room that had been her home for nearly three years, and without wasting another moment hurried out the door and followed Maria to the stairs. She could hear the sounds of other women descending the stairs ahead of them.

As she burst into the open there was no sign that anything was amiss except for the quickly disappearing women who were dodging into alleyways, trying to distance themselves from Madame DeLemerest's house.

A couple of old men lounged on the porch of a tenement up the street; there were no cars in sight, and the spring sunlight beamed down, making it seem a pleasant and peaceful corner of the city.

In front of Louise ran Maria, carrying a suitcase not unlike her own. Maria turned a corner, and Louise heard the sound of brakes squealing from somewhere behind her. She turned in time to see a black car, then a second, then a third, skidding around the corner and then gunning their engines. She cars slid to a halt outside the building they had just vacated. Louise vanished around the corner.

Maria led Louise down alleys and across postage-stamp yards until, half an hour later, they arrived at the railroad station. Breathless, Maria bought tickets for the two of them on the first train out of town, heading anywhere. The train was getting ready to leave as they hurried on to the platform. They threw open the door of a carriage and scrambled inside.

They settled themselves, and only then did Louise look at the ticket that Maria had bought for her. They were on their way to New York.

The next day, the *Riverbend Daily* described two events that had occurred less than an hour apart.

A truck had rammed into a Mercedes owned by a wealthy black woman in her mid-fifties who lived on the outskirts of town. The woman had been killed instantly. The truck was later discovered to have been stolen and was recovered in a supermarket parking lot.

The second event was the burning of an old tenement in the poorer quarter of town. The cause was widely believed to be arson, although as yet there were no definitive clues on the matter. It was thought that the building was deserted at the time of the fire and, amazingly, no one was hurt, although the building was razed to the ground.

Neither the truck driver nor the person responsible for setting the fire was ever found.

New York was in many ways a continuation of life in Riverbend. Maria and Louise continued working as prostitutes. Their pimp this time was male. He seemed likable enough; he took a smaller percentage of their earnings than had Madame DeLemerest, but provided fewer comforts in return. The girls had to find their own living accommodation, but they soon found an apartment on the lower East side and, despite being forced to share it with innumerable cockroaches, they were content enough.

At first, New York overwhelmed Louise. The sheer size of the place, the variety, the crowding, the accents, all made her realize how parochial she was, despite her wide reading.

Gradually, though, she became accustomed to the people: the dirty old men with only one thing on their mind but no money to pay; the immaculately dressed pushers who were beginning to inhabit street corners, flashing $100 bills as if they were confetti; the down and outs whom she, like everyone else, tried to pretend out of existence; the doomsayers proclaiming the end of the world as they roamed the streets with their sandwich boards; the evangelists on soap boxes in the parks proclaiming eternal life; the people with crazed minds who shouted obscenities at everyone; the young long-hairs who wandered the street with beatific smiles on their faces and their hands in permanent "V"s, mumbling, "Love, man, that's all you need" to all and sundry. All these, strange and somewhat alarming at first, soon became part of the daily cycle of her life.

The seasons passed, and winter arrived. Snow began to fall sporadically, and a coldness settled over the city — a coldness that was a new and unpleasant experience for Louise.

She discovered a soup kitchen not far from their apartment, a place where a hot meal could be had for a nickel, or for nothing if you told them you couldn't pay. Louise was never short of a few dollars, but she ate at the kitchen for the simple convenience of it. It was a warm, comforting, easy start to the evening to pay her nickel and eat the generous ladle of hot, hearty soup and the hunk of dark bread. After eating, she would take to the streets in search of clients.

Of the mission that provided the soup, she took no notice whatsoever: it occupied a narrow frontage between a used bookstore that she frequented during daylight hours and a somewhat dubious barber's shop outside which transactions involving large-denomination bills and small paper bags were conducted openly by young blacks — "brothers," they were beginning to call themselves — wearing sunshades, leather jackets, and ill-concealed hand guns.

During the daytime, she continued her reading, but she also liked to stroll alone through the parks and the open areas of the city, especially on weekend mornings after a snowfall. On such days a white integument hid the grimy reality of the city and gave it a kind of grand splendor all its own.

It was on such a morning — Saturday, December 11th, 1965; the date was burned indelibly into her memory — that her life was changed.

It was just on nine when she entered the park. The sound of bells chiming the hour carried clearly on the cold, still air. She disturbed a flock of pigeons pecking at the snow near a bench. From somewhere not far away she heard a voice, loud and insistent but not quite shouting.

She headed towards the place whence the voice came. It was not unusual for half a dozen people, usually preachers or students aspiring to be politicians, to be spread around the park haranguing small knots of onlookers. But this cold weekend morning only one speaker had braved the weather. He was wrapped in a heavy coat, and a red scarf wound around his neck. His breath was visible with every sentence, hanging in the air and mistily catching the early morning sun. He was preaching fervently from a park bench to a crowd of two who were watching him wordlessly, occasionally stamping their feet to keep warm.

The preacher was black; both members of his audience were white. The listeners glanced at Louise as she approached.

Louise knew instinctively that the two white men were aware of her profession, although she doubted that the young preacher, who spoke in the plum tones of a sheltered Yankee, would have guessed.

She took up a position several steps behind the two men. Louise stood there for some time, not listening to what the speaker was saying, but wondering instead what could have driven such an obviously privileged young man to waste his Saturday morning. She noticed him glancing at her speculatively, and wondered whether he fancied her or whether he was belatedly wondering how she earned the money to dress warmly on a day like this.

The two listeners were dressed in thin coats. One man's shoes were split at the side. Every now and then, the men blew into their hands to keep warm.

The young man paused for breath, and one of the men took advantage of the pause to call out, "Thank you, preacher. Merry Christmas. God bless you."

"Aye, merry Christmas," the other said, and the two of them turned to leave.

They had taken about half a dozen steps when the preacher suddenly called out: "Wait a minute."

He stepped off the bench and hurried after them, taking off his overcoat as he went.

Louise watched as the preacher removed his heavy coat, then his long woolen scarf, and finally a deep, thick, sweater. He held them out to the white men.

"Take them, please. You need warm clothes."

"No, man. We don't take no charity," one of them said.

"It's not charity. I'll take your coat and his sweater in exchange."

The white men looked at one another. One man's coat was thin and threadbare, and the other's sweater sported half a dozen holes.

"Go on. Please," the preacher urged.

"All right. Just so long as this ain't charity."

They exchanged clothes and the two men hurried away, obviously wondering if the crazy nigger was going to call a policeman and accuse them of stealing his property.

The preacher stared after them. Louise watched his face carefully. His eyes closed and she saw his lips move. It took her a moment to realize that the young man was praying.

What she did not know, and did not learn until nearly a year later, was that following a brief prayer for the souls of the two men, the young man was praying for guidance as to what he might do to help the pretty young prostitute who had been listening to his preaching.

She looked at the man with a puzzled frown, trying to fathom the motives that had driven him to give away his warm clothes. She was forced to conclude that he was simply acting out his beliefs. Who but someone either utterly sincere or completely crazy would spend a cold Saturday morning preaching to a crowd of two in a park, and then give them the very clothes off his back when they left? It seemed unnatural

91

for a young man to behave in such a way; especially when he was black and the recipients of his largesse were white.

He began to put on the men's clothes.

"Why?" she asked.

"Why what?"

"Why did you do that?"

He began to speak in a soft, gentle voice quite unlike the one he had used while preaching, and before he had spoken more than a dozen words she realized that she recognized him. She had seen him before, helping at the soup kitchen. She had always thought of him as "the shy one," because whenever she thanked him for her ladle of soup, he always looked embarrassed, as if it were a sin to talk to a woman such as she, and he hurried to serve the next person in line.

Now he looked at her with an expression that she could not read. He clapped his arms around himself, trying to stay warm.

"I'm sorry. I'm cold," he said. "If you'll walk with me, I'll try to explain. Would you mind?"

The cloud of his breath almost reached across the narrow space between them.

"Of course not."

She fell into step beside him as he began to walk along the path.

And as they walked a miracle occurred.

Afterwards, neither of them could exactly recapture the moment, but twenty five years later, as she sat in her living room, telling the story for the first time to her pregnant and scared daughter, she stated the simple and indisputable fact that on that chill winter Saturday morning in a lonely park in New York City, the young man began to speak the very Word of God, and over the course of the next few hours her eyes were opened to the truth that God loved her — God loved *her* — and He wanted her only to realize that fact and then to follow in the path He had chosen for her, rather than the one she was choosing for herself.

The young preacher, as she discovered later in his apartment, was more or less what she had surmised: a scion of a wealthy family from Connecticut, studying tax law at Columbia. He had been brought up as a Christian and felt that God was calling him to a special mission to the poor during his time in the city. What he wisely did not tell her until after they were safely married was that the very first time he had seen Louise standing in line at the soup kitchen, a heavy conviction had fallen on him that this sinning and unsaved woman was the wife whom the Lord had chosen for him since before the beginning of time.

Louise eyed her daughter through moist eyes as she concluded her story. She rarely thought about those far-off events any more, and now that she was reciting them out loud for the first time she was finding it difficult not to cry.

"After your father graduated," she said, "we moved down here because your father believed that this is where the Lord wanted him to be. In all honesty I wasn't convinced, but I never have and I never will argue with your father where spiritual matters are concerned.

"Anyway, we moved down here and eventually you were born. We wanted other children, you know, but the doctors told us it was a miracle that we conceived even one. Ever since you were born I've thought of you as our miracle.

"So listen, Pam: the Lord went to a great deal of trouble to bring you into this world, getting your father and me together like that, then having you conceived inside this barren body of mine. So you just understand right here and now that He loves you, even more than your earthly father and I do, and no matter what you've done, as long as you're properly sorry, He'll take the consequences on Himself."

She rose from her chair, walked around the coffee table, and sat on the sofa next to her daughter. She gave Pam's shoulders a squeeze.

"You understand that, Pam, don't you? That's all that's really important. He loves you even more than we do."

Pam burst into tears.

She sobbed, "Yes, yes, Mom. I understand. Oh, I'm so, so sorry."

Her voice dissolved into a flood of tears. She clutched her mother and cried like a baby.

Hill County — 8:45 a.m.

"What are we going to do now? Any ideas?"

David Williamson asked the question as the car halted at the junction with County Road 12.

"Here. Check the billfold. How much money did he have? And get rid of his gun — just throw it into the trees."

Williamson threw Brewer's gun as far as he could, then took the billfold from McLaughlin.

"Fifty two dollars in ones, fives and tens, a couple of stamps, photos of what look like his parents, an oil company credit card and a Visa card."

"Here; let me take a look at the Visa."

He took the card and turned it over. He examined the signature for several seconds and then he moved his right hand in the air, the movements echoing the inky tracery of the signature on the card.

"Yeah, I should be able to manage that."

He handed the card back to Williamson.

"OK, here's what we need to do," said McLaughlin. "First, we've got to get out of these clothes. Let's find a shopping mall somewhere. I'll go in and buy us new clothes. Then we can decide what we're going to do next. I've got someone who'll probably help me if I can contact her. How about you? Anywhere safe you can go? Anyone who'll help you?"

Williamson shook his head.

McLaughlin continued, "OK. Well, I figure we've got an hour at most before the description of this car gets out, so we need to move. Let's try going to the right. He said that's the way to the closest village."

"OK," Williamson agreed, and McLaughlin swung the wheel around and gunned the engine, spinning the rear tires in the dirt of the track. The car skidded into the road and they drove away.

Two miles down the road they reached the hamlet of Georgestown, which, along with other minor amenities, boasted a service station.

"Might as well spend a few bucks on gas and information," McLaughlin said, braking at the last moment and skidding into the station forecourt.

It was a full service station, and Williamson quickly removed his convict's shirt before it caught the attention of the attendant who was nonchalantly walking across the concrete towards them, a cigarette hanging from his mouth in defiance of the "No Smoking" signs.

McLaughlin got out the car as the man reached the vehicle. He requested a fillup and began to talk to the man, asking about nearby towns and where there was a shopping center.

Five minutes later, they were on their way again.

"About twenty miles away in a place called Greenminster. We turn left when we reach State Highway 43. Can't miss it, that's what he said," McLaughlin said to Williamson. "If we want to be there and out again before that cop reaches a phone we'll have to hurry."

And hurry they did. For the next thirty five minutes, McLaughlin drove recklessly toward Greenminster.

Hill County — 8:45 a.m.

Bill Brewer wasted no time. Once his car had disappeared around the corner in a cloud of dust, he climbed painfully to his feet and stumbled towards the nearest trees. He had to get out of sight: what if the men had a change of heart and came back to finish the job?

Reaching the safety of the forest, he halted and counted slowly to one hundred. Nothing happened. Just to be sure, he counted off another hundred. Then he stepped out from the trees and began to walk along the track.

His only thought now was to reach County Road 12 as quickly as possible. He was hurt, but not seriously. He walked with his left arm raised to his right shoulder, pressing to keep the wound from reopening.

He was forced to halt before he had travelled a hundred yards. His unshod feet were being cut by the small, painful, jagged shards of gravel that were scattered across the track. The winding, half-mile-long track to the road loomed as if it were a marathon. Deputy Brewer had been hoping that he would be able to reach the road inside ten minutes, but now he realized that it was going to take much longer. Then he had an idea.

He sat down and stripped off his bloody shirt, leaving him dressed in only his underpants. He ripped the shirt into two pieces and then wrapped a piece around each foot. He got to his feet and took a few steps. That was better. He could make reasonable time now.

95

Running was out of the question, but he settled into a quick gait. Breathing deeply and rhythmically, he began to distance himself from the place where he had been attacked.

He reached the road about twenty minutes later. County Road 12 was narrow and little used, and the nearest house was about two miles away. He turned right, heading for the house.

The sun was by now rising high in the sky and the day had become hot, and sweat was soon dripping off his almost-naked body as he struggled onward. He blanked his mind, just putting one foot in front of the other, concentrating on reaching the next bend, the next mark in the road, the next tree... anything to keep him moving forward.

A sound percolated into his consciousness: a motor, somewhere behind him. He staggered to the middle of the road and waited. He feebly waved one hand.

Around the corner came a shiny new Japanese coupé with Arizona plates.

The elderly driver looked at the spectacle before him in shocked horror. Some sort of lunatic was standing in the middle of the road, nine-tenths naked, waving one hand and clasping the other against his shoulder where a smear of blood was clearly visible.

The driver braked hard. The car squealed to a halt a good sixty feet from the madman. The driver looked at his wife. The man in the road was shouting something, but they couldn't make out the words. He began to advance towards them, his mouth opening and closing in an inaudible shout, his free hand waving animatedly.

"Good heavens, what's that?" Dolores asked from the passenger seat, as if he could possibly have any better theory than she.

Maybe if he were to throw the car in reverse they would be able to escape the oncoming specter.

But Dolores said, "Listen, he's shouting," and she fumbled to lower her window.

The man's voice floated into the car.

"Help. I'm a police officer. I've been attacked. I'm a police officer. Please help."

He kept repeating the phrase 'I'm a police officer,' obviously hoping to reassure the elderly occupants of the car that he wasn't a crazed killer. Still not quite sure that he was doing the right thing, the elderly driver kept the motor running in neutral until the apparition was standing on the other side of his still-closed window, shouting through it.

"I'm a police officer. Two convicts escaped and attacked me and stole my car and clothes. Please take me to a nearby house where I can telephone for help. It's an emergency. I can show you the way."

Almost before the driver knew what had happened, Dolores had invited the man into the car. He slumped on the back seat and gave them directions to the nearest village.

Seven minutes later, Bill Brewer was in the service station in Georgestown with the telephone at his ear. He glanced at the clock on the wall. He estimated that it was about an hour since his target practice had been interrupted.

Northern Replogle County — 10:00 a.m.

Boss Armitage had set up his temporary center of operations at the scene of the accident. Later in the day he would move to the more comfortable surroundings of the Replogle County Justice Center, but for now this seemed the most logical place. Radio and cellular telephone communication kept him in touch with events elsewhere in the county and, in addition, the crash site was the center of the ever-widening imaginary circle whose boundary demarked the farthest that the escapees could have travelled.

With the clear weather that had arrived overnight, the chopper had been out since shortly after dawn, searching the western quadrant of the circle. Now it was making its last few passes before heading north. He looked at the distant smudge in the sky. What, he wondered, were the chances of finding some trace of the men before they escaped to a more populated region?

He was suddenly aware of a deputy standing at his elbow.

"It's Professor Cagney, the expert on tire marks," the deputy said. "He's been stopped at the barricade and he says he has some results for you if you'd like to see them. He says that if you're busy he can leave them for you back at the justice center."

"No, send him through."

The deputy raised a walkie talkie to his lips as he strode away. The sheriff was left to his own thoughts as he watched the chopper. After a couple of minutes the deputy returned with the expert in tow.

The sheriff and Professor Cagney shook hands. "You have something for me?"

"Yes, Mr. Armitage. I found some tire marks on the road surface partway up the hill before I left yesterday. Can't be certain it's the police car yet of course, but the wheel base is identical and the length of the tracks agrees with what one would expect."

"What one would expect if... what?"

"If the car was going between sixty and seventy miles per hour and then braked hard. On a dry surface he would have rounded the corner safely, but with all the rain we had earlier in the week there was almost certainly a thin layer of water on the road, and the tires simply didn't grip properly. The tires did grip and skid for about four feet before the aquaplaning began, but of course there are no tracks once aquaplaning set in. The tires caught again near the bottom of the hill, where the obvious tracks are, but by then it was too late and the driver had run out of road."

Boss Armitage nodded. The news confirmed what the broadcast reports had been proclaiming as truth since late last night — although heaven only knew how they had got on to it.

He had no doubt that Cagney's theory was right. When he had arrived at his office in Replogle at seven this morning, he had debriefed half a dozen officers who had worked in the past with Deputy Baker. All had confirmed that Baker could be a reckless driver.

Armitage's walkie talkie squawked.

"Excuse me," he said to the expert. He raised the radio. "Armitage here."

The chopper, about a mile away, turned and headed north.

"Boss, this is the communications van. We're getting a fax here you should see."

"What's it about?" asked the sheriff tetchily. "Just read me the damn thing."

"Sorry, Boss, the first part says 'do not discuss over the air' in capital letters."

"For God's sake...."

Shaking his head in disbelief he said, "All right, I'm on my way."

Clipping the walkie talkie to his belt, he nodded towards Cagney.

"OK. Thanks. You've written all this up?"

"Yes." The expert held up a slim manila folder. "Do you want it now, or shall I just take it to the justice center?"

"Take it there; I'm too busy for reading right now. But let me know if you change your mind about any of your conclusions. You can make your own way back through the barricade; I'm wanted elsewhere."

With a dismissive nod Armitage hurried away towards the large blue van with white lettering that spelled "SHERIFF OF REPLOGLE COUNTY," then, underneath, in a pinkish color to which Armitage had taken an instant dislike but had never got around to changing, "EMERGENCY MOBILE COMMUNICATIONS CENTER."

The van was its usual shambles. Inside the rear compartment were four people, several computers and radios linked by innumerable cables, and, the most recent additions, half a score of cellular telephones and a fax machine.

The sheriff barely raised an eyebrow at the sight of a civilian kneeling on the floor of the van, a laptop computer partly dismantled at his feet, a screwdriver in hand, and several cables strewn around him on the floor.

The sight of the local radio hams with their packet radio equipment would once have annoyed him, but he had learned their value two years earlier when a flood had threatened a community in the eastern half of the county. The hams had provided the expertise needed to get radio signals in and out of the remote valley, and ever since then he had looked at their towers scattered around the county with a new respect. In hilly Replogle County, radio experts could make the difference between instant communication and none at all.

"OK, spray me with pings," said the man with the laptop to a companion. The sheriff wondered why hams always seemed to talk in a foreign language.

A deputy standing next to the hams held out a piece of paper. "Ah, sir, here's the fax."

The paper curled tightly in the sheriff's hand, and he made a mental note to look into replacing the old-fashioned fax machine in the van with one that used ordinary paper if the budget would stand it. If he caught the fugitives, he thought wryly, doubtless the budget would stand quite a few such improvements.

He squinted at the blotchy printing. He scanned it once, quickly, to get a sense of its meaning, but then he read it through again, slowly and more thoroughly. Then he read it a third time, to be sure that he had not somehow misunderstood the message.

"You read this?" he asked, looking at the deputy who had handed him the fax.

"Yes, sir."

"OK, then," said the sheriff. "Try to get the word out to everyone. Use beepers and cellular phones. Keep it off the air. Tell everyone... no, wait a minute. You there."

The radio ham who was working on the floor of the van looked up.

"Yes, you. You're a radio ham, right?"

"Yes, sir."

"What license class you got?"

"Codeless tech, sir."

The sheriff looked blank. "Any one here with an extra class license?"

The ham pointed to the man he had asked to spray him with pings. "He does, sir."

"OK." The sheriff heaved himself into the van, reducing the available space almost to nil. "I have a question for you."

He looked at the impossibly young man with the extra class license — he looked more like a teenager home from college for the summer than a fully licensed ham.

"You got an extra class ham license, right?" the sheriff asked dubiously.

"Yes, sir."

"That's still the highest grade of license, isn't it?"

"Yes, sir."

"Well, OK. What I want to know is: if someone was driving around the area with a police scanner, is there any way he'd be able to hear conversations taking place on cellular phones?"

"No, sir," the youth replied without even pausing to think. "They use different parts of the radio spectrum. Even if it was possible, it's illegal to listen to cellular conversations."

"Illegal. Really? I didn't know that."

"Yes, sir. Do you want me to explain it?"

100

"No, no. OK. Forgetting the legal stuff, though, you're certain there's no way someone with some kind of police scanner could listen to a cellular conversation?"

"Not without taking the scanner apart and modifying it, and probably not even then."

"How about walkie talkie conversations? Would you be able to pick those up on the police radio?"

"Ah, yes, that would be much more likely. Could I take a look at your HT a minute?"

The sheriff looked at him blankly. "Huh?"

"Sorry, 'HT' is what we call a walkie talkie. Could I see your walkie talkie please, sheriff?"

The sheriff passed him the radio and the young ham examined it.

"OK," the ham said. "You'd be able to pick up transmissions from this, but of course you'd have to be tuned to the correct frequency. I see that this HT is set for none of your usual communications channels, so anyone with a police radio would have to deliberately tune off-channel to look for transmissions from this. But it could be done, if the person knew what he was doing."

"He wouldn't have to take the radio apart or modify it?"

"No."

"How about distance? How far away could he pick it up?"

The ham looked around as if he were viewing the landscape, although in fact he could see nothing through the metal sides of the van.

"You don't use repeaters to extend the coverage on those walkie talkie frequencies, do you?" he asked.

"No."

"Then you'd be pretty much limited to this valley. These walkie talkies only put out about 500 milliwatts. That doesn't go very far through trees at the best of times, and in this sort of terrain it's unlikely to get past the next hilltop."

"Line of sight, then?"

"Yes, pretty much. Of course, it might go farther, but I wouldn't really expect it to, and it wouldn't be reliable."

"OK, thanks."

The sheriff turned to face the deputy who had handed him the fax.

"All right. Here's what we'll do. Get the word out to the searchers on their walkie talkies, and tell every one else by cellular and beeper.

101

I'm on my way back to the justice center. If anything else comes in related to this, give me a call on my cellular, OK?"

"Yes, sir."

"Here. You keep this, they'll have the original back at the justice center. Thanks."

The sheriff thrust the fax, moist now with yellow sweat, at the deputy, then he clambered out of the van and walked purposefully to his car.

Greenminster Shopping Mall — 10:30 a.m.

Henry Morris did not look in the least like a security guard, which perhaps was one reason why he was so good at his job.

Standing five feet six inches in his shoes, his clothes carefully chosen to minimize the impact of his muscular frame, he peered out at the world through glasses which only he and his employers knew to be of plain glass. Morris looked more like an aging student than a security guard for the anchor store of a regional shopping mall.

What a casual observer of this plain, rather meek-looking individual could not possibly have guessed was that Morris's second job on three evenings of the week was as an instructor at the town judo club. Neither could the observer have guessed that as a high school senior he had set records for the 100, 220 and 440 yard events, the first and last of which still stood, even though they had been set a dozen years earlier.

But a good security guard is made from more than such deceptive talents. Paramount among his abilities, Henry Morris would have said (had he been asked, which he never was) was a good nose, by which he would have meant an uncanny ability to spot trouble as it entered the store. He regarded it as a personal failure when he was forced to rely on his other talents.

So it was hardly unprecedented when he interrupted his examination of the store's stereo systems midway through Friday morning and observed a short, pasty male somewhere between thirty five and forty entering the store.

It wasn't clear why this man was ringing alarm bells in Henry Morris' head. Perhaps it was merely the sum of several things: unaccompanied male strangers rarely entered the store before lunch time on a weekday; the man had a gray stubble of a couple of days' growth on his chin; he looked abnormally tired; the man's eyes darted this way and that, as if alert for unseen watchers, although he had not as yet spotted Henry's gaze (and would not do so, if Henry did his job properly); his eyes drifted to the ceiling and scanned it, noting the overhead video cameras.

Perhaps it was none of these; perhaps it was simply Henry's innate sixth sense going into action. Whatever the cause, Henry's eyes narrowed suspiciously as he watched the man.

His survey of the ceiling completed, the man lowered his gaze to the signs displaying the names of the various departments.

Spotting the board with the word MEN, he made his way past the toddlers' section, then past the cosmetics and jewelry, until he was standing next to a rack of fashionable sports coats.

Now Henry was even more suspicious, for if there was one thing that this man did not need, it was clothing. All his clothes appeared to be new, and he was carrying two plastic bags displaying the logos of other clothing stores in the mall. Henry watched as the man chose a sport coat, then a pair of pants, then a shirt, and then began to move in the direction of the shoes. All the clothes were chosen summarily, almost without thought; all the man appeared to be interested in was checking the sizes.

Henry had seen enough. He sauntered across to the man in charge of the stereo department. Turning his back on the menswear department, he said quietly, "Let me use your phone for a minute, Denny. And keep your eye on that man walking towards Shoes for me, will you? Let me know if he looks like he's about to leave."

"Sure thing, Henry."

Henry dialled 911, and the dispatcher's voice came instantly on the line. Henry was connected to the police department downtown, and he relayed his suspicion that one of the men who had escaped in Replogle County yesterday was in his store picking out new outfits.

The dispatcher assured Henry they would have a car at the mall in less than ten minutes.

"He's paying," Denny said quietly.

Putting the phone down, Henry turned to see the man handing a credit card to a sales clerk.

103

The man's eyes swept the store. They reached the stereo department, landed on Henry, and rested there a moment too long. Damn! Henry had been spotted.

The man gathered his purchases, snatched the card as soon as it was proffered, and hurried from the store. Henry, walking quickly, followed at a discreet distance.

Greenminster Shopping Mall — 10:37 a.m.

David Williamson sat in the passenger seat of the car, waiting. A couple of hundred cars were parked around the olive-green Buick, close to the mall's entrance. David had finished eating the sandwiches that Duke had purchased in the food court, and now he was endeavoring to be unobtrusive while Duke finished buying clothes. The police radio was switched on, but there had been no transmissions since they had arrived at the mall, nearly half an hour earlier.

A cloud of suspicion began to form in Williamson's mind. Shouldn't the police channels be busier than this? He began to tune the radio across its channels with one hand while he opened the glove compartment with the other.

Among the battered maps and knotted lengths of fishing line he found a sheet that listed the channels used by various local law enforcement agencies. Three were assigned to the Greenminster Police Department. He realized that he had been tuned to the wrong channels. Flipping through the channels he halted as he heard a voice saying: "...on our way." The voice was very loud; the channel, according to the list, was a local one.

He left the radio on that channel, then looked at the mall entrance, suddenly anxious for Duke to return.

Another five minutes passed before he caught sight of McLaughlin, hurrying between the lines of parked cars. David could see that something was wrong: Duke was in too much of a hurry. As soon as Duke reached the car, he threw the plastic bags inside and climbed into the driver's seat.

"We've been spotted," he said curtly.

Simultaneously, the radio came to life.

"Five here. We just arrived at the mall."

104

"10-4."

Williamson and McLaughlin looked at one another. A movement in the rear-view mirror attracted McLaughlin's attention. A patrol car had entered the parking lot and was now cruising slowly along the far side, the officers inside obviously scanning the area for suspicious activity.

The man whom McLaughlin had spotted eyeing him suspiciously in the J. C. Penney store suddenly darted out from among the parked cars and ran towards the police car, waving to attract the attention of the deputies inside.

McLaughlin swore and started the car. "Fasten your belt. We're outta here."

McLaughlin pulled slowly away from the parking space. He turned and made his way unhurriedly to the closest exit. As he reached it, he saw in his mirror that the man from Penney's was getting into the police car. The police car pulled away and began to cross the parking lot, heading directly towards them.

McLaughlin gunned the engine; with tires spinning wildly, he skidded on to the road. A moment later, he heard the sound of a siren, and the bar of lights atop the police car began to flash. The radio burst into life.

"Five here. Suspect has left parking lot of Greenminster Mall in extreme haste, driving a dented olive-green Buick four-door with instate plates. Suspect is accompanied by a second person, appears to be male, seated in the passenger seat. We're giving chase, heading east on Sunrise Boulevard. Request backup."

McLaughlin skidded the car around two corners and headed out of town at sixty miles per hour.

Southern Hill County — 11:15 a.m.

"That was close," Williamson said.

He looked across at the man who had just spent twenty minutes driving like a lunatic down narrow country roads. They had settled down to a safe speed now, but Williamson could see that McLaughlin was still breathing deeply and his hands shook whenever they left the wheel.

105

McLaughlin said nothing.

"You know, we can't keep running like this. We've got to do something," Williamson said.

"Yeah, I know, but what? Give up?"

The car was heading south now, back towards the accident. McLaughlin had chosen this direction on purpose, on the assumption that the police would not expect it.

Williamson left McLaughlin's question unanswered.

"What we need is somewhere to lay low for a couple of days," continued McLaughlin. "I've got a friend. If I can reach her, I'm sure she'd help me get away. You say there's no one who'll help you?"

Williamson shook his head. "No."

"Well, you'd better think of someone. We've got to split up. It'll be twice as hard for them to pick us up if we separate. We're making it too easy for them by staying together. I'd like to ditch the car, but then we'd be back on foot, which'd be even worse. Anyway, I can't think of anywhere we could leave it where they wouldn't find it pretty quick. That damned chopper. We have to split up. Maybe one of us could take the car and one of us chance it on foot?"

Williamson considered this for a few moments. He said, "I'd rather we stick together if we could, at least for a while. I need your help. I've never done anything like this before."

McLaughlin shrugged. Williamson had admitted that he needed McLaughlin, but perhaps McLaughlin also needed Williamson — having a man with a Ph.D. at his side had already proven useful. He could never have figured out the radio by himself. Perhaps they should stay together a while longer.

They drove on, putting more miles between themselves and Greenminster Mall. They passed a sign telling them they were back in Replogle County. Traffic was sparse, and none of the cars they encountered paid them any attention. Williamson returned the radio to its original setting, but it stayed silent. Then, suddenly, as they rounded a bend, a police car came into view. As they passed it, they saw the officer inside turn to look at them. A line of red brake lights lit up the rear-view mirror and the radio sprang to life.

"Car fifteen. Battered four-door olive-green Buick containing two males just passed me heading south on County Road 19. Am giving chase."

The police car was lost to view as McLaughlin accelerated wildly around a corner.

He swore. "That does it," he said. "We're going to get rid of this car."

Replogle — 1 p.m.

Boss Armitage was frustrated, and understandably so. Twice within the space of a single hour the fugitives had been spotted, and each time they had given the police the slip. He had to do something to make sure that next time there would be no escape.

It was not a trivial task. Replogle County encompassed some 525 square miles, roughly half the size of Rhode Island. It was hilly terrain, covered with hardwood forest, and almost all the roads were narrow and sinuous. But he had been quick to spot the common theme in the two near-misses: the problem had been that the fugitives had spotted the cops too soon, giving them just enough time to make a getaway.

So he ordered a change in strategy. He recalled nearly all his officers and told them to patrol the roads in their private vehicles. Every driver was issued a cellular telephone so that if the Buick was spotted, the call-in could not be monitored by the convicts.

Roadblocks had been erected at the county line on every road. Unless the convicts got rid of the vehicle, it could not be long before they were spotted again. And this time they wouldn't get away.

He plastered what he hoped was a convincing smile on his face as he walked out his office and headed for the front of the justice center, where the press was gathered in the parking lot.

Southwestern Replogle County — 1:17 p.m.

When McLaughlin made his decision, he did so with no warning.

They had just heard on the radio that all roads out of the county were now blocked. McLaughlin swore and the two men looked at one another.

They rounded a slight bend, and a short distance ahead he saw a two-story frame house set back amongst the trees. The gravel of a driveway snaked to one side of the house and and then disappeared behind it.

He pulled off the road and on to the driveway, and followed it around to a flat concrete pad at the rear of the house, where he parked in front of a wide garage with two doors. Both doors were raised. The right side of the garage was empty. On the left side, boxed in now by the Buick, was a Japanese compact.

McLaughlin said, "They won't be able to see the car from the road. This looks as good a place as any. Let's go in."

As he got out of the car, he pulled his handgun from his belt.

David Williamson stayed seated and looked at the rear of the house. A mælstrom of thoughts and emotions swam and collided inside his head.

McLaughlin hadn't told him what he planned to do next, but he didn't need to: the progression followed as predictably as a law of nature. The car in the garage meant that probably someone was home. It was probably a woman, perhaps eating a late lunch, perhaps preparing her husband's supper, perhaps just having an indulgent afternoon nap. But whatever she was doing, she was about to suffer a rude shock.

Williamson found himself wondering how he would have reacted a thousand years ago, back when he was an ordinary person, a man with a family and a home, if he had come home from work one day to discover his wife and two children held hostage by a pair of armed fugitives. He stared at the house. Hadn't he caused enough trouble already? What right had he to be the source of yet more grief? When would it all end?

The questions piled up, but there were no answers. Why had he agreed to run with McLaughlin? Worse, why had he pleaded with McLaughlin not to leave him? If they separated, he could give himself up without compromising McLaughlin. Why was he running from the law in the first place? It wasn't as if he didn't deserve his punishment. What right had he to run away from those who had simply imposed justice on him?

Williamson looked down and discovered that he was holding Deputy Baker's gun. He gazed at the weapon. His thoughts went back to the last time he had held a gun.

It had been a long, hard winter, the longest and hardest of the four that had passed since David Williamson had turned his back on his former life. Even though it was now March, spring was still undecided about making an appearance.

David was bearded, dirty, pungently odiferous and utterly down on his luck. It was twenty four hours since he had eaten. Dark, heavy rain fell from the gunmetal sky on him and his companion.

The man at his side answered to any name anyone cared to give him, but Williamson had always called him Charlie for the simple reason that he had never been close to anyone by that name, so it evoked no painful memories that had to be suppressed whenever he used it.

It was late afternoon. Somewhere behind the gray clouds, the sun was close to setting. The two hobos were huddled under a street lamp, as if the meager umbrella of the lamp could afford them some protection from the rain.

Neither of them could have named the town in which they stood, shivering, underneath that lamppost. David was unsure even of the state, although he was fairly certain that they were in the south somewhere. If they had been in the north, the rain would have been snow, and the cold would have been unendurable instead of merely unpleasant.

Charlie, as always, would have been hard pressed to say much of anything. David looked at Charlie and wondered when it was all going to end.

Charlie had attached himself to David almost a year ago, when David had come to his rescue in a scrap somewhere out west — Denver, probably, although sometimes David thought it might have been Albuquerque. Since that evening, Charlie had accompanied David everywhere.

Charlie had been waving a gun in a threatening manner — goodness only knew where he had obtained the weapon — at a group of teenage girls who were standing in the parking lot behind a bar, sharing a joint.

Half terrified by Charlie's crazed face and incomprehensible shouts, one of the girls had threatened to call the police. Charlie had begun to advance on her, waving the gun from side to side, when David had appeared around the darkness of a corner. The sudden appearance of a second hobo had given the girls the chance they were looking for, and while Charlie was distracted by his confusion at David's arrival, they scattered and disappeared into the night.

For some reason, Charlie had looked on David as his savior. It was as if he knew that had David not appeared, he would have done something unforgivable. From that moment onward he had attached himself to David as desperately as a dying man clutches at life.

It quickly became apparent to David that, like many of those he had encountered in his wanderings, Charlie was not quite *compos mentis*. Charlie would smile vacantly at passersby and mumble things like "He good" and "He save me" in reference to David when anyone paused and took a momentary interest in the two hobos. When they heard Charlie speak, though, people hurried on their way.

Charlie was far from young. He might have been fifty; more likely, he was nearing seventy, or perhaps he was even older. He carried himself with a kind of hunch, although whether there was a physical reason for this David never knew. Charlie did not smile much, and when he did it was not a pretty sight, for the few teeth that remained were uniformly brown with rot. His nose was large and purple-veined, his cheeks were bulbous, his left eye would not open properly, and his right eye blinked slowly, as if he had to think consciously about moving the lid, and he gave the constant impression that he was on the point of dozing. He was, to put it bluntly, unlovable.

Even though David didn't know how old Charlie was, he was certain that he was much older than himself. In the early days together, Charlie talked about France and Germany and the Second World War in a way that made it clear that he had been there. Charlie had claimed that he was a soldier in the Battle of the Bulge. Of all Charlie's claims, this was the only one that David was sure was the truth. It was the only story which, whenever Charlie told it, was spoken in a clear, steady voice and, although details sometimes varied, these variations could be ascribed more easily to the failing memory of an old man than to imagination.

After Charlie had been by his side for a month, David wondered how Charlie had ever survived without him, because it was obvious that as a beggar he was a lost cause.

He would look vaguely at people in the streets, sometimes holding out his hands for help, but he never asked for money and never, in all the time that David watched, did anyone offer him any. As far as David could tell, Charlie was unable either to read or to write. He refused to answer questions — indeed, he rarely spoke at all, although every now and then he would say a sentence or two, usually in the evening, as if it were a sort of commentary on the day. Occasionally, with no warning he would answer a question that David might have posed an hour, or a day, or a week earlier.

David never did discover much of Charlie's past.

As time went on and he began to understand how thoroughly dependent on him Charlie was, David tried to prise Charlie's story from his companion. Sometimes when David asked him a question, Charlie would provide surprisingly lucid answers. For a while, David thought he was making real progress, but slowly he began to notice inconsistencies in Charlie's answers: one day he said that he had been born in New York; then he would declare that he was originally from England; and in response to being questioned a third time he would say that he was an orphan from Chicago. Slowly, David came to the conclusion that for Charlie all his past lives were equally real.

The handgun that Charlie had been brandishing when David first met him turned out to be unloaded. But even that simple fact took considerable effort to ascertain, and it was never clear to him whether Charlie understood the difference between a loaded gun and an unloaded one. In Charlie's world, a gun was a gun, and there the matter seemed to end.

David had tried to persuade Charlie to hand over the weapon on that first night, but Charlie had refused, saying simply, "No; it's mine," whenever David asked for it. This went on for nearly a week and appeared to be one of the few stable features in Charlie's life. It was almost like an article of faith with Charlie: the gun was his and no one else was allowed to touch it. When David asked if it was loaded, he got whichever answer, either "Yes" or "No," that came first to Charlie's lips. Charlie steadfastly refused to open the chamber so that David could see for himself.

Eventually, one night while Charlie slept, David removed the gun from the pocket of Charlie's coat and checked it. Yet even as a wave of relief swept over him, the relief was mixed with guilt that he had in some way betrayed a trust. David could never decide whether it was his imagination or whether Charlie really did treat him differently from that point on.

———————————

Now the two of them were standing — tired, hungry, penniless and rainsodden — in some unknown southern town at the close of a miserable wintery day.

They leaned against the lamppost, and watched the occasional car as it passed blindly by. The streetlight came on, giving the hobos a yellow pallor and lighting the raindrops as they fell, so that the drops looked like evanescent slivers of gold.

A police car cruised past. The officer inside glanced at them. His eyes momentarily met David's; then the officer looked away and the car continued up the street.

They sat down on the curb, ignoring their sodden backsides and the puddle in which their feet rested. Neither man moved, nor spoke.

They saw fewer and fewer cars. They huddled against the lamppost and dozed intermittently.

Lights came on in the apartments over the stores that lined the street. Later, the lights went off again.

David, inasmuch as he thought of anything, realized that it must be nearing midnight. Soon, the lamp above their heads would be extinguished. That would signal the end of their day: it would be time to find a sheltered doorway in which to spend the night.

Tomorrow, perhaps the rain would end.

Charlie sneezed for the fourth time in as many minutes. In the yellow glare from the lamp, David looked at his friend.

Mucus dribbled down the old man's face. His rheumy eyes looked even more tired and dispirited than usual. All day, Charlie had been particularly uncommunicative. This morning they had trudged around the town in the rain, trying to find someone who would take pity on them. Usually in these small towns there was a church or a pastor who was willing to help. But in this town they had found no one.

"How are you, Charlie?" David asked. They were the first words he had spoken in nearly four hours.

It was a stupid question. It was obvious how Charlie was: old, weak, ailing, penniless, cold, hungry and probably several other unpleasant things besides. But David just wanted to hear Charlie's voice, if only to convince himself that it was no weaker than usual.

The old man looked at him with his trusting eyes, the left eye drooping more than usual, so that it was almost completely closed. The right eye looked at him as a sick dog might look at the master who has protected it from all the hardships of its long life, firm in its trusting belief that the master will make everything right in his own good time if only he will be patient.

Like a dog, Charlie trusted David to look after him. For nearly a year, David had succeeded in that task, but tonight, in a lonely, miserable, wet town somewhere in the south — a town whose despicable inhabitants would rather ignore than help — an icy fear wrapped itself around David's heart, and he knew that for the first time he was failing his friend.

Charlie needed somewhere warm — somewhere where he could rest and be nursed back to health. If the town had had a hospital, or even a clinic, David would have taken Charlie there. But there was no clinic, merely churches with locked doors and policemen who looked away as they drove past.

"How are you doing, old man?" David asked again.

David realized that Charlie hadn't mentioned the war and his part in the Battle of the Bulge for at least a week. That had never happened before.

Charlie looked at him with his one good eye and coughed. The cough turned into a sneeze and then into a coughing fit. His coughs were truncated expellations, as if every breath hurt. Charlie held his ribs with one hand and the lamppost with the other. Gradually, the fit subsided. At last, he answered David's question.

"I'm not going to make it, Davie," he said weakly. "Maybe it's time for you to leave me."

David realized that his friend was sicker — much sicker — than he had thought.

"Never, Charlie. I'll never leave you." And he meant it. "We'll make it somehow."

David was not sure he believed his own words, but he had to say them anyway.

Some part of his mind that had lain dormant for nearly five years slowly began to function, as if it were waking from a deep sleep. *Here, he was thinking, is a problem, and solving problems is something I'm good at — or at least I used to be. I have to attract someone's attention somehow, and make sure that Charlie is looked after, before it's too late.*

Charlie smiled trustingly at David: a thin smile of ugly brown teeth and thin lips that were a sickly shade somewhere between purple and blue. The rain had pasted wet straggles of wispy, gray hair across his face.

"Come on, old man. Let's see if we can find somewhere dry for the night."

David raised himself and helped Charlie to his feet.

Charlie stood, leaning partly against David, partly against the lamppost. His one good eye seemed to glaze momentarily.

"I can't do it, Davie. I'm tired. Let me sit down."

Charlie lowered himself back down on to the sidewalk. His feet, with their holed sneakers and thin socks, landed in a runnel of water.

David looked around for anyone who might be able to help. The street was deserted.

A car turned a corner and approached. For a moment, David thought it was the police car. He nearly stepped out into its path, so that the officer could not ignore him this time, but he realized just in time that it was just an ordinary family car; inside, a smartly dressed man and his wife were on their way home after an evening out.

The driver slowed slightly. The woman looked at them with an unreadable expression as she peered through the rain-streaked glass. Her face was rendered yellow and her lipstick purple by the street lamp.

The car, even though it had slowed, still ran through a puddle and sent a splash their way. David, standing, caught it on his feet and the lower part of his pants; Charlie, seated, caught the full force of the splash. The car accelerated and sped away.

Watching the receding vehicle, David noticed a light a hundred yards away on the opposite side of the road. *Convenience Store —*

Open 24 Hours a flickering neon sign proclaimed in silent winks. It had been there all this time, but he had not noticed it before. Suddenly, he felt a glimmer of hope.

He turned to Charlie. His friend was moving to lie down on the sidewalk, assuming a fetal position on the hard concrete.

"Charlie, there's a 24-hour store up the street. Maybe they can help. We could get some hot food and something to drink. Maybe they'd even give us some money."

"You go without me. I'm going to stay here and rest."

Charlie closed his good eye with glacial slowness.

Desperately, David looked at his companion, then at the flickering light up the street, trying to decide what to do.

Charlie's left hand went to the pocket of his coat, where he fumbled for a moment before withdrawing his gun. For a moment he held it to his face and caressed it as if he were a child and the gun was a soft, much-loved teddy bear. Then he opened his hand and offered the gun to David.

David looked at it with a sinking feeling in the pit of his stomach. The gun was the one thing about which Charlie had always been possessive. If he were now offering it to David, it could only mean that the old man thought it was time for someone else to look after the part of him that the gun represented.

The muscles in Charlie's face relaxed, and for a moment David thought that his companion had gone.

David bent down and placed his ear near to Charlie's mouth. He sighed with relief: Charlie was still breathing.

He thought that he heard Charlie say something. He couldn't be sure, but it sounded like "Thank you, Davie"; then the breathing, although shallow, became regular as the old man slipped into sleep.

David straightened and looked down the street at the neon sign. Then he leant down and said quietly into Charlie's ear, "Charlie, you stay here. I'm going to get us some food and some money. I'll be back in a few minutes. Don't worry."

The only response was the weak, regular, barely audible sound of Charlie's breathing. David could hear the sound of râles.

David stood and, looking down at an unaccustomed weight in his hand, discovered that he was holding Charlie's pistol. He had no conscious recollection of removing it from Charlie's hand, but now, as he held it, it firmed his resolve to do whatever was necessary to help his friend.

He stepped boldly into the road and began to walk towards the beckoning light.

The store was thoroughly unremarkable: a convenience store in a shabby neighborhood of liquor stores specializing in cheap wines; "adult" bookstores; video stores with large stocks of "artistic" and "foreign" movies.

It was a Sunday, and the convenience store was the only store on the block permitted by law to open its doors. Ordinarily at this time on a Sunday evening, the proprietor, a swarthy man of mixed Hispanic, Indian and Caucasian blood, was doing a distinctly profitable business supplying surreptitiously the needs that the other stores were barred from supplying on this one day of the week. But this evening the day-long rain had put a damper on his business.

It had been half an hour since the last customer had left the store when a shadow at the window caused him to lift his head hopefully from the screen of the portable television on the counter.

It was impossible to distinguish more than the overall shape of the person peering through the window. Then an unwashed, unshaven face pressed against the window. He began to worry. The last thing he needed was trouble with a homeless bum; business was tenuous enough already.

David looked through the window into the store. He paused for a moment, then moved to the door and pushed his way inside.

He looked at the proprietor. In his pocket he stroked the contours of the gun. He moved away from the door and began to wander up and down the aisles. For perhaps half a minute, he completely forgot the reason why he had entered the store. He had forgotten what a well-equipped food store looked like.

The proprietor watched him, his eyes narrow with suspicion. David looked up from the rows of cans and returned the gaze. In front of the counter was a display of soft porn. Harder stuff was wrapped in plastic bags behind the proprietor's head.

The flickering television screen attracted and then held David's attention. The sound was turned down but the pictures on the screen stirred a dim memory. After a moment he recalled the movie. *Beverly Hills Cop*. Eddie Murphy was giving a fast-talking pitch about cigarettes to some crooks who did not yet know that he was an under-cover policeman.

Oh yeah, that's good, he found himself thinking.

"Can I help you?"

The proprietor's voice jerked him back to the present. David shook his head and wandered away down the aisle.

For about two minutes, he simply looked, touching nothing. The food made his mouth water. At last he began to think coherently. To help Charlie, he needed just a few simple things: a loaf or two of bread; maybe some apples; a carton of juice or hot coffee from the vending machine buzzing noisily in one corner. And some money, he mustn't forget that.

He walked up to the man behind the counter, whose attention had not wavered from the smelly hobo ever since he had entered the shop.

"I need some bread..."

For an awful moment the proprietor thought that the hobo meant "money" and he was being robbed, and he heaved an audible sigh of relief as the man continued with his shopping list — "...and some juice and a couple of cups of coffee. Do you have those mugs with tops so they won't spill?"

The proprietor nodded. But then, his suspicions getting the best of him, he asked, "And you can pay for this?"

He knew it was a mistake as soon as the words slipped out of his mouth, for a momentary frown crossed the hobo's face. Then, ponderously, almost as if he had hoped that it would not come to this, the hobo lifted his hand from his pocket. In it was a gun.

"And I'd like whatever you have in your cash register, please."

The man behind the counter swallowed hard.

"Most of the money's in a safe."

He moved to one side and pointed to the floor behind him. A sticker on the front of a safe declared: *Time Release Safe; Cashier Cannot Open At Will.*

David did not even glance at the safe. He had no interest in such things; he had no interest in anything other than getting food, drink and money for Charlie.

"Just the cash from the register and some bread, juice and coffee," he said.

The proprietor kept the relief from his face. There was a little over fifty dollars in the cash drawer. He never let it get less than fifty for this very reason: if a robber came into the shop and there was less than fifty dollars on hand, the robber might try to take his disappointment out on him — not that this one looked as if he cared very much; the proprietor was almost certain that the hobo was either drunk or on drugs; his vacant stare was little different from the dilated, uninterested look shared by more than a few of his customers.

"Let me get the other stuff first, then I'll get you the money," he said brightly. He bustled his way from behind the counter. "Any particular kind of bread?"

"What? No; I don't care. Anything. Just something to eat. Don't forget the juice and coffee."

For a moment, the proprietor almost felt sorry for the hobo. It was obvious now that he must be cold and hungry and thirsty. He was drenched. The man must have been out in the rain all day. Perhaps none of this was the man's fault. After all, a man had a right to live.

Firming his resolve, he reminded himself that the hobo had threatened him with a gun. He grabbed a couple of loaves and two cartons of orange juice. He brought them to the counter and retrieved some change from the cash register. He went to the vending machine and bought a cup of coffee.

"Another one," the hobo said as he placed the coffee on the counter next to the bread and juice.

The proprietor repeated the trip to the vending machine. Returning to his station behind the counter, he triple-bagged the items so they wouldn't fall out on to the sidewalk as soon as the thin paper of the cheap bags got wet. He held out the bag and the hobo took it.

For a long moment, he thought that the hobo had forgotten about the money in the cash register. The hobo half turned to leave before a look of irritation crossed his face and he turned back to face the man behind the counter.

"And the money. Whatever you've got. Money, I need money." Then he added, as if it were an excuse, "It's not for me."

With a great show of reluctance, the proprietor opened the cash register. He slowly retrieved the bills and counted them out on to the counter. Fifty three dollars in bills, a further three dollars and 73 cents in change. The hobo took the money wordlessly, stuffing it carelessly into the pockets of his coat. Then, without another word — with no admonitions not to call the police, no threats of what would happen to the proprietor if he did — the hobo put the gun in his pocket and walked out the store.

The police found the hobo fifteen minutes later, in full view of any passersby (not that there were any), kneeling on the sidewalk in the spill of a street lamp no more than a hundred yards from the store that had reported the robbery.

The hobo did not raise his head from the bundle on which it was cradled as the police car stopped on the opposite side of the street. He paid no attention when the two police officers got out of the car with their guns drawn.

The officers approached warily, their guns pointing unwaveringly at the hobo. It was only as they came near that the policemen realized that the hobo's body was heaving in great, grief-filled sobs.

The shadow of one of the officers fell on the hobo.

The hobo slowly turned to gaze up vacantly into the silhouette of the man whose form was limned by the lamp. The officer's uniform glistened in the wet rain, but there was no flicker of comprehension in the hobo's eyes. Slowly, it dawned on the officer that what he had taken for a bundle of clothes on which the hobo had been resting his head was in fact a man, lying on the sidewalk, his knees bent tightly into his chest.

The hobo spoke, his words coming from a face soaked not with rain but with tears.

"He's dead," the hobo said.

Replogle — Noon

Usually, George Ellsworth's sermon was all but finished by Friday afternoon. This week he had barely started. He sat in his study, reading and re-reading the notes he had jotted on the pad before him.

It was no good: he couldn't concentrate.

He closed his eyes to pray for guidance, but instead a heavy conviction came over him that somewhere, at this very moment, David

Williamson was facing a crisis, and that the fugitive was about to make the wrong decision and be lost for ever.

His lips began to move in fervent prayer.

The McGuire House — 1:24 p.m.

David Williamson looked at the rear of the house behind which McLaughlin had parked the Buick.

The building was impressive, at least by the standards of rural Replogle County, and it was obvious that the owners had substantial means. It was a two-story frame house, well maintained, with the stained wooden siding in good repair. The window frames were pale blue; the rear door was a glossy burgundy. It was a home on which patience and care had been lavished. It seemed a pity to desecrate it with his presence.

"Are you coming?" Duke asked impatiently from near the door.

McLaughlin couldn't mean the question to be taken seriously, for where else could Williamson go? The radio had said that the county was cordoned off, and the roads were probably full of cars prowling in search of the battered Buick.

Yet, for a moment, David wondered.... Was there really any need to enter the house? Couldn't the two of them try to make a run for it? Or hide in the hills?

McLaughlin made his decision for him by simply turning his back and putting his hand to the handle of the door. Reluctantly, David concluded that he had no choice. He got out of the car and joined Duke by the door.

Loud, violent barking suddenly erupted inside the house.

David swore loudly: never fond of dogs, his aversion had swelled to full-blooded hatred after the death of his wife and children.

"You don't like dogs?" McLaughlin asked.

Not trusting himself to speak, David shook his head.

"Neither do I. But look on the bright side: the dog has a bark and mebbe a bite... but we've got guns."

McLaughlin opened the door.

What happened next occurred too quickly for David to take it in until it was over.

McLaughlin entered the house with David a pace behind. The room into which they walked was the kitchen. For a perhaps as long as a second, the two convicts were alone, but before the men had sufficient time to orient themselves, a large, noisy brown mass hurtled through a doorway. One glance at the animal was enough to render David immobile: it was a mastiff, the very breed that had caused the death of his wife and children.

The dog skidded to a halt on the slippery vinyl of the kitchen floor and barked menacingly at Duke. Duke raised his arm. In his hand was the gun he had stolen from Deputy Palmer. The dog stopped barking and emitted a deep, low-pitched growl.

Looking along his arm, Duke pulled the trigger.

The shot momentarily stunned David. As the sound died away, replaced by a ringing in his ears, David realized that the dog was no longer growling.

The creature gave a long, anguished howl and then collapsed, spilling red liquid over the white vinyl. The dog was still alive, but blood seeped from an ugly wound near its left shoulder. The dog wavered, then slipped to the floor.

After his initial shock, the only emotion David felt at the sight of the wounded and helpless animal was a warm satisfaction.

"That'll bring anyone in the house," Duke said quietly into the silence.

For a few moments they heard nothing. Then they heard people — definitely more than one person — hurrying down stairs.

A sheen of sweat appeared on David's brow and he grasped his gun; then two women burst through the doorway.

They halted in shock. Frozen almost into immobility, only their heads moved, flicking between the dog and the two strangers.

David felt a momentary burst of surprise, followed instantly by shame. Why should he be surprised that the people who lived in this well-to-do house were black?

There was no time for further introspection. Duke stepped forward and raised his gun menacingly.

The two women looked like mother and daughter. The mother was perhaps forty five, wearing no make up and simple but not inexpensive clothes. Her hair was long, and shone silkily. Her figure was slim and looked set to remain that way for a good many years to come. The daughter, half hidden behind her mother, was slightly the taller of the pair, perhaps five feet seven to her mother's five feet six. She wore her hair shorter but none the less attractively. She appeared to be in her late teens, and the tone of her skin looked so healthy that it almost seemed to glow. David wondered if perhaps she was pregnant.

For five seconds no one spoke. Then Duke said, "Is anyone else in the house?"

His words acted to shatter the illusion of a *tableau vivant*. The daughter shouted a single word of exclamation that sounded like "Murphy!" and, pushing past her mother, she knelt beside the wounded animal. She embraced the dog's head.

The girl looked up from the animal and stared at the men, first at Duke, then at David. Then, apparently having decided where responsibility lay, she looked back at Duke.

"How could you?"

With startling swiftness, her eyes glistened and then overflowed.

"Get away from the dog," Duke snapped, his voice hard and uncaring.

He made a jerking sideways gesture with his gun.

For a moment, David thought that the young woman was going to disobey, and he wondered how Duke would react. The daughter repeated her question without moving away from the wounded animal.

"How could you?"

"Simple," Duke replied with a menacing calm. "I pointed the gun and I pulled the trigger. If you don't move away from the mutt, I'll be forced to give you a demonstration." His tone was utterly without emotion. The matter-of-factness in his voice was terrifying, even to David.

The thought flashed into David's head that he should never have left the car wreck. By doing so, he had inextricably bound himself to Duke McLaughlin, setting in motion a trail of events that might lead anywhere. They were wanted men, known to be armed and believed to be dangerous. Duke had little to lose by using his gun. The whole thing was out of David's control. While they had been in the woods it had seemed more like a game, a sort of dangerous, adult version of hide and seek. But now it had become real, and the prospect that someone might get hurt — or worse — was all too evident.

The daughter looked into Duke's eyes for several seconds and then, responding to something she saw there, she stood and moved a couple of paces backward. The dog whined half-heartedly at her infidelity; then it lowered its head on to its front legs to conserve what remained of its strength. The girl looked at the dog through her tears, then at Duke with undisguised venom.

"I hate you," she said through gritted teeth.

Duke ignored her.

He said, "We may as well establish a good working relationship from the beginning. We may be here for some time. You can call me Duke, and this is David. What are your names?"

"Louise," said the mother, who had neither spoken nor moved since entering the kitchen. "Louise McGuire. And this is my daughter, Pam. We know who you are. Was that really necessary?" she asked, nodding towards the dog.

"Yes, it was. Now, who else is here?"

"There's no one else here."

"Other family members. Who are they?"

"Just my husband, Alan. He works in Replogle. He's at work now."

"No others?"

"No."

"What kind of work does your husband do, Louise?" Duke's voice was suddenly unexpectedly gentle.

"He's a tax accountant."

"A tax accountant. I see. When will he be home?"

"Half five or so."

Reflexively, four pairs of eyes looked at the red plastic of the kitchen clock. It stood at just after half past one.

"So we have plenty of time before he comes home, right?"

Louise nodded.

"What about the weekend? Are any of you expected somewhere in the next couple of days?"

"Oh, God!" exclaimed Pam. "You aren't going to stay? Just leave, can't you?"

Her mother turned and suddenly slapped Pam hard on the cheek.

"Don't you ever take the Lord's name in vain again." Turning towards Duke, she continued, "We're good Christian folk in this house, Mr. Duke, and I will not permit the breaking of the third commandment

within these walls. And I'd be much obliged if you'd both have a mind
to remember that as long as you're here."

"I'm sure I'll do my best, ma'am." A tolerant smile suffused Duke's
face. "Now, answer the question."

Louise thought for a moment, then shook her head.

"Our only commitment is church on Sunday morning."

"No golf games on Saturday for your husband?"

"No."

"You're sure? Because if you're lying, I still have plenty of bullets."

"Sir, I would no more think of lying than I would of taking the Lord's
name in vain. I would not lie to you, not under any circumstances."

Her eyes thrust a challenge at Duke McLaughlin, but he simply
looked away and let his gaze wander around the kitchen.

Eventually, his gaze returned to Louise. "What do you all have
planned for tomorrow?"

"Nothing special. Normally we might go to Greenminster Mall and
do some shopping, but there's nothing we need urgently. Alan usually
spends Saturday working on projects around the house and in the yard.
He's not expected anywhere, as far as I know."

"OK. So there's nothing until Sunday morning. Well, maybe we'll
be gone by then and you'll be able to go to church and pray for my
soul."

He laughed as if he had told a joke, but no one else joined in. Louise
opened her mouth to say something, but she thought better of it and
closed her mouth again, leaving the words, whatever they were, unsaid.

"Is anyone likely to come calling? Any dates for — what's your
name? — Pam here? Any boyfriends who might come by?"

Pam said, "No. There's no one."

Louise, for a fraction of a second, assumed a look somewhere between question and surprise. Pam's answer was obviously unexpected,
meaning that perhaps it was not truthful; or maybe it was not the
whole truth. David wondered whether Louise would permit her daughter the luxury of the lie she had forbidden herself. He stored away the
possibility that a visitor for Pam *was* expected sometime in the next
day or two.

Duke continued the interrogation.

"How about dinner arrangements tomorrow? Going out somewhere?
Guests coming here?"

Louise replied, "No. No one will miss us until church on Sunday morning."

Duke nodded. "All right. Good. Now, show us around the house."

"What about Murphy?" asked Pam, her eyes welling.

"Murphy here can get along fine for a while without your help."

"But he's hurt, just look at him."

Murphy was now lying on the floor, his eyes closed and mouth open, panting weakly.

"He needs help," continued Pam.

"Forget the effing dog. It's not my problem. I just want to get outta here safely. Now, your mom is going to show us around the house and you're going to come with us. You... Mom, go first. David, you follow her; then Pam, then I'll come last. And remember, any tricks and I won't hesitate to use my gun. Got that?"

Louise said, "Please. You don't need to threaten us. There won't be any tricks. I swear it."

"Lady, it ain't you I'm worried about. It's this spirited filly of yours."

Pam glared at McLaughlin.

"Come on. Let's get started. This is obviously the kitchen. You eat in here?"

"Only breakfast and sometimes lunch, at that table there. We eat supper in the dining room. I'll show you."

Louise led the way out of the kitchen.

The tour took nearly half an hour. In every room, Duke stopped and cross-examined the McGuires. He opened closets and drawers; he paced the entire perimeter of each room, moving bookcases and cabinets where they could be moved, looking behind them. He asked questions about everything: were they wired for cable television? (No) How many phone lines were there? (One) Was there a fax machine? (No) Where were Louise's cosmetics? (I don't wear any) What? Never? (Never!) Was the telephone on a party line (No, not since last year) Are any of the radios in the house capable of picking up the police? (I don't know, we've never tried) — but David knew the answer to this question after just a glance at each radio: none of them could intercept police transmissions.

After trooping through every room in the house, they descended the stairs to the hallway.

"Back to the kitchen," Duke ordered.

Pam, desperate to see how Murphy was doing, hurried ahead of the others.

David halted in the hallway. He was looking at a small, ornate plate that was decorated with yellow and blue flowers intertwined around the circumference; in the center of the plate were the words: "As for me and my house, we will serve the LORD."

Seemingly without thinking, David recited woodenly: "And if it seem evil unto you to serve the LORD, choose you this day whom ye will serve; whether the gods which your fathers served that were on the other side of the flood, or the gods of the Amorites, in whose land ye dwell: but as for me and my house, we will serve the LORD."

Nearby, Louise looked at him with a puzzled frown.

Before the birth of their first child, Alice had worked in a Christian bookstore not far from their rented house near the university in Virginia. After Danielle was born, Alice gave up her job in order to care for the baby. But money became tighter and tighter, their income never quite matching their expenses.

Then she became pregnant again, and for the first time the Williamsons began to be truly worried about the future. Neither of them wanted Alice to go back to work, but there seemed to be no other option. They prayed about the matter with an increasing sense of desperation. Then it had all been settled for them — as so many things seemed to be settled in those easy days — by a series of circumstances that they could ascribe only to the hand of God.

David had always been happy in his position at the university. The pay was mediocre, but their rented house was nice enough, and they lived in a crime-free, middle-class neighborhood. There was every expectation of slow but steady advancement for David in the years to come. His research was going well, and he published a steady stream of research papers. In addition to being a competent researcher, he was a good instructor. Students enjoyed his classes and did well.

Then, without his ever having applied for it, came the offer of an interview for an opening and promotion in Trenton, Mississippi.

There was little to discuss: the offer seemed like an answer to prayer. David went to Mississippi for the interview and was soon offered a tenure-track position as an associate professor of astronomy in the physics department at the University of Trenton. In the seventh month of Alice's second pregnancy, the Williamson family said goodbye to their friends and moved south.

The cost of living was much lower in Mississippi, and David's pay was slightly higher because of the promotion, and so it seemed that all their financial concerns were over.

Alice no longer needed to work. The cost of housing was low enough that, although they rented for the first year, by the time David started his second year of teaching, they were actively looking for a house to buy.

It was a slow, unaggressive search; Alice and David were quite happy to continue renting until they found exactly the right house: the house that would become a true home; the house that God had already chosen for them and was merely waiting for them to find. They found it just before Christmas.

There was nothing particularly distinguished about it: it was a tract house in an unremarkable subdivision, thirty years old but well maintained by the family that had lived in it since it was built. The carpets showed a few patches of wear, but the exterior paint was new last summer. The roof had another year or two in it, and although a few things would need fixing in the not-very-distant future, there was nothing that required immediate attention. The asking price was reasonable, and without the demeaning haggling that usually accompanies such transactions, the house became the Williamsons' shortly after noon on Christmas Eve.

They slept that night in their rented house, but they rose early on Christmas morning to spend the day in their new home. The children discovered that Santa had left presents in the front room, and they fell on the packages and opened them with squeals of delight.

David took the following week as vacation, and during the break they painted and wallpapered most of the rooms, and moved their belongings into the new house. By the time New Year arrived, the house was warm, lived-in and full of joyous love. Already, the house was well on the way to becoming a true home, a fact that was evident to their pastor when he made a surprise visit late in the afternoon of New Year's Day.

Evren Mills was a tall, slightly overweight man in late middle age. His hair, what remained of it, was halfway between dirty gray and white. He arrived on the Williamsons' doorstep at four thirty on the first afternoon of the year, smiling his usual disarming smile. David ushered him into the living room, and the pastor held out a wrapped gift while David asked if he could get him anything.

"No, no, David. I just dropped by to give you this. A housewarming present for your family."

David smiled as he accepted the thin package. It was surprisingly heavy.

"May I open it?"

"Yes, yes. Please do."

Under the watchful eyes of his wife, David carefully unwrapped the gift. It was a piece of slate on which was a stylized painting of a colonial New England mansion. Underneath were the words: "As for me and my house, we will serve the LORD."

Evren explained, "I wanted you to have something to remind you and your visitors that all our material things, houses included, are always at the service of our Lord."

Alice's eyes glowed with pleasure.

"Oh! it's beautiful, Evren, and so appropriate. We'll hang it in the hallway; it'll be the first thing visitors see when they come in the house."

"That would give me great pleasure," said the pastor. "And now I must be going. But perhaps, if you don't mind, before I go we could say a prayer for your new home?"

"Yes, please. If you would."

The three of them stood. Alice's arms were weighed by the sleeping form of fourteen-month-old Derek. David put his arm around his wife while Evren Mills prayed that the Williamsons' new home would be dedicated not to the glory of humans, but to the service of the Lord. David and Alice's amens were heartfelt and sincere. Both of them knew that the house was a gift from the Lord, and they both fervently desired that they would always be ready to place it in His service whenever He needed them to do so.

For five years the slate hung on a nail in the hallway, the very first thing that greeted David every day when he walked into the house after work. And for five years he and Alice tried to live up to the quotation on the slate's surface — until the day when his life was shattered beyond repair.

That day, when his eyes landed on the slate the words mocked his misplaced trust in the One whom he had declared he would serve.

A terrible calm fury seem to rise from the core of his being.

He took the slate from the nail and held it in his hands for an eternity.

Then, taking a deep breath, he lifted the slate high above his head and smashed it down against the corner of a table. The slate shattered. Half lay in pieces on the floor; the other half, the lower half, remained complete in his hand.

"We will serve the LORD," the writing continued to mock him.

He carried the remnant into the garage, where he removed a hammer from his tool rack and pounded the slate into smithereens. Dropping the hammer on the workbench, he walked away.

Six weeks later when he left the house for the last time, the shards of slate still lay on the floor of the hallway and on the surface of the workbench in the garage.

The McGuire House — 2:10 p.m.

David turned from the plate and looked into Louise's eyes.

"Joshua, chapter 24, verse 15," he said.

"Yes," agreed Louise, puzzled.

"When you two are finished...," said Duke.

David's eyes focused on his companion, and he wrenched his thoughts to the present.

He nodded vacantly. Louise followed him into the kitchen, wondering what sort of man carried a gun and quoted scripture from memory. Duke brought up the rear; he wondered if David Williamson was going to be more trouble than he was worth.

In the kitchen, Pam was kneeling beside Murphy, who was now asleep. She stroked him and muttered soothing sounds while her mother poured disinfectant into a bucket of hot water.

For a while, the two men watched the women clean the floor around the dog. No one spoke until the task was complete.

Then Duke asked suddenly, "Pam, how many telephones in the house?"

Pam counted. "Four."

"Where are they?"

"One in here with the answering machine; one in my parents' room; one in my room; and one in the living room."

"And what about the one in the storage room?"

"What? There isn't a telephone in there, is there, Mom?"

She turned to her mother, who was measuring coffee.

Louise paused and said, "Well, there's an old phone, but it's not connected to anything. There's no phone outlet in there."

She went back to preparing the coffee.

"I didn't ask about outlets, I asked about phones," Duke said testily. He waved his gun belligerently, causing both the women to shrink back in fear.

McLaughlin continued, "Listen to me. When I ask a question, you'd better answer it. If I think you're trying to pull a fast one, you'll regret it. Understand?"

He pointed the gun at Pam.

"OK," she said.

Louise said, "It was an honest mistake. I'd have said the same thing. It's just an old phone."

McLaughlin pointed the gun at her.

"Understand?" he repeated.

Louise nodded. "OK. I understand."

"One more question. You don't have any of those fancy new cellular phones, do you?"

"Do we look like...," Pam began.

Her mother interrupted.

"No, Mr. McLaughlin. My husband has been thinking of maybe getting one for his work, but we haven't bought one yet."

"OK. David, you go through the house and check that they didn't 'forget' to tell us about any more phones. Bring all the phones here."

David nodded and left on the errand. Three minutes of uneasy near-silence passed in the kitchen. The only sounds were the regular rhythm of the dog's breathing, the noise of the coffee brewing, and the noises made by Williamson as he moved around the house.

He returned to the kitchen and dumped the phones on to the counter with a ringing clatter.

"Can you disable them, or should I just smash them?" asked Duke.

David examined one of the phones.

"You want them so they can be made to work again, or do you want them broken forever?"

"Broken. I don't want anyone thinking they can hook one up and make a call. We'll just leave the one in here working."

"I'll need a screwdriver, but it's an easy enough job."

"All right. You saw the workshop in the basement? Get whatever you need and disable the phones."

The coffee finished brewing, and Louise poured four mugs of the dark, steaming liquid.

David was gone for a couple of minutes. When he returned, he opened a phone, inserted a screwdriver into a harness of wires and pulled. Four color-coded wires ripped out of their sockets.

"That good enough?" he asked. "It could be made to work again, but it would take some time and the right tools. And they'd need to know what they were doing."

"Yeah, sure, that's good enough. Do the same to the rest of them."

One after another, the other phones received the same treatment, until the useless remains of four phones were heaped on the counter.

"Next...," said Duke, "we need to get that radio in from the car. And we need to put the car in the garage. We don't want that chopper to see it." Duke gestured to the women. "You come with us."

They all trooped outside. While Duke kept his gun on them, the two women watched while David maneuvered the car into the empty half of the garage. Then they sat among the detritus on the rear seat while the two men labored to remove the radio from the dash and the battery from the engine compartment.

They brought the radio and the battery inside. David connected the radio to the battery and fashioned a makeshift antenna. He flicked through the available channels. The radio remained silent.

"You sure it's working?" asked Duke.

"Yes. It's just the squelch."

David turned the squelch control and the hiss of static filled the kitchen. He turned the control again and the radio fell silent once more. He scanned the channels again, but still there were no signals.

He said, "I think the problem is that they know we've got a radio, so they're keeping all their traffic off the air. This valley is probably a pretty lousy place for reception, but we should be able to hear *something*."

"Then how're they talking to one another if they aren't using the radio?"

"Who knows? Other channels that this radio can't pick up? Cellular telephones? Ham radio? There's plenty of ways they can communicate without us knowing about it."

Duke swore. "So now we've lugged this thing in here, it may not be any use?"

"Maybe not. But it's all we have."

Duke swore again. He glanced up at the kitchen clock, then he turned to the women.

"All right, you two. The ground rules. You will obey us without question. If you don't understand an order, get us to explain it. Neither of you will attempt to escape. If one of you tries, we will shoot the other one. Understood?"

The women nodded. At the mention of shooting, Pam flashed a glance at the still-sleeping Murphy.

"I don't know how long we'll be here," Duke continued. "We need to work a few things out. Maybe we'll be gone tomorrow, maybe not. You just treat us right and we'll do the same by you, and no one will get hurt. OK?"

The women nodded again.

"All right. You, Louise, you say your husband gets home around five thirty; right?"

Louise nodded and elaborated: "I'd forgotten this was Friday. Fridays he sometimes gets home a bit earlier."

"How much earlier?"

"Any time after about four o'clock. It depends on when he finishes at the office."

"OK. Well, in the meantime, David and I are hungry. You ladies fix us something to eat while we talk." He stopped for a moment as a thought struck him. "Do you have anything to drink? We're mighty thirsty."

"You mean alcohol?"

"Yes, I mean alcohol."

"Alan doesn't hold with strong drink. But there might be some beers in the refrigerator. He sometimes has one on hot days."

Duke opened the refrigerator and triumphantly held up a can.

"Want one?" he asked David. "There's a couple more."

David shook his head.

"Fine by me" Duke said. "All the more for me. All right, you two, get to work."

He beckoned David to join him in a corner where he could keep an eye on the women while they worked.

"OK, David," Duke began, "I don't know about you, but I'm going to call an old girlfriend and see if she'll drive down here and pick me up. She lives in Boston, so she'll take a while to get here. But in the meantime, you'd better figure out what you're going to do when she arrives. You're not coming with me. If we split up we'll both stand a better chance of getting away. Right now, we're sitting ducks."

David nodded, but said nothing.

"Do you have anyone you can call? Anyone who would hide you for a while until it all blows over?"

David shook his head wordlessly and his eyes took on the glazed look that they had worn in jail.

Duke looked at David. David was a strange and disturbing mixture, full of paradoxes. That glazed look could mean only drugs or alcohol or something wrong with his head. David had refused a beer, and he'd had no chance to get his hands on any drugs, which seemed to leave only the third possibility. And yet the man was undeniably clever: he knew a lot about how things like radios and telephones worked. His unlikely claim to a Ph.D. might even be true. If so, at one time he must have been capable of intense concentration, yet now his mind seemed to wander off into nothingness at the slightest provocation.

With a mental shrug, Duke concluded that it was not his problem. He doubted that David would last six hours once they separated. Perhaps he had already told David too much about his ex-girlfriend. Half an hour in police custody, and they would know everything David knew. He'd better be more careful about what he told David.

To make matters worse, it was obvious to Duke — although he hoped not to the women — that David wouldn't use his gun no matter what the provocation.

"Your food's ready," called Louise from the other side of the kitchen.

Her voice woke the dog. Murphy tried to get to his feet and promptly let out a yelp of pain as his front left leg collapsed. Pam ran to the dog and cradled its head.

The two men ignored her and sat down to eat.

Replogle County Justice Center — 4:25 p.m.

"The reporters are waiting for you, Boss."

A deputy had poked his head around the door of Boss Armitage's office to give him the message. The sheriff was kneeling on the floor with a large-scale map of the county spread out before him. Without looking up, he raised the index finger of his right hand.

"Tell them I'll be with them in one minute."

"OK, Boss."

The deputy retreated and closed the door behind him.

Sitting on a chair in one corner, watching the sheriff and unseen by the deputy who had just intruded, was a man in his early fifties dressed in a polyester suit, white shirt and muted tie. The man's shoes were glossily polished.

He said, "What are you going to tell them?"

Armitage looked up from the map.

Theoretically, the man from the FBI outranked the sheriff, but they were both professionals, each aware of the usefulness and the limitations of the other. Circumstances had brought them together, uniting them in a single cause, and both men were determined to use their combined strength to bring their collaboration to a successful conclusion. Boss Armitage was a homespun who probably knew the county better than any other man alive; Nate Painter had a razor-sharp mind and more than twenty years' experience at catching fleeing fugitives.

Painter could have taken the case from the sheriff; but he was too intelligent to pull rank unless it became necessary. Here in Replogle County, the sheriff was the man to direct operations. If the fugitives escaped the confines of the loosely drawn net that the sheriff had established, then the FBI agent would move on to another county and determine whether the man in charge there was competent to organize the chase. He had no doubt that as long as the men were in Replogle County Boss Armitage was the man to lead the hunt.

But Armitage was dissatisfied with the way things were going. Every road out of the county was sealed, and there were now a dozen cars checking the outlying roads. So far, though, there had been no trace of Bill Brewer's Buick since the two sightings earlier in the day.

That disturbed him more than he cared to admit. The county was large, over five hundred square miles, but between the cars and the helicopter over half the roads in the county had already been checked, and as yet there was no sign of the stolen vehicle. He had a nasty feeling that by the time darkness fell, virtually the entire county would be covered and still no trace of the car was going to surface.

He realized that the man in the corner was still waiting for an answer.

"What'll I tell the reporters? The truth," the sheriff said.

"All of it?"

"No. But enough."

"You think the men are still in the county?"

Armitage raised himself awkwardly with the assistance of the corner of his desk.

"My heart says 'yes'; my head is less sure," he admitted. "If I was trying to escape, I'd ditch the car and cross out of the county on foot. But I know this area like the back of my hand, and I know what resources the sheriff has at his disposal. These men don't have either of those advantages, so my guess is they're still holed up somewhere."

"With hostages?"

It was a question that had been bothering the sheriff for some time. He had been wondering if the FBI man had also thought of the possibility. Evidently he had.

"Probably," he said glumly. "If not now, then in an hour or so when people get home from work."

Painter nodded his agreement and asked, "You going to tell the reporters that?"

"I don't know. I'll try to avoid the issue, but maybe they'll work it out for themselves. You want to come out and face the firing squad with me?" There was no hint of a smile on his face: he was not joking.

"No thanks, I'll just watch from in here."

Painter added, as if it were an afterthought, "You going to mention me?"

Now Armitage did smile. "Only if I think I need a scapegoat."

"Thanks a lot."

"Any time."

Armitage turned and left his office.

Replogle — 4:25 p.m.

Alan McGuire eased himself comfortably into his car. He mentally checked one last time that there was no unfinished business that had to be dealt with before he left for the weekend. His face clouded for a moment as he recalled that his cares at the moment centered on his home life, not his work.

Three times during the afternoon he had nearly picked up the phone to call Louise.

They had had a long talk in bed last night, and Louise had promised to try to have a serious discussion with Pam today, to see if she could discover what was bothering their daughter. All afternoon, Alan's mind had been wandering, half praying, half worrying about what kind of trouble Pam might have got herself into. Once, a long time ago, he had heard a pastor on the radio say: "If you are the parent of a son, you worry; but if you are the parent of a daughter, you pray." He had felt the truth of those words many times, but never as strongly as today.

He kept telling himself that if Louise had made progress, she would have called to tell him the news — unless it was something so awful that she could not bring herself to talk about it over the telephone.

Alan shook himself and turned the key in the ignition. The motor erupted into life, and the sound of the radio filled the interior of the car. A sermon was just coming to an end. He turned the volume down slightly, then eased the car out of its space between a pair of trucks.

The drive home usually took about twenty five minutes, and generally the time passed agreeably, especially at this time of year. Some days, he was forced to run the air conditioner, but most days he drove with the window down, the breeze bringing the scents of the hardwood trees to his nostrils and helping him shed the burdens of the day before he arrived home. Often, he would only half concentrate on the winding road as he drove, while his mind relaxed and he thanked the Lord for his many blessings.

But this was a day for the air conditioner, and his cares about Pam kept any thanksgiving from his heart. Although he did not notice the fact, he drove rather faster than usual.

The sermon on the radio ended, and a half-hour news broadcast began. Generally, Alan paid little attention to the news. Events in Washington or the world beyond the United States were things which held little interest. Sometimes stories of atrocities in some distant corner of the world would move him to pray for half a minute, but otherwise the news usually meant little to him.

But today was different. The headline story on the local Christian radio station was still about the prisoners who had escaped yesterday while being transported to the state penitentiary. After recapping the latest in the story, which was the shooting and wounding of an off-duty deputy and the theft of his private car in Hill County, the announcer said: "And now we can go live to the parking lot of the justice center in Replogle, where sheriff Bradley Armitage is about to begin a news conference."

The announcer's voice faded and Alan turned up the volume slightly. The background murmur of a crowd of reporters diminished, and Boss Armitage's voice authoritatively filled the car.

"Good afternoon, ladies and gentlemen. I'd like to make a brief statement, after which I'll take a few questions.

"To bring you up to date with the events of the day: first of all, I would like to take this opportunity to assure the citizens of Replogle County that my department, along with the sheriffs' departments from surrounding counties, is giving this matter its highest priority. These men are now known to be carrying weapons that they are not afraid to use, and we are working as hard as possible to apprehend them and get them safely behind bars again.

"One ray of hope is that our forensic expert has concluded that, with the evidence we have in hand, there is no reason to believe that the men caused the crash. I stress that there may be other evidence that has not yet come to light which may cause us to change that judgment, but as of right now it is our opinion that the escape was opportunistic rather than planned."

There were several shouted questions at this point, but the sheriff ignored them.

"At approximately eight thirty this morning, the men were seen in an isolated spot in the southern portion of Hill County. The man who saw them was an off-duty deputy from my department. One of the fugitives fired a handgun, believed to be one of those that were taken from the officers who were killed in yesterday's crash. The deputy was wounded, but not severely. The deputy believes that the shot was intended to wound and not to kill. The fugitives stole some of the deputy's clothing as well as his automobile."

Until now, the sheriff had essentially been recapitulating information that had already been disseminated. Now he began to report on more recent events.

"The deputy's automobile was spotted approximately two hours later in the Greenminster shopping mall in Hill County. At the same time, one of the men, Duke McLaughlin, was identified inside the shopping mall. Shortly afterwards, the car carrying the fugitives left the mall parking lot with a Greenminster PD car giving chase.

"Unfortunately, the fugitives managed to evade the police. The Buick was seen approximately thirty minutes later in northern Replogle County, heading south on County Road 19. That was the last positive sighting. As of right now, there are checkpoints on all roads out of the county. We are confident that the vehicle has not left the county and we expect to find it within the next twelve hours."

More questions erupted, and this time the sheriff said loudly over the babble, "That's all I have for now, but I will take a couple of questions. Yes, Sherri?"

"Sheriff Armitage, you said that you are confident that the vehicle hasn't left Replogle County. How can you be sure that the fugitives themselves are still in the county? Surely there's a good chance that they've ditched the car by now?"

"Yes, certainly there's a chance they've crossed into another county on foot. But we believe that because of their close calls earlier in the day, they are more likely to be lying low somewhere waiting for the search to become less aggressive. Yes, Todd?"

"Boss, if they *are* in the county, they must by now be pretty tired and they're probably getting anxious about their situation. So how concerned are you that they might have taken hostages in a private residence?"

There was a pause while the sheriff weighed his answer to the question he had hoped nobody would think of asking.

"Of course that is a concern," he said, "and it's becoming more of a concern as time goes on. Let me just say that we will deal with that eventuality if and when it becomes necessary. And now, ladies and gentlemen, if you will excuse me...."

There was a clamor as the sheriff hastily concluded the news conference, but he was not to be drawn into answering any more questions. The hubbub on the radio faded, to be replaced by the calm voice of the studio announcer moving on to other items. Alan McGuire lowered the volume.

He arrived home a few minutes before five. He was surprised to see that the right-hand side of the garage was closed. The left-hand door was open, and Louise's car was in its usual spot. Suppressing a momentary flash of irritation, he pressed the button on the opener to open the right-hand door. The garage door did not move. Tossing the opener on to the seat beside him, he switched off the engine and eased himself out of the car.

Strangely, the handle of the garage door was in the locked position. He rotated the handle to unlock the door, then hefted the door upward.

He stopped, puzzled. In the place where his car usually stood was a dirty green Buick several years past its prime, sporting many dents and several rust spots.

A Buick. He turned and ran for the house.

Before he reached it, a man opened the back door and stepped outside. In his hand was a gun.

Before Alan could assess probabilities — was the gun loaded? could he take a flying leap at the man and hope to disarm him? could he simply run and try to put his car between himself and the man with a gun? — Duke McLaughlin said in a quiet, matter-of-fact voice, "This gun is loaded, Mr. McGuire, and so is the one that my friend is pointing at your wife in the kitchen."

Alan's eyes darted wildly for a few seconds, then his shoulder slumped.

"Inside," said McLaughlin. "Your family's unharmed. I can't say the same for your dog."

Alan walked past Duke into the kitchen and took in everything at a glance: the dog on the floor with its coat matted red; his daughter standing anxiously in one corner; his wife standing next to a stranger who looked at him with a vacant expression and held a gun that pointed vaguely at Louise. Alan rushed to his wife and clasped her tightly in his arms.

"Honey, are you all right?"

Tears of relief welled up in Louise's eyes. She nodded, sniffing back the tears.

"We're both all right; just shaken, that's all."

"They haven't hurt you?"

"No; we're OK."

Pam moved from the corner and joined her parents. Alan put an arm around her.

After a few moment, Pam said quietly, "They shot Murphy."

Alan removed himself from the clinch and looked at the dog. It was a wretched, woebegone sight. As Alan watched, it got awkwardly to its feet. It held its left front paw crookedly clear of the ground. On three legs, the dog hobbled to Alan and licked the leg of its master's pants. Its tail twitched. Alan bent down and examined Murphy's wound.

He gently moved the limb that hung limply from the dog's shoulder. The dog reacted with a sharp yelp, baring its teeth and emitting a growl that seemed to come from the depths of its stomach. Alan made soothing noises and gently stroked Murphy's back. Slowly, the dog quieted. Murphy eased himself to the floor until he was lying at Alan's feet. The dog closed its eyes.

Alan looked up at the fugitives.

"Did you have to do this?" He looked from one to the other.

David opened his mouth to reply, but he was forestalled by Duke.

"Rule number one, Mr. McGuire — Alan, isn't it?"

Alan nodded.

"Well, rule number one, Alan, is that we ask the questions. Rule number two is that you answer them. You got that?"

Alan nodded meekly. "Yes; I understand."

His hand sought his wife's. They squeezed hands tightly.

Duke turned to David. "Now they're all here, we need to figure out our next move. You seem to know about phones and stuff. How quickly can they trace an incoming long-distance phone call on a tapped phone?"

David shook his head. "Sorry. I have no idea. Just a few seconds, I think. But I think I read once that they can trace local calls even if no one answers, so maybe they could do the same for long distance calls. Why?"

"I'm going to call my friend Katie, and by now they might have figured out that it might be smart to tap her phone. Well, I guess I've gotta risk it. You take these people into the living room where they won't hear anything. I'll join you in a minute."

Boston — 6:30 p.m.

A taxi, its yellow paint glossy after a day of rain, crashed through the broad pool of water that had gathered on the uncambered road, sending a sheet of spray skyward.

Katie Murcheson saw the arch of water heading towards her and she tried to move away, but her high-heeled shoes were not built for speed and the filthy water splashed on to her legs, soaking the exposed pantyhose below the hem of her plastic raincoat. She turned toward the retreating cab, raised a finger and let rip a stream of abuse. The cab driver returned her gesture. Uttering a final epithet, she turned away.

The building in which she lived rose six stories above the sidewalk. In good weather, the building looked dilapidated, unkempt and impoverished. The day's rain had added a sheen of bleak despair. She climbed the steps and went inside. A wet, heavy smell greeted her. She fiddled with the mailbox key. Somewhere on the floor above a couple was fighting: Spanish cries wafted down the stairwell. In a room across the hall, a stereo was playing some hit of years gone by that she vaguely recognized. The metal of the mailbox vibrated in time with the bass. A whiff of stale urine, perhaps animal, perhaps human, meandered sharply across her nostrils.

There were two items inside the mailbox: a bill from the utility company and a four-color flyer from a supermarket chain whose closest outlet lay nearly a mile away up Peoria Street. Several copies of the flyer were strewn around the floor near the mailboxes, most of them marked with dirty footprints. For a second she hesitated, then she let her copy of the flyer fall to the ground. Purposefully, she stepped on the advertisement as she headed for the elevator. Her shoe left a muddy mark on a misregistered picture of a pack of tomatoes.

The elevator was working (for a change) although as it creaked to the building's penultimate story it seemed to resent every inch of the journey.

What a day! thought Katie Murcheson. *What a lousy, wet, miserable, stinking, effing day.* And to cap it all, the day was not yet over.

She had lived here now for more than three months, ever since the night she had come home early to find Duke in bed with a "friend".

At first, when she had stormed out of his apartment, bummed around for a while, and then ended up here, it had been easy to convince herself that this, at last, was *freedom*, and that finally she had done away with the emotional shackles that had bound her to the no-hope loser for so long.

But then she had received an anonymous newspaper cutting (probably, she thought, sent by Duke's "friend"), saying that Duke had been caught after holding up a liquor store. Given his past transgressions, he was bound to receive a stiff sentence.

The trouble was, she still loved him. And life without him was so *dull*. If it weren't for his arrest, it would have been so easy to go back to Duke and his unpredictable ways, his violent temper, his tempestuous lovemaking, his neverending schemes for making the two of them wealthy beyond measure.

She had sent him a letter, care of the police department in the town in which he had been arrested. The letter said nothing much: it just gave him her new address in Boston and said she wanted to hear from him. She never received a reply.

She tried to put Duke out of her mind and to think about tonight instead.

Ever since landing her job she had known that it was only a matter of time before her boss, a forty-five-year-old insecure male attorney, would proposition her. It had finally happened yesterday, and tonight Mr. Glotz had arranged to meet her at *Antonio's* at eight thirty for dinner, after which they would go back to his house for drinks, drugs and a romp in the bed that Glotz shared with his wife when she was not "visiting her parents."

Did people *really* do that? she wondered as she pushed open the battered door of her apartment. Did adults really go halfway across the country to visit their parents? His wife must be in her mid forties. What woman in her mid forties would willingly visit her parents for a long weekend?

Mrs. Glotz was probably nowhere near her parents: much more likely that she was enjoying herself somewhere with another man. So that was what Katie Murcheson had descended to: she had become revenge for a wife's infidelity.

She left a trail of drops on the vinyl floor of her apartment. Taking off her cheap plastic raincoat, she looked for somewhere to put it, gave up, and threw it on the threadbare sofa. After resting precariously for a moment, the raincoat slid off the sofa and slipped wetly to the floor.

Katie plopped down on the sofa and kicked off her shoes. She sighed pleasurably as her feet regained their freedom. She rubbed them through the pantyhose.

The telephone rang, making her jump. For a second, she considered ignoring it. But the most likely caller was her boss, calling to tell her that his wife had "returned early" (or some such euphemism for cold feet) and they would have to postpone their "dinner meeting." Katie stretched out her hand and lifted the instrument.

"Katie?"

She nearly dropped the phone. It couldn't be.

"Katie? Are you there? This is Duke."

Emotions swam through her mind, too ephemeral and too inconsistent to be identified.

"Duke? I thought...."

"Katie, listen carefully. I'm going to ring off now and call back in one hour. When I do, give me the number of a nearby phone that isn't yours. I don't care if it's a pay phone or a phone at a friend's place. Just give me another number. I'm sorry I can't talk to you now, but I'll call you in an hour. I need your help, babe. Please do this for me. I love you. I always have."

The line went dead.

"Duke? Duke?"

She looked at the phone, partly in anger, partly in confusion. She suddenly laughed out loud. He had done it again; nothing had changed. He'd talked for no more than a few seconds, and now she was feeling the same absurd farrago of emotions. Excitement, desire, frustration.

She hung up the phone and stared at it blankly for a long eternity.

The sound of a car backfiring brought her back to her senses.

So Duke, whom she had thought had left her life for good, had reentered it with a vengeance. Was she pleased or devastated? She couldn't tell. But she did know that she loved him as much as ever. And he needed her.

Well, of one thing she was glad: she would no longer have to go through the charade of dinner with the insecure Mr. Glotz.

She thought about calling Glotz to cancel. No, she decided with a smile: let him stew. She was going to lose her job anyway, that was the way these things always worked out. Let her lose it for something worthwhile. And with that she dismissed Mr. Glotz instantly and (she thought) irrevocably from her mind.

Now... what had Duke told her to do? Find another phone somewhere where he could call her. Now why would he want her to do that? He knew her number. Why not just call her again...? Of course! Duke thought her phone was being tapped. And that's why he had rung off so abruptly.

She guessed what must have happened: Duke had escaped. The authorities would have a list of his close acquaintances and she was probably on that list.

Feeling suddenly ten years younger, she stood. *Duke!* she thought with satisfaction. *You are something else.*

Replogle County Justice Center — 5:30 p.m.

Duke and Katie were right to worry that her phone might be tapped. But they had overestimated the speed at which bureaucracy moves. Even as Katie heaved herself off the sofa after her brief conversation with her once and (she hoped) future lover, a man in a crumpled polyester suit slammed a stack of papers down on Boss Armitage's desk.

Nate Painter said, "Here you go. Here's a list of their known friends and acquaintances, hot off the fax machine, along with contact details."

Armitage looked at the sheaf of paper, fully half an inch thick, with a sinking feeling in his stomach. Each sheet contained a thumbnail sketch of someone whom one of the fugitives might reasonably be expected to contact, courtesy of the FBI computers.

"It's better than it looks," Painter assured him. "Half of these people are behind bars, and most of the others are indirect acquaintances, just friends of friends. I went through them all and by my reckoning that entire pile has only two promising candidates, and they're both friends of McLaughlin. We have almost nothing on Williamson except some data related to his 'missing person' status. And none of the police records we've been able to track down are any better."

"A loner?"

"More like a bum, actually, although it seems like that wasn't always the case. But let's not waste time; I put the two most likely reports at the top." He leant over the desk and read the names upside down. "Katie Murcheson and Hillary Starr, real name Erma Stricknos. They were the last two loves of his life."

The sheriff scanned the biographies of the two women as Painter continued.

"Starr is basically a whore who caters to the upper middle class. You know: expense account types. It's not obvious what she ever saw in McLaughlin. Or how McLaughlin could afford her. Anyway, he left Murcheson for Starr about two months before he was arrested. I've already got a warrant from a judge; her phone will be tapped within the hour.

"Murcheson is a bit more problematical. He was with her for nearly two years, and off and on for much longer, before ditching her for the Starr woman. We're trying to find her. We think she moved out, headed north maybe. My people say there are 65 phones registered in variations of her name scattered throughout the U.S. We should know which one is hers, if any, later this evening. Our judge will sign the papers for us the moment we know which number is hers. Until then, all we can do is wait."

Armitage pushed the papers away and corrected Painter.

"Wait and worry about what two armed fugitives can do to a family if they decide to start taking hostages."

The McGuire House — 6:30 p.m.

The first frightening surge of adrenalin was now long gone. The fugitives were beginning to feel more at home in the McGuire's house, and as they started to relax, so too did the McGuires.

They were all seated in the living room, handguns tucked discreetly into the fugitives' belts, having just finished a meal of ham and boiled potatoes. Now they were watching the television. To a stranger, it would have looked almost as if they were an extended family.

The McGuires were seated on the sofa, slightly cramped; the two fugitives were in armchairs from which they could keep an eye on their involuntary hosts. Across the lap of all three McGuires sprawled Murphy, his eyes closed.

McLaughlin had been switching channels, surfing from one news program to another. But nothing useful had been added to what the sheriff had said during the news conference that Alan had heard on his way home from the office. The sheriff was still sure that the stolen Buick was somewhere in the county, and reasonably certain that the fugitives were still nearby. He reiterated several times that the men were armed and dangerous, and emphasized that under no circumstances were they to be approached by a member of the public.

A pleased smile had crossed Duke's face the first time he had heard the warning; but his pleasure had been dampened by its frequent repetition — the sheriff made it sound too much like he and Williamson would start shooting people for no reason. On the TV, the sheriff closed an interview with yet another repetition of the warning, and the scene transferred to a news studio.

"That's the last of the local news now until ten o'clock," volunteered Pam as the camera receded from a pair of news anchors chatting smilingly under the sound of martial music. The screen faded, and an advertisement for a soft drink appeared on the screen. McLaughlin lifted the remote control and the screen died with a click.

McLaughlin looked at his watch.

"You look after them for a minute, David. I have to make another phone call."

David nodded vaguely.

Alan McGuire watched McLaughlin leave the room, then let his eyes rest on David.

David Williamson was a real puzzle.

The media painted him as Duke's twin, but it was obvious that that was simply not true. There was too much about David that did not add up. Oh, the vacant stare that came and went was genuine enough. The man seemed preoccupied, and he gave the impression of being only partly aware of where he was and what he was doing. It would have been easy to jump to the conclusion that David was mentally deficient, but the more Alan watched him, the more certain he was that David's problem lay elsewhere.

Shortly after Alan had arrived home, Duke had ordered the family to take them on a second tour of the house, this time permitting only Alan to speak, so he could compare what Alan said with what Louise and Pam had told them. Alan noticed that it was always Duke who asked the demanding questions, and Duke who carried his gun belligerently, pointing it at one of the hostages for emphasis whenever he wanted to make a point.

But as they wandered from room to room, Alan found himself wondering more and more about David. Once, he caught David's gaze running along a bookshelf, his eyes scanning the titles. He stretched out a hand and ran a finger along the spines of a line of Bibles. Alan wondered why, of all the books in the house, David had chosen to touch the Bibles.

And yet he carried a gun, and seemed willing to obey any command that McLaughlin issued.

No matter how he looked at it, Alan could make no sense of David Williamson.

Boston — 7:30 p.m.

Duke's suggestion to Katie that she use a friend's phone was pointless. She had no friends and nowhere to go except her apartment and the office where she worked.

Ten minutes after Duke's call she found herself wandering the neighborhood in the rain, circling her apartment at ever-increasing distances until she realized that half of her allotted hour had passed and she was no closer to finding a telephone.

But there was one place where she knew there was a phone. Time was running out. It would have to do. She hated to go into the store, but she had no choice. She trudged a block and a half and halted outside the window.

Pavel's Corner Grocery, the signboard read; in smaller letters in the corner: *Owner: Pavel Shah*. The yellow letters glistened in the rain.

She hesitated. Perhaps she could simply look up the number in the phone book? Then she need come here only once. But no, Duke's voice had had an edge of desperation to it. She could not take the chance that the number had been changed or that the phone service had been cut off or that the phone was out of order.

She pushed the door, a bell jangled tinnily, and Pavel Shah's head rose predictably from the magazine before him on the counter.

The look of bored disinterest disappeared from his face in a flash, replaced by the look that made her want to shudder every time she saw it. Why, oh why, had she let herself in for this? Couldn't she have found a phone someplace else? But it was too late to change her mind now. In twenty two minutes Duke would be calling her apartment, and there was no time to waste.

She glanced at Pavel Shah and was relieved to see, standing on the counter near his left hand, the old, black, Bakelite telephone she had remembered. She walked determinedly towards the counter. Shah grinned at her. She could feel his eyes removing her clothes.

"Hello, most heavenly miss."

His head dipped up and down appreciatively. Even though she was wearing a cheap plastic raincoat that she would have thought would deter anyone, he addressed his words to her body rather than to her face.

"It is long time since you have honored my humble store with your heavenly presence. Your coming is like... like breath of fresh air to this lonely man."

Katie ran her hand through her hair, causing it to fall about her face in bedraggled strands. She had intended to convey an air of desperation, but Mr. Shah seemed to think that the distraught look merely increased her attractiveness, and perhaps her helplessness.

"I was wondering if you could help me?"

She tried to sound desperate, but the only desperate feeling she had was an almost insurmountable urge to slap the grinning proprietor.

"Heavenly miss, for you I would do anything. Anything." The man gave the word an undercurrent of meaning that Katie did not want to think about.

"My telephone is on the fritz."

The deliberate use of the slang word stopped him. Katie struggled hard to keep her malicious pleasure from showing as the man's grin was replaced by puzzlement.

"It's broken," she elaborated. "Not working. Kaput."

"Ah, yes. I understand. Most distressing."

"So I was wondering if I could use your phone. I'm expecting a call."

The lascivious grin was replaced by a frown of thought. He tore his eyes from Katie and transferred them to the ancient instrument at his side. Several times he looked first at one, then at the other, as if trying to make a weighty decision.

For God's sake. He's going to refuse! I don't believe it, Katie thought. She sent a prayer to a God in whom she did not believe. *Come on, God, just this once, do something nice for me.*

Mr. Shah looked at Katie, reached a decision, and his brow cleared.

"Yes. Of course. Anything to help, heavenly miss. I am always pleased to help such a pretty lady, yes?"

"Yes. Thanks."

She thanked the man; she did not bother to thank the God in whom she did not believe.

The owner pushed the phone across the counter, allowing her to dial her work number on the old, slow rotary dial. As the phone in her office rang, she pointed to the number typed on a circular piece of paper in the center of the dial.

She asked, "Is this the right number?"

"Right number? Yes, that is right number."

The answering machine at work answered; to it she said, "This is Katie. You can call me at 555-3984. I'll be expecting your call. Thanks. Bye."

She put the phone down. Katie explained that she needed to leave for a while, maybe half an hour, but she would be back soon to receive an important call. Murmuring her thanks, she backed towards the door and escaped.

She hurried back to her apartment, then dialled the office and replayed the recording of her voice. She jotted down the number she had recited, and then began a long quarter of an hour, waiting for Duke to call.

The phone rang within thirty seconds of the appointed time.

"Katie?"

"Duke?"

"Do you have a number where I can reach you in a few minutes?"

"Yeah, sure."

"What is it? Quickly, please."

In her mind's eye, she could imagine Duke's hand writing the numbers as she dictated them. But where was he? It sounded like a local call, but these days the lines were so good that he might have been on the other side of the country, or even the other side of the world.

Duke had said something. What was it? She tried to collect her thoughts, to stop them drifting. He repeated the numbers back to her.

"Yes, that's right," she said.

"OK. Be at that number in fifteen minutes. I'll call you then, babe. Thanks."

She found herself holding a dead instrument. She kept the receiver at her ear, listening for any clicks or buzzes. But maybe that just happened in stories. She heard nothing suspicious: just a long, almost-inaudible, faraway sea of endless waves crashing into cliffs.

She put the phone down. Seven minutes later she was on the opposite side of the street from the store, watching Mr. Shah through the rain-streaked window.

She paced nervously up and down the sidewalk, halting now and then beside a lamppost. A police car turned on to the street and headed towards her. The last thing she wanted was for a police officer to stop her on suspicion of soliciting. She moved away from the lamppost and walked slowly down the sidewalk until the car turned a corner and was gone.

She glanced at her watch. One minute to go. She ran across the street and into the store.

Pavel Shah's head rose from the magazine on the counter. He broke into a grin.

She asked, "Did I get a phone call yet?"

"Not yet, heaven...."

He was interrupted by the strident ringing of the old-fashioned bell. Katie lifted the handset.

"555-3984."

"Katie?"

"Yes."

"Are you alone?"

"No, but it's OK."

"Not the police?"

"No; I'm in a convenience store and the storekeeper is nearby, that's all."

A moment's hesitation, then: "OK. Katie, babe, I need help."

For a second anger flared and she nearly retorted: "Oh, so now that you need help, you come to Katie Doormat Murcheson. You didn't seem to need me when Hillary Starr came on the scene with her bottled platinum and implanted tits." But she bit back the words. There would be time enough later to tell Duke what she thought of him. Right now, only one thing mattered: he needed her. Whether he had already approached Hillary Starr and been turned down was a matter for later, when the two of them were face to face. Or, more likely, body to body.

"I'm here. I'll do what I can, Duke."

"Thank God. Listen, there's no time to explain. Let's see, first things first.... You still own a car?"

A car? That was one expense she had cheerfully discarded when she had moved to the city, and she said as much to Duke.

"Shit! Well, could you get one? Borrow one from a friend or something?"

"Duke, I don't have a whole lot of friends here, you know. Cities can be very lonely places."

"Maybe you could steal one? No, stupid idea. Forget I said it."

"Right first time. Where are you anyway?"

"What does it matter? It doesn't sound like you could get here. Say, is there somewhere you could rent a car for a day or two?"

"I guess there must be somewhere....Wait a minute. Perhaps I might be able to borrow a car after all, but it wouldn't be for a few hours." A delightful idea had just occurred to her.

"You sure?"

"Yes, I think so."

"OK. Well, give it a shot. Here's a number to call: 501-447-9524. You'll get an answering machine with a woman's voice. Don't worry, babe: it's just a place I'm staying; I don't know her. Anyway, leave a message. Let me know whether you got the car. But remember, don't use your own phone to make the call."

"Hang on. Let me find something to write with."

How stupid could she be? she wondered as she fumbled in her purse. She should have had a pen and paper ready before the call came through. Giving up the search, she grabbed a pen from beside the cash register. Mr. Shah was trying determinedly to look down the front of her raincoat. She grabbed the magazine he had been "reading," flicked across several pages of airbrushed models until she reached a page with a margin, and said, "OK, give me that again."

Duke repeated the telephone number while she scrawled it in the margin.

"Call me when you've got the car. It doesn't matter what time of day or night, just do it. I'll call you right back, wherever you are. Leave a number."

"OK. I'll do my best. And Duke?"

"Yes."

"I love you."

There was an awkward silence. She had not meant the words to slip out. She was not even certain they were true. Maybe *need* was a better word than *love*.

"Me too, babe. Talk to you later."

"Yes. Bye."

She replaced the phone. Without asking permission, she tore the page from the magazine.

"Thank you," she said. "Thank you very much."

"You are very welcome, heavenly miss. It is my pleasure to help young ladies in distress."

He looked at the unsaleable magazine. She could tell that he was wondering if she had been worth it.

"Right. Yes. Well. Thanks again."

She turned and almost ran from the store.

Boston — 8:15 p.m.

Phil Glotz straightened his tie and turned to look at his profile in the hinged mirror. He turned back and examined his reflection face-on. Yes, even though he was now on the wrong side of forty, he didn't look half bad. And anyway, weren't women supposed to be attracted to older men, as long as their success was commensurate with their years?

Anyway, Katie was only a secretary. Even though in theory she had a choice, they both knew that the truth was that he was the boss, and if she wanted to keep her job.... Really, she should be pleased he was interested in her.

He winked at his reflection. Yes, the old devil-may-care, let's-have-some-fun glint still came readily to his eye. Tonight should be fun.

Antonio's Restaurant, Boston — 9:00 p.m.

She was late.

Well, of course she would be, wouldn't she? She was playing the dating game. Although it was a bit surprising that she was playing so hard. Half an hour was pushing it. One more drink, and then he'd leave. And Katie Murcheson would be out of a job. He raised his finger to signal for another Manhattan.

She entered the restaurant, scanning this way and that, looking for him. His face brightened. Now the evening could start properly.

She slipped into the booth, perkily apologizing for being late. He was silent for several seconds, simply looking at her, drinking her in.

She had done him proud. She had never worn anything like this to the office, and a good thing too. It was a simple outfit, all the more startling for its simplicity: a short skirt of some maroon material that stopped well above her knee; a white blouse with some sort of lacy trim, one too many buttons unfastened; black leather boots; just a hint of eye shadow and blush.

She leaned forward as she kept talking — something about being unable to get a taxi — and he nearly spluttered into his drink. Good God! Maybe they should just skip the meal and leave right now. He couldn't remember the last time he'd wanted a woman so much.

But she leaned back in her seat and picked up the menu. "What's good here?" she asked.

Dinner came and went and he remembered very little of it. Neither did he remember any talk following the meal, for the simple reason that there was none. It was all like a dream. Afterwards, he couldn't remember whether his conversation had been scintillating or tedious. But it didn't matter. She flirted all through the meal, and it was obvious that she was as hungry for him as he was for her.

After the meal he must have driven them to her apartment, although he had no recollection of the drive. He had intended to take her to his place, but somehow they had ended up at hers. He felt a pang of concern as he surveyed the neighborhood. This was obviously not the wisest place to park a Porsche, but it was too late to do anything about it: Katie was already climbing the steps, opening the door, turning, holding it open for him, smiling encouragement.

Burying his anxieties, he locked the car and hurried up the steps, nearly tripping over the uneven stones in his hurry to be with her.

Boston — 11:30 p.m.

He fell asleep afterwards, succumbing to a wave of blissful fatigue. By his side, with his hand draped possessively across her breasts, Katie forced herself to lie quietly on her back, her eyes open, watching the movement of lights reflected on to the ceiling by the puddles outside. Every few minutes, she turned first to the digital alarm clock by her head, and then to her boss, trying to judge how deeply he was sleeping.

She waited a full hour before moving. His breathing was quiet, shallow, regular; his eyes moved under his eyelids: Phil Glotz was dreaming.

She extricated herself from his hand, which had moved downward and now lay across her pelvis. Then she moved from under the bedclothes, and finally got out of the bed itself. She pulled the bedclothes carefully over him, keeping him warm. The rhythm of his breathing did not change.

She tiptoed from the room, stopping only to lift his pants from the floor. She carried them into the living room where, still naked, she

searched the pockets and removed his keys and wallet. She took a wad
of bills from the wallet. She did not bother to count them.

Silently, Katie dressed in the warm clothes she had stashed behind
the couch on which they had passed all of two minutes on the way
to the bedroom: underclothes, jeans, socks, sneakers, a man's shirt
(Duke's, actually, she remembered with an odd feeling of things going
full circle). She picked up her purse from the place where she had
surreptitiously dropped it near the door, and stuffed Glotz's bills inside.

Ninety seconds later, she was seated in the Porsche, looking for the
ignition. She turned the key. The car started first time.

Well, what did you expect, you idiot? It's a Porsche, she thought.
Then, *I sure hope Duke didn't want an inconspicuous car. Well, if he
did, he can steal one.* And with that thought, she pulled away from
the sidewalk.

It was still raining, and she drove defensively through the sheets of
water, unsure how the car would handle. The swish of the windshield
wipers was louder than the car's engine. As she drove, she felt an
unaccustomed feeling of quiet superiority. She passed two police cars
patrolling the night-time streets. One of them followed her for a while,
spawning a nervous feeling in the pit of her stomach; but after a while
the car turned on to a side street and she breathed a heavy sigh of
relief.

She drove for nearly an hour before stopping for gas at a large, busy,
all-night service station. Four pay phones hugged a wall across from
the window where she paid for the gas. She looked at her watch in the
unnatural glare from the overhead fluorescent lights. Ten minutes to
midnight. Well, she thought with a smile, he had told her to call at
any time of day or night.

The phone rang. Even though it was no more than three feet from his
head, the instrument had started its third ring before Duke blearily
lifted his head from the kitchen counter. He looked at the phone
groggily. After a few seconds, he picked up the telephone a moment
before the answering machine kicked in.

"Yes?" His voice was tired, unrecognizable.

"Duke?"

He cleared his throat. "Yes. Sorry. You woke me."

"You said to call any time."

155

"Yeah... you got a car?"

"Sure did."

"Rented?"

"Not exactly. Let's say it's on loan."

"Does the owner know?"

"Not when I last saw him. I suppose he might by now."

"That's my babe. Give me a moment; I need to think."

He rubbed his face, trying to get the sleep out of his brain.

He continued, "When he realizes it's gone, will he know who took it?"

"Er, yes..., probably; I'm pretty sure he'll figure that out."

"What'll he do?"

Katie paused and considered. What would Mister Philip up-and-coming-lawyer Glotz do when he realized that both his car and his one-night-stand had gone missing? Would he go to the police? Would he wait for a couple of days hoping that they would turn up somewhere? She hadn't a clue.

"I really have no idea."

"OK. I guess we'll have to assume he'll call the police. We'll need to deal with that somehow. Now, where are you?"

"About an hour south of the city. I've just filled the car with gas. I've got plenty of money for several more tanks of gas, easily enough to get me across the country, unless the car drinks like its owner."

"Great. Now, let me give you the address of the house where I'm at. You have a pen and paper?"

"Yes."

"The street address is 10673 Valley Road, Replogle, Arkansas. Replogle is a small town in northwest Arkansas. You'll need to buy a map to find it. We're about ten miles out of town in the foothills of the Ozarks. Right now there are roadblocks up at the county line on all the roads in and out of the county. They're looking for two of us who jumped ship when the ship was wrecked, if you get my meaning. We're both holed up here. Don't worry about the other guy: he's going to have to make his own plans. Now, if you can get to an adjacent county and give me a call, I should be able to slip across the border on foot and meet you somewhere safe. Then we can get out of here. Any idea how long it'll take you to get down here?"

"Depends on how many tickets you want me to risk. I'm driving a Porsche."

There was a moment's silence, then Duke laughed a throaty laugh of genuine pleasure. He stifled it quickly.

"I love you, babe. I always said you've got style. No crummy Japanese job for you. No, when you steal a car, it has to be a Porsche. All right, well, take it easy, try not to draw attention to yourself, if that's possible. Drive with the traffic, no more than five miles an hour over the limit. If you see a cop car, don't give him a reason to stop you. Stay off the highways as much as you can. Get yourself a good set of maps."

"Yes, *Mein Herr*. Anything else?"

"No, I guess not. Wait. Yes. There is one thing. Did you mean what you said earlier, about loving me?"

Katie exhaled a "pah!" of exasperation.

"Of course not, you idiot. I'd steal a car for anybody."

"Babe, you're a saint. I wasn't sure you'd come through. I'm sorry about what happened...."

"Stow it, Duke. We're gonna talk about that later."

"Yeah; I guess we are. But I want you to know I love you. After this, it'll just be you and me. I promise. See you in a day or two, I guess. Take it easy."

"Yeah. Take it easy yourself."

She put the phone down. Arkansas? *Arkansas?* She really must be an idiot, stealing her boss's Porsche and agreeing to drive it all the way to Arkansas just because someone who had thrown her over for a bottle blonde had asked her to. She needed her head examining.

She walked away from the phone, got into the car, and began to drive. She felt happier than she had done for months.

Saturday

Boston — 2:30 a.m.

An insistent, rhythmic knocking intruded on Phil Glotz's consciousness from somewhere far away. He shifted uneasily in the bed, willing the metrical tapping that had no place in his dream to go away. It didn't.

In his dream, he looked at the dinner table that separated him from his wife and noticed a woodpecker near the edge, tapping away at the wooden surface. Its head bobbed rhythmically. Tap, tap, tap.

He turned to look at his wife, but she had gone; he was alone now except for the woodpecker. The tapping continued, louder now and more insistent. Slowly, his eyes opened and he realized dully that his wife and the table and the woodpecker had been nothing but a dream; but the tapping was real.

He stretched his arm out toward Katie. She wasn't there. Where had she gone? Maybe she was in the bathroom. He called her name several times. There was no answer except the insistent knocking.

Clumsily, he got out of bed and, naked, wandered into the living room. The tapping was coming from the door of the apartment. The living room was dim and gloomy; the only light was the diffuse, middle-of-the-night glow that filtered through the thin drapes at the window. He peered around the room. There was no sign of Katie. Perhaps, he thought dubiously, she was in the kitchen. He saw a heap on the floor and, looking more closely, realized that it was his pants. He called her name again, loudly now, and turned on the light.

The knocking suddenly stopped. Whoever was in the corridor must have heard him calling Katie. He picked up the pants and rifled through the pockets. His wallet was missing. No, there it was, on the sofa. He opened it. The money was gone, but the other contents — the credit cards, the driver's license, the insurance cards — all those seemed to be there.

"Miss Murcheson?"

The voice was quiet yet penetrating, and very male. Holding the pants in one hand, Glotz padded into the kitchen. She wasn't there.

He turned and called pointlessly into the empty apartment: "Katie?" His voice held a forlorn note of undeserved betrayal.

The knocking returned, louder and more urgent.

"Miss Murcheson? Are you in there? Please open the door."

He hurried to the door.

"Hang on a minute. I'll just be a moment."

Silence fell while he wrestled with his pants and pulled them over his nakedness. He opened the door.

It was unlocked. Whoever was in the corridor could simply have walked in. As he opened the door, a drunken memory came of Katie closing the bolt when they had entered the apartment together.

Two men were standing in the hallway. They were cleanshaven and young, one still in his twenties, the other not yet thirty five. They stood respectfully away from door, trying not to appear threatening. They wore cheap off-the-peg polyester suits, but it was impossible to make out any detail in the light of the single naked 40-watt bulb which glowed at the far end of the corridor.

One of the men reached into the pocket of his jacket and retrieved something small and rectangular. He thrust a badge towards the lawyer.

"Federal Bureau of Investigation. Is Miss Murcheson at home?"

Somehow, Phil Glotz found himself back inside Katie's apartment, sitting on the threadbare couch. He was still naked from the waist up as he waited for the mug of coffee that the younger of the two men from the FBI was brewing in the kitchen.

The older of the two was seated on a hard dining chair, his hands in his pockets and his legs stretched out before him. His eyes ruminatively wandered the apartment. He said nothing until his colleague returned with the coffee.

The younger man shook his head a fraction of an inch. The older man inclined his head. Without a word being spoken, the younger one disappeared into the bedroom. He closed the door behind him. Glotz could see a light showing under the door.

The older man looked at Glotz. "Now then, let's take it from the top. You are?"

Without being aware of how it happened exactly, Phil Glotz began to talk.

Replogle County Justice Center — 4 a.m.

Sheriff Armitage was woken for the third time in as many hours by the telephone close to his head. It also woke the other man in Armitage's office. Just as on the last two occasions, Nate Painter was out of his chair, across the room and had lifted the handset before the sheriff was fully cognizant.

"Sheriff's office. Painter here."

The sheriff listened to one half of a conversation, which was conducted entirely in monosyllables and wordless grunts. The clock on the wall stood at just after four o'clock. He stood up and stretched: there would be no more sleep tonight. Maybe by the end of today he would be able to sleep in his own bed; surely some trace of McLaughlin and Williamson would be found today?

Painter put the phone down.

"Coffee?" offered Armitage.

He nodded toward the coffee maker that stood on the counter next to the tiny sink that hugged one wall of his office.

He continued, "I'll make some fresh. The first shift of deputies will be here in half an hour, and I need to be awake when they arrive."

Painter nodded. "Sure. And I have some news. From Boston, of all places."

It took the sheriff a moment to remember the importance of Boston.

"Oh, yes, one of the girlfriends."

"Right. Katie Murcheson, the one that got ditched. Well, evidently she's unditched. Either that or she's suddenly gone off her rocker."

"Why? What's happened?"

"She had a one night stand with her boss last night at her apartment. She went out while he was sleeping it off, sometime between ten and two. She took all his money." He paused meaningfully. "And his car keys."

"And his car?"

Painter nodded. "And, as you say, his car. The woman has style, I admit that."

"What do you mean?"

"Every police department between here and Boston is now on the lookout for a white Porsche with Massachusetts plates."

Armitage pondered this news while his hands automatically went through the routine of making coffee.

"Good news and bad news, then," he ventured as a stream of dark liquid began to pour into the flask.

Painter considered this for a moment. "In what way bad? It sounds like all good news to me. It's hard to hide a white Porsche."

"Well, maybe she will lead us to them, or at least one of them...."

"But?"

"But if Duke McLaughlin has contacted this girlfriend, then that means he's been able to use a phone. And presumably she knows how to contact him. And that means..."

"...that he's in someone's house."

Armitage nodded. No more words were necessary.

The McGuire House — 7 a.m.

The sun rose that morning at seventeen minutes past five. Its light did not immediately penetrate the thick canopy of leaves that surrounded 10673 Valley Road, and for some time the five forms that were scattered around two rooms on the first floor remained asleep.

In the living room, and sleeping most comfortably, were the McGuires. Louise McGuire lay on the sofa with her head resting on a cushion. Pam, hunched in a pair of armchairs that had been moved together to create a wide, flat-bottomed "U" of a bed, slept with her knees pulled into her chest, while her head rested uncomfortably on a cushion which lay in the crook between one arm and the back of one of the chairs. On the floor, in the center of the room, between the two women, slept Alan McGuire, his breathing stertorious and troubled, his head on a pillow purloined from his bed upstairs.

Blocking the doorway slept David Williamson, his face the most restful of all of them, his breathing shallow but regular. His head lay on the pillow from Louise McGuire's bed; underneath the pillow was Deputy Baker's handgun.

Duke McLaughlin dozed in the kitchen. Since Katie's call his sleep had been fitful and unsatisfying.

Duke was the first to wake, when the sun poked above the trees and its rays slanted through a window to land on his face. His eyelids flickered troubledly; giving up the struggle, he opened them.

He eased himself to a sitting position and massaged his legs to restore the circulation, then he dragged himself to his feet and looked at David, still asleep in the doorway between kitchen and living room.

He heard sounds coming from the living room. David stirred and opened his eyes. A new day had begun.

The McGuire House — 7:30 a.m.

Louise lay with her eyes closed, remembering. She hadn't thought about the way she and Alan met for years, but her conversation with Pam yesterday had brought it all back.

It was so easy to take one's husband for granted; so easy to forget that he had changed her life that morning when they first met.

For whatever reason — probably incredulity that anyone would simply give away his coat in such frigid weather, she found herself walking at the young man's side as they headed for the gates of the park.

It was obvious that he wanted to say something, but each time he opened his mouth to speak, a cloud of vapor issued forth, a doubtful look entered his eyes, and he closed his mouth again, leaving whatever was on his mind unsaid.

They reached the park entrance, and stopped. The man fidgeted, but still he said nothing. Louise was forced to take the initiative.

"Why did you give them your coat and sweater?"

"If you'll walk with me, I'll tell you," he said with obvious relief that she had initiated a conversation. "If that's all right?"

He gestured to the right, up the street. She nodded, and they began to walk quickly along the sidewalk.

"Those men needed warm clothes," he said. "I have plenty of clothes at home. They don't even have a home."

"And that's it? That's why you gave them your things?"

"Can you think of a better reason?"

She didn't reply immediately; instead she studied his profile as he hurried along beside her.

"I've seen you before, haven't I?" she said.

"Yes. At the soup kitchen. You have a home, though, don't you? You're not homeless?"

"No. I just go to the soup kitchen because it's easy and convenient. I always pay," she added, defensively. The kitchen charged a nominal

164

fee of a nickel for its meal, for those who could afford to pay. She realized that she had never thought of paying more than the nickel the kitchen asked.

"You a college student?" she asked.

"Yes, Columbia, studying tax law. You...," There was a pause; then with an obvious effort he said, "You're a prostitute, aren't you? I'm sorry. I shouldn't have said that."

"No, you're right. That's what I am."

They walked for a while in silence.

Suddenly he asked, "Do you enjoy it?"

"What?"

"Do you enjoy it? Being a prostitute, I mean."

She paused to think. The man deserved an honest answer, and she needed to think for a moment what she really thought of her life.

"On the whole, yes, I do. Life could be lot worse. The money's good, and so are the hours, and it gives me plenty of time to be by myself to think and to read."

"You read?" he said, obviously surprised. "What kind of things do you read?"

"Books. I guess I like reading about other places and times. Books remind me that there's more to life than this." She swept her hand around in an expansive gesture, indicating the city. "I like the classics, the kind they don't write any more: Hardy, Jane Austen, the Brontë sisters... books like that."

The man halted and looked at her with raised eyebrows.

He held out his hand towards her.

"I'm sorry; I never introduced myself. Alan McGuire."

"Louise Brown."

They shook hands and smiled at each other; the handshake was the first physical contact between them.

"Look," said McGuire, "it's cold, and my apartment is only a couple of blocks away. How'd you like to come up for a cup of coffee or something?"

It was the "or something" that gave Louise pause. She knew what men meant when they said that. She hesitated.

"Come on," he urged. "It's cold out here, and I'd enjoy talking with you."

"Just talk?"

"What? Oh! Oh, yes, just talk. I'm sorry. I guess you must think of men as swine. Really, we're not all like that. Honestly."

He crossed his heart with his hands as if he were a child.

Louise said, "OK, then. Sure. I'd like that."

And so she found herself in Alan's apartment. It was on the fourth floor of a well-maintained building in a middling neighborhood. His apartment was about the same size as hers, but of a decidedly different character. Posters hung on the wall, most of them bearing a religious message: a stream meandering through a field with a green copse in the distance and underneath the text: "He leads me beside still waters"; a glass of wine and a loaf of bread set against a black background, with no accompanying words. One poster was completely black except for a single bright, four pointed star, and at the bottom the words:

> *A star looks down at me,*
> *And says: "Here I and you*
> *Stand, each in our degree:*
> *What do you mean to do?"*

She frowned for a moment, trying to place the poem. "Oh!" she exclaimed. "Thomas Hardy, isn't it?"

"What?" Alan asked, glancing at her from the closet where he was hanging her coat.

"Thomas Hardy," she repeated. "That stanza on the poster of the star. It's from one of his poems, isn't it? *Waiting Both*, I think."

"I don't know. I just got it because I liked it. I didn't realize it was a quotation."

He smiled at her.

Alan's simple statement came as a shock to Louise. Alan was an urbane college student and obviously from a wealthy family, and yet he happily conceded that she knew more than he about the origin of an obscure quote from a dead British poet. But of course it was just chance that she happened to recognize the poem. She was nothing but a prostitute with no formal education worth speaking of.

She corrected herself. Surely she was more than that. She was a person with feelings, a person who loved good books and the pleasure they gave her.

She looked at him with renewed interest. She couldn't remember the last time someone — especially a man — had treated her as a person instead of an object. Just what sort of man was he, who gave away perfectly good clothing, who accepted her superior knowledge without question, who didn't just think of her as a prostitute?

"Coffee, then?" he asked.

"Yes, please. Black."

"Right. Make yourself comfortable. I'll be back in a few."

Alan disappeared through an open doorway into the kitchen.

Louise wandered around the living room, looking for clues as to what made this strange young man tick.

The room was decorated in light shades of eggshell and cream. The carpet's pile was tight and deep. There were no signs of poverty here, no threadbare patches in the carpet, no thin patches on the upholstery.

A bookcase, tall and wide, filled one wall. Next to it was a construction of planks and bricks that served to accommodate even more books. Most of them had titles like *Theory of Microeconomics*, *Tax Law*, and *The Management of Small Businesses*, but there were fiction books as well, mostly modern fantasy and science fiction.

One and a half shelves were devoted to theological texts. Louise picked one out and opened it at random. She read: "The relationship between the Tetragrammaton in MT and the use of the emphatic form ἐγώ εἰμι in such phrases as 'I am the bread of life' is one that would have been as obvious to the contemporary readers of the Johannine account as it is obscure to modern readers." She closed the book and replaced it without reading further. Alan's library contained none of the books in her own treasured collection, which she kept hidden away in the closet so that her "clients" would not feel intimidated.

Alan returned with the coffee and a plate of Oreos. They sat and talked through one mug of coffee, and then a second, as the Oreos gradually disappeared.

She'd never met anyone like him.

He told her about his faith — how certain he was that nothing happened without a reason, and that God loved everyone, no matter what they had done.

167

"Not prostitutes, though," she said.

"Of course prostitutes. Even thieves. Even murderers."

She smiled politely, not wanting to argue even though she thought him naïf.

Somehow, the time passed and it was suddenly lunchtime. He made them cheese on toast. Lunch time became early afternoon, and then the window began to darken with the oncoming dusk, and somehow the incredible happened.

Louise should have left long ago: she needed to get ready for the evening's work, but instead she was still seated on the sofa, listening to Alan McGuire. A softcovered Bible was open in his hand as he sat next to her, a finger following the words on a page as he read aloud a passage from the gospel of John.

She knew the story. At least, she thought she did. Yet somehow hearing it from Alan seemed to make it so much more real. Somehow, it wasn't just a story any more.

Alan's voice rose and fell with emotion as if he were reading today's news, and he was somehow personally involved in this death of an innocent man.

Alan paused and looked up from the book. "So far, really, nothing extraordinary has happened. If that was where the story ended, then all we could say was that Jesus was a great teacher, perhaps a bit misguided, and that in the end he was doomed to suffer, like so many, at the hands of injustice. But, praise God, that is *not* where the story ends."

He continued to read.

And Louise was changed forever.

Something happened as he described the events of that first Easter morning. Something wonderful, and powerful, and *true*. How had she never seen it before?

It wasn't just some sort of story designed to keep oppressed people in their place, giving them the illusion of hope in a hopeless world. No — it was the ultimate triumph of good over everything that stands against it. A single, world-shattering event that took place in a garden thousands of miles away and nearly two thousand years ago. An event that changed everything. Everything.

A dead man had been placed in a tomb — a tomb guarded by two Roman soldiers. And two days later the guards were gone and the tomb was empty. And Jesus had returned.

And at that moment and forever afterward, she believed.

Someone was stirring nearby, and Louise opened her eyes.

For some seconds she was confused: she wanted to be back with Alan, back at the moment when she had first believed, when everything had seemed so clear... so clear and so simple.

But there was no escaping into the past. She opened her eyes to the reality of the here and now.

Alan was seated on the floor, rubbing his calves, restoring his circulation. Pam, bleary eyed and looking slightly ill, was slowly extricating herself from the two armchairs that had been pushed together to make a bed for her. Murphy was mewling piteously as he hobbled from one member of the family to another. David was rubbing the sleep from his eyes.

"Rise and shine, everyone," said Duke from the doorway in a loud, sarcastic voice. "Let's get with the program. I have some news for you. Someone's coming to pick me up, and she should be here tomorrow. So this will be our last day together. Shouldn't be any problem. We've all gotten along so far, haven't we?"

No one answered.

"Haven't we?" Duke repeated angrily.

Alan grunted, and Duke nodded. "Good, that's better. Now, breakfast. Eggs, bacon, hash browns and orange juice for me. What about you, David?"

Before David could respond, Alan interrupted.

"Excuse me. In this house we spend some time in private devotion before we start the day."

There was an eerie silence, punctuated by the ticking of a clock in the corner of the room.

Eventually, Duke said, "Devotion? What the hell is devotion?"

"As we told you yesterday, we are Christians in this house. We believe it's important to spend time every day in Bible study and prayer. In this house we do that first thing in the morning, before breakfast, so we can give the whole day to the Lord before it starts."

Duke's mouth opened half an inch. He couldn't believe what he was hearing. He turned to David.

"A whole county to choose from, and we wind up with a bunch of effing religious zealots."

He pulled his gun from his belt, and aimed it in the general direction of the McGuires.

"Now get this, and get this good, because I'm not going to repeat it. While we're in this house, we give the orders. We don't want to hurt any of you, but we aren't going to take any of your religious crap. There'll be plenty of time later in the day for you to pray or whatever else you want to do. Right now, me and David here are hungry, and you people are going to get us some breakfast. Got it?"

Alan opened his mouth to protest, but Louise laid a hand on his arm.

"It's all right. We'll do as you say. And we'll pray for your souls later."

Duke glared at her for a moment, but decided not to make an issue of it. "Make mine two eggs, sunny side up. What are you having, David?"

Louise, assisted by Alan and Pam, made them all breakfast. They ate quietly and afterwards they took it in turns to shower and change into clean clothes. The McGuires repaired to the living room where they read their Bibles under the watchful eyes of the two fugitives, and for the better part of an hour there was almost complete silence in the house. Occasionally, the quiet was broken by a sudden squawk from the police radio in the kitchen, but most of the time passed in silence as the McGuires tried to concentrate on God's word and the fugitives alternated between watching the hostages and re-reading the morning newspaper for clues about how the search for them was progressing. They briefly checked the TV, but none of the stations seemed to carry local news so early in the morning.

The only break in the monotony came when Duke took Murphy outside to relieve himself. It was obvious from the strained look on her face that Pam was worried that Duke would finish the job he had started the day before, but after a few minutes Duke returned with the dog and with obvious relief Pam went back to her reading.

After devotions, Louise said that she needed to clean the house and do some laundry. Duke dogged her footsteps as she worked around the house while Pam and Alan read in the living room and David sat nearby to keep an eye on them.

After a few minutes, Alan put down his book and looked at David. David had become bored and was staring through the window at nothing in particular, his thoughts obviously far away.

"Excuse me," said Alan softly.

David's head slowly turned and he struggled to focus on the man on the far side of the room.

"I've been watching you," said Alan gently. "I'm sorry, but you're different from Duke. He's a criminal, but you're not. Why are you doing this?"

"Be quiet," warned David.

Alan ignored him.

"You're educated. That's obvious from the way you speak and the way you look at our books. You know, it's not too late to give yourself up. I'd vouch for you. You haven't done us any harm and...."

David abruptly removed his pistol from his belt and pointed it at Alan.

"Shut up," he snapped.

Gradually, David lowered the gun.

"I'm sorry," David said. "I just don't want to talk about it."

"Would you mind if I prayed for you?" asked Alan, so quietly that it was almost as if the question had risen spontaneously from the air.

"There's no point. But if you want to, I'm not going to stop you."

Alan closed his eyes and for a couple of minutes his lips moved silently as he prayed for the man sitting on the opposite side of the room.

"Amen," he said out loud.

He smiled at David, who turned abruptly away; then he picked up his book to continue reading.

At length Louise returned with Duke still following close behind.

Duke said, "I guess it's not too early for lunch."

There was a bustle of movement as they all headed for the kitchen, where Duke guided David to a corner.

"Look," Duke said, "my ticket out of here is on its way. How about you? I'm not taking you with me. What are you going to do when I've gone?"

David shrugged. "I don't know. I guess I'll leave and try to make my own way. I've done it before."

"You're sure there's no one who'll help you?"

"I'm sure."

Duke sighed. "OK, then. Well, good luck. You'll need it."

"I think we'll both need it, don't you?"

Duke ignored the question; he had already decided that David wasn't going to last an hour alone.

He turned to the McGuires and demanded: "Get a move on, we're hungry."

Soon after lunch, everything changed.

Until now, the McGuires had thought they were in no real danger as long as they obeyed the fugitives' — and especially Duke's — commands. The illusion of security was shattered in a sudden, unexpected and thoroughly unpleasant manner.

Behind the living room was a sun room, and they were all seated there with the windows open while a fan drew a steady breeze through the room. Louise and Pam were struggling to stay awake while they read; Alan was stretched out on an old couch with his eyes closed, apparently asleep.

David was idly flicking through a book about the Civil War, stopping now and then to read a sentence or two. Duke was slumped in a rattan chair doing nothing in particular, his eyes roaming the room and the trees outside, boredom written all over his face. Murphy, his shoulder now bandaged tightly, snoozed in a patch of sun. A TV was on in the living room, the sound turned low, in case a news report came on.

Duke's eyes settled on Pam.

For perhaps thirty seconds he watched her. His eyes stayed on her as she finally succumbed to sleep.

Abruptly shattering the calm, he stood up, looked directly at Pam, and said loudly, "You're coming upstairs with me."

Her eyes flickered open, "Wha...?"

Alan's eyes jerked open, but no one moved.

"I said upstairs. Now."

"Why?"

"Because I say so, that's why."

Slowly she levered herself out of her chair.

Alan said, "You aren't going to do anything to her, are you?"

"Why? What are you going to do about it? Pray? I've never had a black girl, and I've been sitting here thinking that this here's about as good a chance as I'm likely to get."

A shout came from Pam and Louise. "No!"

Seemingly out of nowhere, Duke's gun appeared. He pointed it first at Pam, then at Louise, and finally at Alan.

"Listen, and listen good. All you effing goody-two-shoes get one thing straight. Me and David here are the ones with the guns, and what we say goes. If I want to take your effing daughter upstairs and show her how a white man does it, then that's exactly what's going to happen. Understand me?"

"Sir."

Into the monosyllable Alan put all the subservience of a slave who has seen that his master is about to do something unwise and has to be stopped.

"Please, there's no need to wave your gun around. But we've done you no harm. We've obeyed every order you've given us. Can't you see? This is asking too much."

"Why? You afraid I might infect her or something? I've been in-car-cer-at-ed. Jailed. Behind bars. I'm clean. I haven't had the chance to be anything else. Now, you, come along upstairs. David, watch the other two for me. This will probably take a while. I've got a lot to teach her."

"No... please don't," said Alan, rising.

Duke pushed him back down on to the couch. He waved his gun in Alan's face.

"I mean it, nigger. Your God can't save her, and neither can you. If you force me to, I'll shoot you. But I'll still have her afterwards."

Pam was standing by her chair with panic in her eyes. "What if I refuse?"

Duke pointed the gun at Louise. "Bang," he said.

Pam looked at her mother, then at her father, who was looking at her in turn with a desperate hopelessness. Finally, she looked at Duke.

"All right," she said, "I'll come with you."

"No!" shouted Alan.

"Yes, Dad. I have no choice."

The others watched in silence as Pam left the room with Duke close behind, his gun still in his hand and a triumphant smile on his face.

In horrified silence, they heard them climb the stairs, then their footsteps were obscured by the sound of the fan. Louise looked at David, who returned her gaze with a miserable helplessness.

Alan implored him, "For the love of God, stop him, man. Maybe he'll listen to you."

David's eyes, although they looked at Alan, did not see him. The vacant stare had returned.

"Come on," Alan insisted. "It's not fair. She's our only daughter. This will scar her for life. She'll never get over it."

"Shut up. I'm thinking," David snapped.

Alan opened his mouth to argue, then thought better of it. Louise turned off the fan. From upstairs there was an ominous silence. Louise closed her eyes and her lips began to move in prayer. Alan was incapable of prayer; he was wondering how long it would take Duke to remove Pam's clothes.

Suddenly, David's eyes focused sharply on Louise. She must have sensed his gaze, because her lips stopped moving and her eyes opened. For a long moment they stared at one another. Alan watched them, mystified. It was as if his wife and this dangerous stranger were somehow speaking to one another in a language that he could not understand.

David said to Louise, "There's only one thing you can say that will make me interrupt what's going on up there. And I think you know what it is. Is it true?"

Unflinchingly, Louise returned David's gaze.

She said, "She's pregnant."

For an eternity there was silence.

Then Alan blurted, too loudly, "Of course she's not."

Louise ignored her husband. "How did you know?"

"This is insane," said Alan to no one in particular.

"I was pretty sure the first time I saw her," said David. He pulled the gun from his belt. "Neither of you move from this room until I get back. Understand?"

"Yes," agreed Louise.

Alan nodded, not trusting himself to speak.

David brandished the gun dangerously at Alan and said, "Say it, you. Swear in the name of your God that you won't move from this room. I want to hear the words."

"I won't leave this room. I swear it. In the name of Jesus Christ our Lord. Neither of us will."

With his knuckles white with the strength of his grip on the gun, David stalked from the room.

The door of Pam's bedroom was open. David stepped through the doorway with his gun raised. Inside, he paused, observing the scene before him. Pam was on the bed, naked, eyes closed, her mouth moving but producing no sound. Duke was beside the bed, naked from the waist down, and was in the process of unbuttoning his shirt. Duke swore with impatience at a button, then ripped it off.

Sensing David's presence, he stopped. He turned and saw the gun in David's hand.

"What the...," he began.

"She's pregnant. Leave her alone."

"What?"

"You heard. I said the girl's pregnant. Leave her alone."

"She's pregnant?"

Duke swivelled to look at Pam. He smiled.

"Why, you cunning bitch. And I thought you were unused."

"Leave her alone, Duke. You're not going to have her."

"Why the hell not?"

"Because it's not right."

"Because she's pregnant? Give me a break. You can't be serious. Maybe she can teach *me* something."

"I'm not going to argue about it. Leave her alone."

"Or what?"

"Or I'll shoot you. Here and now. In cold blood."

"You wouldn't dare. You haven't got the balls."

"Try me."

Duke made a move to get on the bed. David's grip on the gun tightened as he lined up the weapon with Duke's body. Duke stopped and looked at David's face. It wasn't hard to read. David wasn't bluffing.

Duke said, "Look, you can have her first if you want."

The gun began to tremble in David's hand as rage welled up and threatened to spill into action.

"Pam, get your clothes and go downstairs. Now!"

With the two men angrily facing one another, she scrambled off the bed, gathered her clothes from the floor and hurried, still naked, from the room.

"I'll get you for this." Duke said. There was hatred in his eyes.

David shook his head. "I'm sorry, Duke. I couldn't let you do it. I could never have lived with myself afterwards. I had a daughter once."

"Who the hell cares? I hope that when the effing cops catch you they put you away and throw away the key. I was looking forward to that."

David tried to mollify him. "Come on, Duke. We need each other, at least for now."

"Speaking of which, do you realize that right now you and me are in this room alone? No one's guarding them. The whole effing family has probably called the cops."

"I made them promise they wouldn't leave the sun room."

"You what?" Duke shrieked. "You made them promise they wouldn't leave the room? I don't believe it. What kind of mush do you have for brains? Get back down there. Now." Duke picked up his pants and began wrestling them on.

David turned and went back downstairs.

As he reached the sun room, Pam was buttoning the final buttons of her blouse, and Alan and Louise were in the midst of an angry exchange.

"I'm sorry, honey," Louise McGuire was saying to her husband in a raised voice, obviously trying to justify herself. "I haven't had a chance to tell you. I only found out myself yesterday lunchtime. We haven't been alone since then."

The dog Murphy, who had been woken by the argument, for some reason decided that this was the moment to have another go at one of the strangers who had been responsible for the pain in his shoulder. He heaved himself to his feet and ran three-leggedly across the room towards David, barking as loudly as he knew how.

David raised his gun and, as the mastiff lopsidedly launched itself at him, he fired.

No one moved.

Duke arrived, breathing heavily from running down the stairs three at a time. He halted beside David. All eyes were on the dog. Or what remained of him — for the shot, fired at point blank range, had ripped open the animal's skull. Blood and brains mixed in a nauseating mess on the floor. It was as grisly a sight as any of them had ever seen.

Pam and Louise winced and turned away. Pam closed her eyes tightly and retched several times. Then she threw up over her chair.

Duke was the first to speak.

"This house is mad. Absolutely effing crazy. A pregnant virgin and a kamikaze dog. What is it with you people?"

He shook his head angrily and stalked out of the room.

Central Replogle County — 7:30 a.m.

Jim Brewer looked at the clock in the dashboard of the police car. It was seven thirty. At the next junction, he performed a three-point turn and started to drive slowly back the way he had come, heading back towards Replogle.

He had arrived at the justice center shortly before four thirty. The news was that there was no news: his brother's Buick still had not been found, and there was still no trace of the fugitives.

He wondered whether they were going to find the men. Had they already evaded the roadblocks and the prowling vehicles and crossed into another county? Or were they lying low somewhere in the hills, waiting for the searchers' enthusiasm to wane? Boss had looked distracted and tired as he gave the men their orders not long before dawn: "I want every inch of public roadway in this county covered by at least one police vehicle before seven thirty this morning, and I want you all back here at eight."

It was an impossible order of course, but the deputies had set about the task with a will, determined to cover as much ground as possible before eight o'clock.

The sheriff hadn't given the men detailed instructions or specific itineraries. Each man was free to go wherever he wanted within a specific portion of the county. In this way, the sheriff had thought that the search pattern would be unpredictable, so that the fugitives would not be safe if they moved to some part of the county that had already been searched.

In Brewer's case, his instructions were simply: "take a look to the south and south west, Jim."

About half the cars were marked. Perhaps a third of those were from the Replogle County Sheriff's Department; the others were a mixture from surrounding departments: Hill County, Faraday County, a few from nearby cities that could spare them. The enforcement agencies in surrounding counties were being stretched thin, and there was some concern that if the fugitives managed to cross the county line they would find it easy to slip away completely out of the area.

The road blocks were still in place, though. If they crossed into another county, they would have to do so on foot. Then they would have to steal another vehicle if they wanted to get very far.

He wondered who the odds favored: the police or the fugitives?

He passed an unmarked car travelling slowly in the opposite direction. The driver of the other car lifted a hand in acknowledgment. Neither of the deputies smiled.

Jim Brewer arrived back at the justice center a little before eight. Inside, officers from several departments were milling around in the conference room and spilling out into the corridor, waiting for the morning briefing.

He joined the line at the coffee machine. Someone had brought a supply of doughnuts and he munched one gratefully while waiting his turn at the machine. There was muted conversation all around, but no one really knew anything: it was simply conversation for the sake of it. Some of the men were discussing a rumor that there had been some sort of a break in the case overnight and that Boss was going to share something he wanted to keep from the press, but although there was plenty of speculation, none of them knew for sure what the break might be.

The sheriff had held a press conference at seven thirty in the parking lot, and several of the deputies had noticed that his dealings with the media had been uncharacteristically terse and his answers peculiarly unhelpful. The entire conference could have been summed up in one sentence: "We haven't found them yet, and I have nothing else to say."

Brewer finally reached the front of the line. He poured a mug of coffee and carried it into the conference room. With so many officers from other departments around, he was not sanguine about the sheriff's chances of keeping anything from the media if there really had been a break.

The furniture had been moved to make more room for the deputies. A table was at one end of the room; fifty-odd chairs filled the rest of the space. A couple of clumps of officers were talking in a small space free of chairs at the rear of the room; a few were already seated. There was no sign of Boss.

Brewer selected a chair near the center of the room. Almost as soon as he sat down, he heard a strident "Good morning, men," from the doorway; as an afterthought, Boss added, "and women."

Conversation ceased and there was a general movement towards the chairs as the sheriff strode to the front of the room. Walking almost in his footsteps was a man in his fifties wearing a remarkably crumpled civilian suit. Brewer didn't recognize him. The two men went directly to the table at the front of the room. The man in the suit sat, but the sheriff remained standing, looking out over the sea of faces, waiting for everyone to find a place. Slowly, the room fell silent. Brewer heard the sound of someone closing the door. The air conditioner seemed unnaturally loud.

Boss looked out over the officers, his eyes slowly sweeping from one to the next, until he had examined the face of everyone in the room.

"Deputy Stewart," he said to a man at the rear of the room, "perhaps you would be so good as to escort Mr. Livingstone from the building. Make sure that the receptionist knows what he looks like and make it clear that he is not to be allowed into the building again unless accompanied by a *bona fide* officer."

There was a momentary silence while the words sank in, then someone laughed as Todd Livingstone, Channel 7's investigative reporter, rose from a seat near the rear of the room. He was dressed in the uniform of a deputy of the Hill County Sheriff's Department.

The reporter lifted his hands in mock surrender and said with a grin, "It's a fair cop."

The room broke into laughter and there was scattered applause. Livingstone bowed to the sheriff and then made his way towards the door. Officer Stewart put a hand under the reporter's arm and escorted him from the room. Boss shook his head as they left, although on his face was a grin as wide as Livingstone's.

He turned to the gathering and addressed the officers.

"Good morning, ladies and gentlemen. Before I say anything, I want you all to know that everything I am about to say is confidential.

That goes for those of you not directly under my jurisdiction as well as those who are. I have been in contact with your commanding officers, and they have all assured me that anyone who breathes a word of what we are about to tell you will face a severe reprimand. If there is anyone who can't live with that, they'd better leave the room now.

"And the same goes if there is still a representative of the media skulking around here somewhere. If a word of what I am about to say gets out, someone is going to be skinned alive, and I don't want to hear any bellyaching about First Amendment rights while I'm doing the skinning, understood?"

There was neither a smile nor a frown on his face as he spoke. He was simply stating facts, and there was not a person in the room who did not understand that Boss Armitage meant exactly what he said.

The sheriff's eyes scanned the room methodically, from left to right, front to back, a challenge in his eyes. Some eyes met his, some looked away. No one rose to leave.

"All right," he said. "First, let me introduce Nate Painter of the FBI, who has some words he wants to share with you."

The sheriff sat and the FBI man stood.

When Painter spoke, there was a gravely authority in his voice that surprised most of the people in the room. In his cheap, crumpled suit, Painter looked like a desk man who spent his life filling in forms, not someone who actually understood anything about catching bad guys.

"As Sheriff Armitage has indicated, my name is Nate Painter and I am an agent with the Federal Bureau of Investigation. Although you are all taking your orders from Mr. Armitage here, it is the Bureau that is ultimately responsible for catching the two men whom we are seeking. But I would like to take this opportunity to thank Mr. Armitage, if not exactly publicly then at least in front of this august group, for his wholehearted cooperation and support in this operation."

There was a smattering of applause, led by Boss's own men. It subsided as Painter continued.

"Now, to business, ladies and gentlemen. We cannot be certain, but overnight we have received strong evidence suggesting that Williamson and McLaughlin are still somewhere in Replogle County, probably in a private residence.

"At this time of year, as you are all aware, a percentage of homes in the county stand empty while the owners are away on vacation.

Today, however, as I'm sure you all realized as you dragged yourselves out of bed this morning, is a Saturday, and so at least some of those who have been away will likely be returning today. And one of those families may be returning to find some unexpected house guests.

"However, we have no reason to believe that our men were particularly choosy about finding a house in which to lay low. It is quite possible, even likely, that somewhere in this county our men are holding a family hostage. In response to that possibility, today we will be changing our tactics.

"There are approximately fifty of you in this room. Ten of you will continue to drive unmarked cars along the roads of the county, looking for signs of anything suspicious. The rest of you have a different job. You will visit as many houses in the county as possible, looking for any signs of the men's presence. There are a total of 5,652 dwelling units in the county. We have printed 6,000 one-page flyers that show the men's pictures and include phone numbers for members of the public to call if they see the men whose pictures are on the flyers.

"Individual routes have been designed for each of you and for your replacements who will take over this afternoon at five o'clock. If you do the arithmetic, you will see that we have quite a task ahead of us. With just forty of you out there at any given time, each of you has to visit a hundred and fifty houses. We are hoping that every home in the county will have been visited before we lose daylight this evening. As you leave this room, each of you will be given a stack of leaflets to give out, as well as sheets and maps on which will be marked every house you are to visit.

"If you need assistance at any time, we recommend that you use the nearest public phone if at all possible. Use the radios in the cars only as a last resort. As you know, the fugitives stole a vehicle yesterday inside which was a police radio; we must assume that the fugitives are using the scanner to listen in on any conversations that take place on our channels. A few of you will be issued with cellular phones, but they are unreliable because of the hills. Don't assume they will work unless you are close to a transmission tower.

"If you see anything suspicious, do nothing; but call it in as soon as possible. Don't take any unilateral action unless forced to do so. Remember, these men are dangerous. If they're in a house that's occupied, we must assume that they've threatened the family. So don't assume that anyone who talks to you will tell you about the men if they're inside the house. They may be too scared to talk. Don't push. If you see something suspicious, simply call it in, and we'll take it from there.

"If you go to a house and no one is home, make a note of it, along with anything else you think might be important, next to the address on the sheet. Don't leave a flyer at any house that is unoccupied. Watch for signs of stress or strain in people's faces. Try to engage people in conversation. Don't be in too much of a hurry. I'd rather we don't finish before sundown than that we let them slip through the net because we weren't careful enough.

"Meet back here at five o'clock this evening to hand over any remaining work to the next shift. If for some reason we need to end the operation, the dispatcher will broadcast a message in which the phrase 'a heavy wind is expected' will be used. If you hear a message containing those words at any time during the day, return here immediately. Do not respond to the message. The message will be transmitted several times on orange channel, as necessary. Any questions?"

There were none. All the officers were grim. As Painter regained his seat, Boss Armitage stood once more.

"All right, ladies and gentlemen. Each of you pick up a packet as you leave. Good luck, and be careful. And remember, use the radio only for routine messages; if you see anything suspicious, use a telephone unless you have no option."

Jim Brewer stood with the others, and lined up to receive his stack of addresses, along with the key to a vehicle. The deputies filed out the room silently, with an air of grim determination.

The air was damp and heavy, and Brewer was sweating before he had walked halfway across the parking lot. His car was number 21, painted in the livery of the Replogle County Sheriff's Department. He dumped the papers on the passenger seat, started the car, and switched on the air conditioner.

He picked up the top sheet. It was a hastily drawn map with his route marked in black. His stack was thinner than most, and now he saw the reason. His route lay in the southwestern quadrant of the county, which was particularly sparsely populated.

Leafing quickly through the papers, he counted only one hundred homes, but all bore rural addresses like 10253 Woodside Road or 19732 South County Road 9. He would need to drive to every house individually; there would be no walking from one house to the next. He put the car in gear and nosed his way into the stream of vehicles trickling out the parking lot.

The first address on his list was 1005 Hillside Lane. It should have taken him no more than twenty minutes to reach the house, but he got lost and added a quarter of an hour to the journey. At one point he nearly radioed the dispatcher for help, but he fought down the impulse to air his stupidity in public and eventually he found the unmarked track that was Hillside Lane.

He bounced down the pitted road and finally reached the end, where stood a ramshackle house in an advanced state of disrepair. A labrador jumped to its feet and pulled at its chain, barking viciously in his direction. Jim Brewer sighed. It was going to be a long day.

The morning went slowly, even more slowly than he had feared.

Replogle County people were an independent bunch. The word "ornery" might have been coined especially for them. Few houses displayed numbers, and often the tracks leading to them were, like Hillside Lane, devoid of any road signs. Dogs outnumbered people, and not a few guns were in evidence when people came to the door in answer to his insistent knocking.

At last he broke off for lunch. He dropped over the county line into Faraday and grabbed a burger and a root beer float from an A & W. By one o'clock, he was back in the routine.

By three o'clock, he was exhausted. The last four houses had taken over half an hour: each of them had been difficult to find and then turned out to be unoccupied. He had prowled around them, looking for anything out of the ordinary: tire marks that might have belonged to his brother's Buick, or the telltale oil leak it always left whenever it was parked for more than a couple of minutes, or curtains drawn closed in the middle of the day, or sounds coming from inside the apparently deserted building.

But there was nothing, and next to each he had dutifully marked "apparently unoccupied" on his sheet, and handed the problem to someone else.

He looked at his watch. Only another two hours to go. Ninety minutes if he allowed half an hour for the drive back to Replogle. He looked forlornly at the stack of paper on the passenger seat. He was not yet half way through. He supposed he should feel a pang of pity for the officer who would be taking over at five, but instead he just wanted to go home, drink a beer, and go to sleep.

As the day had progressed, the nature of the houses on his list had slowly changed. Gradually, the ramshackle hovels had given way to tidy homes in which retired couples lived and then to ranch houses hidden deep in the trees, and now, as he entered the hilliest portion of the county in the extreme south west, he was beginning to visit some quite fine homes.

He looked at the next address on his list: 10673 Valley Road. Well, this one at least should be easy to find. Valley Road was marked on his map as being an alternative name for County Road 13, which was the road along which he was currently driving.

He saw the house two minutes later, in a valley between two tall ridges. The house was set back a short distance from the road, half hidden by the forest. Its gravel driveway disappeared around the rear of the building. In keeping with county fire regulations, the house address was marked on the siding in contrasting colors, easily visible from the main road. It was one of the few houses Brewer had seen all day that obeyed this particular regulation.

Brewer slowed and pulled off the road, bringing the car to a halt on the driveway beside the house. Grabbing his clipboard and the topmost flyer from the stack, he made his way to the front door. He strolled slowly, trying to appear casual.

Things were certainly looking up. The house had two full stories, and there was what looked like a circular swimming pool fenced off at the rear of the house. The siding was recently stained and the lawn and the flower beds were neat and tidy. He thought he saw a movement inside the house at one of the upper windows. Pausing to look up, he was less sure: perhaps it had simply been a bird's reflection as it flew overhead. The sound of birds in the trees was loud here, and as he watched a flock took flight and circled once before disappearing behind the trees, heading northward.

He reached the front porch and spotted the doorbell, the house address repeated in small digits above it. He pressed the button and heard a faint, genteel, two-tone bell somewhere deep inside the house.

He began counting slowly. By now he had established a procedure that he repeated at each house as necessary: first the doorbell or a knock on the door; count to thirty; try the doorbell again; another count to thirty; rap loudly on the door; amble slowly all the way around the house, returning to the front door; one more press on the bell and, on the count of ten, a flurry of hard raps on the door; then return to the car and note that the house was vacant; then on to the next house.

Brewer reached his first count of thirty. In response to the bell there had definitely been movement inside the house, but no one had come to the door. Perhaps it was just a family pet. He pressed the doorbell again. The chimes sounded. He heard movement again. This time he was sure that the sounds were human: the footfalls, indistinct though they were, were too heavy for a house pet. They were coming closer.

The door was opened by a well-preserved woman in her forties. She returned his smile, but only with her mouth. It was the sort of greeting he had seen all day, although expressed more politely than most: a willingness to say "hello" to the uniformed officer but not to offer any warmth. By now he was becoming accustomed to that look.

The woman's eyes were a little bloodshot and she seemed distinctly tired. He wondered if she had been drinking. She was blinking as if something was troubling her eyes.

"Sorry to bother you, ma'am." He nodded politely and consulted his clipboard. "Are you Mrs. McGuire?"

"I am."

Jim Brewer began the liturgy he had perfected hours before.

"I'm sure you've heard about the two fugitives who escaped in the northern part of the county on Thursday morning, ma'am?" A pause for her assent. "We were wondering if you've seen anything suspicious at all? Strangers prowling around in the forest? Anything unusual?"

"Strangers in the forest? No, I don't think so."

She drew the thumb and forefinger of her right hand across the uppermost parts of her cheeks, across the bridge of her nose, then across her eyes. Perhaps he had woken her from an afternoon nap.

"Anyone else in the house, ma'am?"

"My husband and daughter are here, but they can't come to the door right now."

"Well, please make sure they call us if they see anything suspicious. Here's a flyer with pictures of the two men and a phone number you can call anytime, day or night. We'd be grateful if you'd take a look at this and show it to the other members of your family, and if any of you sees anything out of the ordinary, anything at all, or if you catch sight of the vehicle that's described on the flyer, call us immediately. And don't try to approach the men yourselves. As I'm sure you've heard, they're armed and dangerous. Just call us if you see anything suspicious, and we'll take it from there."

The woman, her eyes still bothering her, accepted the flyer.

"Thank you, officer. You can count on us to do what we can."

"Thank you, ma'am. Good afternoon."

Deputy Brewer made his way back to the car, his mind already on what route he would take to the next house.

The McGuire House — 3:10 p.m.

While Duke sulked, Alan and David took Murphy's remains outside and buried them under a nearby tree. Louise cleaned up the blood and gore and filled the sun room with the scent of air freshener. Pam sat and stared sightlessly through the gauze of the window screens at nothing in particular.

Alan and David came back inside, and in an effort to restore normality Louise went into the kitchen to make coffee. Then they all stopped and looked at one another: a vehicle had come up the driveway and stopped beside the house.

Upstairs, Duke was in the spare bedroom at the front of the house, distancing himself from everyone else's craziness and trying to figure out what he was going to do when Katie arrived.

He heard the sound of a car on the gravel of the driveway.

The car's engine stopped. Duke looked outside to see who had chosen this unlucky moment to visit the McGuires. Shit! A uniformed police officer was walking slowly along the path which edged the front of the house, his gaze wandering all over the building.

Duke drew himself back from the window, hoping he hadn't been spotted. He raced down the stairs, and met David in the hallway just as the two-toned chime of the doorbell rang out.

"A cop!" Duke exclaimed in a sharp whisper.

He hurried past David into the kitchen.

"Why is a cop here?" he demanded.

The McGuires looked at one another in consternation.

David walked into the room. "Perhaps someone reported the shot when I killed the dog," he suggested.

"No. There aren't any houses close enough for anyone to hear," said Alan.

The chimes rang out again.

"OK," Duke said desperately, "here's what we're gonna do. Louise, you go and answer the door. Be nice to him. Say whatever it takes to get rid of him. We'll be listening to every word you say. If you do anything to raise his suspicions, anything at all, there'll be no warning. I'll simply shoot Pam the way David shot the dog, Understand?"

Trembling, Louise nodded.

"OK; now go out there and get rid of him."

Louise, trying to control her fright and dabbing at her eyes, unsteadily walked past the men and into the hallway. David and Duke withdrew into the living room, out of sight. They listened intently.

Louise answered the door, and they heard the officer explain that they were checking all the houses in the county in case anyone had seen any sign of the fugitives. Louise assured him that she would be sure to call the number on the flyer if she saw anything suspicious.

Louise closed the door. Duke and David relaxed as their breathing returned to normal.

"Good girl," said Duke as she walked past them into the living room. "I'm glad at least one person in this house isn't completely crazy."

She looked at him with eyes filled with pity.

Southwest Pennsylvania — 2:30 p.m.

Officer Dan Kowalski returned his attention to the latest John le Carré paperback. The book was certainly more interesting than real life. For the past three hours, excepting only the occasional bursts of activity when he gave chase and presented an unhappy driver with a ticket (or, if the driver was a good-looking young woman, a warning and an ingratiating smile) his Saturday afternoon had been wasted on speeding duty.

This was one of Kowalski's least enjoyable assignments, not so much because of the amount of work it entailed (which was slight) but because of the sheer boredom. Not many cars travelled this part of State Highway 44 because the Interstate ran parallel to the highway only five miles away. But those that did drive along this stretch of road almost invariably broke the 55 mph limit.

There were good clear shots for the Doppler beams in both directions, even though his car was reasonably hidden, parked a few yards from a junction near the middle of the two-mile stretch of ruler-straight highway. He clocked every car as it entered the straight stretch, and it was a rare vehicle that did not accelerate past the legal limit within seconds.

Most of them he ignored. But if a vehicle was doing more than 65 he would watch it as it passed; then, depending on how he judged the attitude (or the looks) of the driver, he would either ignore it or pull out and give chase.

The last such vehicle had been a little over half an hour ago: a red Camry driven by a pretty young blonde in her early thirties which he had clocked at sixty eight. He had chased after her with his lights flashing but, after a brief struggle with his conscience, let her off with a warning.

That meant he was further behind his quota than ever; but the smile she had thrown him had made it worthwhile. Lowering the paperback, he stared out the window and remembered her smile....

A beeping interrupted his reverie. Placing a finger on the page to keep his place, he saw a low white sports car approaching at fifty seven miles per hour.

He watched as the car came closer. Its speed didn't change. That meant it carried either a radar detector or a remarkably cautious driver. The car passed by, its speed still barely over the limit. As it passed, three things registered almost simultaneously.

The first was that the driver had obviously spotted him, for she glanced at his half-hidden car as she drove by. The second was that she was extraordinarily pretty, or at least gave that impression in the fleeting glimpse he had of her. The third took a moment longer to register: the car was a white Porsche with Massachusetts plates.

He hesitated a moment while he processed this last fact. Then he started his engine and reached for the microphone.

"Dispatch, this is car 14, Officer Kowalski. Please confirm for me the description of that vehicle with Massachusetts plates we're looking for."

"Good afternoon, Dan. Please stand by. We'll get that for you."

For perhaps thirty seconds, he watched the Porsche recede. Its speed didn't change.

The dispatcher came back on the radio.

"OK, Dan; here's the description: white Porsche model 911, three years old, clean, excellent condition. 32,000 miles on the clock. Massachusetts plates, tag number 290 KAF. Registration in the glove compartment in the name of Philip Glotz. I have his address if you need it."

Kowalski scribbled the information on the pad on his dash.

"No thanks, dispatch; that won't be necessary. We may have a live one here. I'll report further in a few minutes."

"10-4, Dan."

He put the car in gear, pulled out on to the highway, and executed a tight turn, the tires squealing in protest. In the distance, the Porsche passed out of sight as it reached the end of the straight section of the highway. Kowalski floored the accelerator. He had reached ninety before he had to brake to take the corner. As he turned the wheel, the radio came to life.

"Car 14, this is Captain Taggart."

He rounded the corner and picked up the microphone.

"Fourteen, sir."

"Just a reminder that we are not to interfere with the vehicle unless it's absolutely necessary."

"Yes, sir. A white Porsche 911 with Massachusetts plates passed me about a minute ago. I'm in pursuit to try to get a look at its plates."

"Was it speeding?"

"No, sir."

"Then don't interfere unless the driver gives you cause to do so. Just check the plates."

"10-4, sir. I see it up ahead now. Wait a minute."

The Porsche was not far ahead now. The highway had narrowed and was beginning to wind its way around the base of a hill, and the driver of the Porsche was still proceeding cautiously. Kowalski slowed his vehicle until it was travelling only slightly faster than the Porsche. The distance between the two vehicles slowly diminished. After about a minute, Kowalski was close enough to read the license plate.

"290 KAF, sir. That's the one."

He slowed, allowing the Porsche to pull away.

"OK. Where are you?"

"About two miles west of Lambourne on Highway 44. The driver is a youngish white female, mid twenties to mid thirties at a guess. She appears to be unaccompanied. She's driving carefully, about the speed limit. My guess is she's trying not to attract attention."

"OK, Kowalski. Take the next turning. Our instructions were simply to note the vehicle's progress, preferably without the driver knowing we were doing so."

"10-4, sir."

At the first opportunity Officer Kowalski turned off the highway, wondering as he did so what the pretty young driver could possibly have done to attract such unusual orders.

Southern Replogle County — 4:30 p.m.

Two hours later and some eight hundred miles to the southwest of Katie Murcheson, Deputy James Brewer of the Replogle County Sheriff's Department was driving slowly along narrow, rural roads. The long day was almost over, and he was exhausted as he headed back towards the justice center for the five o'clock handover. Brewer turned the wheel lazily to the left, then to the right, drifting around corners.

The sun was still high in the sky; the day was still hot, well over ninety, but at least the air conditioner was keeping the car comfortable now that he wasn't stopping every few minutes.

His eyes roamed the surrounding hills, which rose steeply on both sides. He found himself thinking how fortunate he was to live in such a beautiful place.

Houses were scattered among the trees, but for the most part they were hidden behind layers of jungle-like growth. It always came as a shock when the first chill days of fall arrived and the trees began to lose their mantle of greenery, exposing the houses salted away in their midst.

He turned a corner and a glint at the corner of his eye momentarily attracted his attention. Atop a hill the sun reflected off a ham radio antenna. Somewhere below it, invisible behind the greenery, must be the house to which it was attached.

Then, as sometimes happens when one is thinking about nothing in particular, a quirky series of associations flashed through his head: antenna; ham radio; radio communication; emergency; Morse code; SOS — and then, reflexively, his foot slammed the brake pedal to the floor. The police car skidded to a halt.

Jim Brewer closed his eyes and tried to remember.

Was he simply imagining it? Was his mind playing tricks with him, remembering something that wasn't true?

He played the scene over and over again in his head. Sometimes he was sure he was right, then, a moment later, he would be more than half convinced that his imagination was simply making it up.

He had been standing at the front door. The woman had been rubbing her bleary eyes as she opened the door. Throughout their brief conversation she had kept blinking her eyes, trying, so he had thought, to remove some sort of irritant.

But had there been more to it than that? Were the blinks random? Or had there been a pattern, a well known pattern: three short blinks, followed by three long ones, followed by three short ones?

"Yes!" he shouted.

He reached for the microphone.

Without thinking, he identified himself. "Car 21."

Then, just as he was about to blurt out his suspicions, he remembered the order to keep radio silence.

"Sorry, dispatch. I'll call it in in a couple of minutes."

"10-4, car 21."

He replaced the microphone, put the car in gear, and drove until he saw a driveway threading away through the trees.

Replogle County Justice Center — 4:38 p.m.

Jim Brewer's telephone call was routed directly to Boss Armitage's office, where it was fed to the speakerphone so that both he and Nate Painter could listen to what the deputy had to say.

When Deputy Brewer had finished speaking, the sheriff crisply ordered him to say nothing to anyone and to return immediately to the justice center.

Pressing the button that killed the line, Armitage turned to the FBI man, who had been scribbling while Brewer spoke. The sheriff raised his eyebrow interrogatively.

"One hour, max," said Painter.

"OK. I'll go out and tell the media how little progress we're making, but how we're going to keep looking until we find something. Then we'll get the SWAT team in here for orders."

Painter nodded; he was already on the telephone.

The McGuire House — 5:00 p.m.

They all watched the news. Strain was etched on every face.

David Williamson had retreated inside himself and he had been sullen and uncommunicative most of the afternoon. As suppertime approached, Louise asked what he wanted to eat, and he snapped at her with an angry vehemence that bordered on the violent.

She went into the kitchen and left him to fend for himself.

Duke seemed more relaxed. Following the foiled rape, he appeared to put the incident out of his mind, as if it had been no more than a scheme to inject a little interest into a monotonous afternoon. The visit by the police officer had made him anxious for a while, but he seemed to recover from that incident too.

Alan sat restlessly in front of the television while Louise and Pam busied themselves preparing supper.

Alan got up and wandered into the kitchen. Pam looked at her father apprehensively. His face told her that the moment she had been dreading had finally arrived.

"Do you want to tell me about it?" he asked.

Louise intervened before Pam could say anything.

"Now's not the time, honey. The baby's Craig's and she's not going to have an abortion, and I think anything else can wait until a more appropriate time."

"But...."

Louise shook her head, warning him not to press.

He looked closely at Pam, and realized that she was close to tears.

And then he did one of the hardest things he had ever done. He crossed the kitchen, put his arm around his daughter, and kissed her lightly on the cheek.

"It's all right, Pam. I don't need to know. Not now, anyway. And it'll all turn out all right in the end, you'll see."

He wished he could believe his own words.

Pam sniffed back the tears and nodded.

"How touching," said Duke from the doorway.

All three McGuires glared at him.

The fugitive shrugged and said, "About time for the news. Let's see how the cops are doing."

Pam and her father followed him into the living room. On the TV, ads were still running. The ads faded and the news began. David wandered in from somewhere.

The hunt for the fugitives was the first item; Boss Armitage was about to hold a news conference outside the Replogle Justice Center.

The camera zoomed in unsteadily on the sheriff. A caption giving Boss's name and status appeared for several seconds then faded. The sheriff spoke extemporaneously.

"Gentlemen, ladies. I know you're all anxious for news of what's happening in our search for the two fugitives, McLaughlin and Williamson."

Photographs of the fugitives came on the screen.

"I want to assure you all that we're still working full time on the case. We have men from several counties and municipalities assisting us in the hunt for these men. It is our intention that before nightfall we'll have visited every home in the county, and presented each one with a description and photographs of the two men, along with our contact information."

Superimposed on the photographs, a pair of telephone numbers appeared.

Over the photos the sheriff continued, "These men are going to discover that there's nowhere they can hide from us. We've been working on this all day, and as soon as I've finished here, I will oversee the change of shifts. We're going to keep at it until we're done. From the progress reports I've received so far, my best guess is that we'll be finished by nine o'clock tonight at the latest."

The camera returned to the scene outside the Replogle County Justice Center. A microphone at the bottom of the screen moved as a reporter asked a question.

"Then you think they're still in Replogle County, sheriff?"

The sheriff said, "As yet, we haven't found either the men or the vehicle in which they were last seen. An APB has gone out to every police department in the state to keep a lookout for the car, but it has not yet been sighted."

Another question was shouted at Boss Armitage: "Do you think they could have gotten the car through your roadblocks? Are the roadblocks still up?"

"The roadblocks are still in place on every road out of the county. We don't think the fugitives could have driven the vehicle we're looking for across the county line. Now, if you'll excuse me, I have to go talk to the next shift before they go out."

"What's the prognosis, Boss?" the voice of Todd Livingstone asked. "When do you think you'll have them safely in custody?"

The sheriff turned to face the camera. His face filled the screen.

"I don't know when we'll get them. But rest assured that we will."

For a long moment, the sheriff's eyes bored into the viewers from the screen. As the sheriff turned away from the camera and the news conference faded to a shot of the news anchors in the studio, Duke had the uncomfortable feeling that not only did the sheriff know that he and David had been watching the broadcast, but that he had a good idea of where they were watching it from.

Sheriff Armitage would have been pleased to know that his quarry was worried. But in fact the sheriff had not yet allowed himself to become optimistic about Jim Brewer's report. Most likely, it was all a product of the deputy's imagination. But they had to follow every lead.

When the sheriff reached his office, Jim Brewer was inside, sitting in front of the sheriff's desk. Nate Painter was in his habitual place in the corner.

Painter said, "Deputy Brewer arrived while you were out bamboozling the press. We haven't spoken, except to introduce ourselves."

Armitage nodded; as he took his seat he said, "OK, Jim, tell me all about it."

It was over quickly. Really there was little to say, and as Brewer told the story he was aware of how thin it sounded. It sounded so melodramatic to be talking about messages blinked out in Morse code. A few minutes ago he had been sure that there was something to it... now he almost wished that he hadn't said anything.

But neither the sheriff nor the FBI man seemed to share the deputy's anxieties.

Armitage asked Painter: "What do you think?"

"Sounds promising to me. The phone tap should be in place very soon. I've told them to route the call to this office to let us know as soon as it's installed. The SWAT team should arrive here in plain clothes and unmarked cars within the hour. I think the important question now is how to verify what Jim's told us without Williamson and McLaughlin realizing we're on to them."

Armitage nodded. "My thoughts exactly. I was wondering... what about a chopper taking a slow pass over the area before it gets too dark? The pilot will have to spend some time scanning a fairly wide area, so that if they really are in that house they don't get suspicious."

"Good idea. How long would it take to arrange?"

"Shouldn't take the chopper more than a few minutes to get out there once I file the order."

"OK, let's do it. And we should get a couple of cars out there, out of sight but not too far away. Just in case our men decide to make a run for it."

"Right. Brewer, show me this place on the map, will you?"

Brewer crossed to the wall map and jabbed a finger at a small gray oblong. "That's the house, sir."

Armitage frowned. "OK, well, thanks." He was obviously displeased about something, but he did not elaborate. "Would you be able to guide a chopper in if you were aboard?"

"I should think so, sir."

"OK. Get to it, then. Tell my assistant to make the arrangements. Remember, don't use the radio. Now, you'd better be going."

Brewer raised his hand in a gesture that was half salute, half wave. With a nod toward Painter, he hurried from the office.

As soon as the door closed, the sheriff continued, "We'll have a problem with ground communications, Nate."

"Why? Can't we use the cellular phones?"

"No, for several reasons. First of all, we're relying too much on them already. Phones are point to point. Although that means that McLaughlin and Williamson can't listen in, it also means we can't get information out very easily. It's not like the radio where everyone can listen in on one channel.

"Then there's a problem with the number of incoming lines we have here. If things start happening, we'll be inundated with officers calling in, and everything will just be mass confusion.

"And finally there's the topography. If we put a couple of cars out here along Valley Road" — he stabbed at the map near the oblong that Brewer had indicated — "I doubt they'd be able to use cellular phones anyway. Look at the contours on the map. Valley Road is well named; there are tall hills all around, and cellular coverage in Replogle County is patchy at best. Out there it'll be almost non-existent."

Painter grimaced. "The radio that was in the car they stole: was it a wide-band scanner, or did it just cover your own channels?"

"Wideband. It covered the fire and ambulance and the VHF ham bands and all the channels used by the surrounding police departments as well as our own. If they've set it to scan then they'll pick up anything within range that's transmitted on any of those channels."

Painter though for a moment. "How about if we tied up one channel with a lot of traffic? Then wouldn't the scanner stay stuck on that channel? So we could use a different channel to carry the real traffic?"

"Maybe. You're right, the scanner would lock on to the busy channel. But as soon as they figured out that it was just a bunch of chatter, they could lock that channel out. Or they might even be able to set the scanner so that it simply remained on that channel for a few seconds and then continued scanning."

"They don't have an instruction manual or anything." But Painter recognized the flaw in that argument as soon as he made it.

Boss said, "According to the history file we got from your people, Williamson has a Ph.D. in physics; we can't rely on technical incompetence."

"Well, how about this? We could set up a phony series of conversations on a couple of channels. Make it sound like we think they're somewhere else entirely and we're closing in on them. Surely they'd want to listen to us make fools of ourselves as we closed the net on the wrong place. Then we could use other channels for the real operation."

The sheriff shrugged unhappily. "I suppose it might work. But it would take men off the real operation, and there's still the chance they would figure it out. Maybe there are other scanners in the house; they're not illegal. They might be able to listen to several channels at once."

Silence fell for several moments. An idea began to form in Armitage's mind.

"Hmmm..., I wonder."

He crossed to a filing cabinet, opened a drawer and riffled through the tightly packed folders. He withdrew one and opened it on his desk.

"I thought of something. It's something the hams use. They had it set up at the scene of the car crash and it seems to work pretty well. Packet radio, I think they call it. It allows computers to communicate with one another over the radio. It sounds like a modem — maybe it *is* a modem — anyway, I'm pretty sure it wouldn't make sense to anyone listening in. And even if that won't work, maybe the hams can think of something else. They're pretty good at figuring out how to communicate around the county. Let me make a call and see what they have to say."

"Computers? I don't understand," said Painter, but the sheriff ignored him while he dialled and waited for someone to answer.

"Come on, come on...," the sheriff willed someone to pick up.

After the fifth ring, a male voice said, "Hello?"

"I'm trying to reach Don Watts. He's a radio ham. His radio callsign is..." — he looked at a sheet of paper from the folder — "...NQ0I."

"This is Don Watts. What can I do for you?"

"This is Sheriff Armitage. Are you still the head of the Replogle County Amateur Radio Emergency Service?"

"That's me, sheriff. What's up?"

"I'm sorry if these are stupid questions, but I was wondering if you can answer some questions about radio communications for me."

"Sure. Glad to help any way I can."

"OK. But before I say anything more, I need your assurance that you won't tell anyone else about this conversation."

There was a momentary hesitation, then, "I guess that's OK."

"Right. I want you to consider a hypothetical situation. Suppose there's a scanning VHF wideband receiver in a valley in the southwestern part of the county. Now suppose that I want to place a transmitter close to the scanner, maybe a couple of hundred yards away, and I want its transmissions to be audible at the justice center in Replogle, but not at the scanner. Is there some way to do that?"

The amateur radio operator considered the puzzle. After about half a minute he replied, "OK. I can think of a couple of things you could do. The first is simply to go to a different part of the frequency spectrum. You'd need to know what frequencies the scanner can receive. For example, if it's a scanner that covers only VHF frequencies, then you might use either UHF or even HF instead. Would you be thinking of having hams provide the communications in this hypothetical scenario?"

"Well, hypothetically, let's suppose so."

"OK. Then I'm afraid we'd have to use HF. We don't have sufficient repeater coverage in that part of the county to use UHF. HF doesn't require repeaters, but it suffers from other problems."

"Such as?"

"Well, it's very public: anyone can listen in if they have a shortwave receiver, and the quality of the communication is not as clear as on VHF. Also, it requires relatively high power and might conceivably interfere with appliances like televisions or telephones inside the house. They wouldn't know what you were saying, but it's possible that they'd know that some kind of communication was taking place."

"Hmmm..., OK, well, I guess we could risk that. But you mentioned there was another possibility?"

"Yes. That depends on what you mean when you say that the scanner mustn't be able to pick up the transmissions. We could use packet radio. Those transmissions would certainly be audible, but they wouldn't be understandable. On a scanner it would sound like a kind of electronic buzzing."

"I was wondering if packet radio might work. But you're sure there's no way they would know what we're saying?"

"No. They'd need a lot of specialized equipment for that. Packet radio is basically a way of tying computers together over the air instead of by wires. It's like using a radio channel instead of a telephone line. Whatever is typed on one computer is transmitted as a sequence of tones. A special receiver decodes the tones at the far end and displays the text on the other computer.

"There are a couple of other advantages too. Packet radio gives you guaranteed 100 per cent accuracy, and you also get a time-stamped log of everything that's sent, so afterwards you can see exactly who said what to whom, as well as when they said it."

"What about speed?"

"Pretty slow. You wouldn't want to send a novel. But for ordinary communications it would be fine."

"And is it possible for several computers to listen in on the channel and decode the transmissions?"

"Sure, if that's what you want."

"OK. Now the big question: do you hams have the resources to set up something like this? The computers and suchlike?"

"How many do you need? We could probably put half a dozen computers on the air inside of ten minutes. If you gave us half an hour, we could maybe double that. Here in my garage there are three complete portable units packed and waiting to go."

"Great. I'd like whatever it takes to put three complete stations on the air as soon as possible. One will be here at the justice center, the others will be in cars at the site."

"OK. I'll be on my way as soon as I've made a couple of calls to get some more operators. I should be at the justice center in about twenty minutes."

"I'll tell reception to expect you. They'll buzz me when you arrive. Thanks; and don't forget: don't tell anyone, especially the media. Make sure your men understand that. It's important."

As the sheriff put down the phone, the sound of the helicopter engine starting up penetrated into the office. Armitage looked at Painter.

"I don't want to tempt fate, but I think maybe we're getting somewhere at last."

The McGuire House — 6:30 p.m.

The telephone rang. Duke McLaughlin looked up from his supper and eyed the instrument. It was too soon for the call to be from Katie: she couldn't be more than halfway; she wouldn't arrive until tomorrow morning at the earliest.

The phone continued to ring. McLaughlin looked at the others, who were ranged around the kitchen table. All eyes except David's were on him: a sort of nervous desperation in Louise's, blank resignation in Alan's, and who-knew-what in Pam's, for she instantly lowered them to look at her food as soon as he looked at her. David didn't even seem to have noticed the telephone: he continued eating as if nothing was happening.

The answering machine kicked in.

Louise's voice said, "Hello. You've reached the home of Alan, Louise and Pam McGuire. We're sorry, but we can't take your call right now. Please leave a message and we'll get back to you as soon as we can. God bless you, and have a nice day."

A man's voice came on the line.

"Yes... er... Mrs. McGuire. If you're screening calls, please pick up the phone. My name is Painter, and I'm working with the Replogle County Sheriff's Department."

Duke's heart started racing. Even David paid attention: he stopped, fork in mid air, and looked quizzically at the machine.

Louise asked, "Should I?"

"No," barked Duke. "Leave it."

For ten seconds there was silence. Then the voice continued evenly, "Well, I guess you're out. I'm sorry to disturb you all. One of our officers visited you earlier. We're trying to reach every home in the county about the escaped convicts, and he reported that you were going to ask the other members of your family if they've seen anything.

"We'd like you please to call 555-2345 as soon as you've talked to the other members of your family, even if they haven't seen anything unusual. We would appreciate hearing from you as soon as possible. That number again is 555-2345. We look forward to hearing from you soon. Thank you."

There was a click as the connection was ended. Duke sighed with relief.

They heard a distant drone. McLaughlin pushed his chair back and moved to the kitchen window. Cautiously removing his gun from his belt, he scanned the sky several times. Then he moved to the door, eased it open, and stepped outside.

The sound seemed suddenly much closer. The chopping sound of rotor blades slicing through the air was mixed with the throb of an engine. McLaughlin came back inside and closed the door behind him.

He leaned his back against the door and looked at the others. "Chopper," he announced, unnecessarily. "Not far away. Sounds like it's searching the area."

"You think they're on to us?" asked David.

"I don't know. It could just be a routine scan of the area. And the phone call might have been just what it claimed to be: a follow up from this afternoon. On the other hand...."

Duke was interrupted by a sudden noise that startled them all. It lasted for perhaps half a second: a strange sort of squeaking electronic beep coming from somewhere nearby. It was followed a fraction of a second later by a quieter and shorter version of the same sound, like an attenuated echo.

Williamson jumped to his feet, looking for the source of the sound. Another long burst came, and this time both men realized that it was coming from the scanner.

McLaughlin looked at the radio in horror. The phone call, the helicopter, and now this. Three coincidences in a row was too much.

Williamson frowned at the scanner as if puzzled.

The sounds continued, some weak, some much stronger, some short, some lasting for perhaps a second or two. This continued for half a minute until silence fell and the radio started to scan the channels once again.

"It was on 145.01 megahertz," David said. "I don't remember for sure, but I think there's a ham band somewhere around that frequency."

"Any radio hams live near here?" Duke asked the McGuires.

"Not as far as I know," said Alan.

David mumbled, "That noise... it was like we were listening to a modem...." He seemed to be thinking aloud.

"Modem?" asked McLaughlin.

"Yes, you know, a box that allows two computers to talk to one another. Usually they're used on telephone lines but it wouldn't take much work to adept them to use radio instead."

"So you're saying that we were listening to computers talking to one another?"

"Yes, I think so."

"Could we listen in? Is there any way to tell what they're saying?"

David shook his head. "Not without special equipment, no."

"What kinds of things could they be talking about? Us?"

"They could be talking about anything. I imagine it's set up so that whatever is typed on one computer is being transmitted through those sounds we heard and then displayed on the screen of another computer some distance away."

"You," McLaughlin pointed his gun at Alan. "Do you have a computer and one of these modem things?"

Then, without waiting for an answer, he asked Williamson, "Could you wire it up so we could intercept the messages?"

Williamson replied before Alan could speak. "No. I don't think so. It would take special hardware and software to decode the information. We could waste days on it and still not get it to work."

A heartfelt expletive fell from Duke's lips, just as the throb of the helicopter became a roar. It flew directly overhead.

The chopper was very low and it was moving slowly — very slowly indeed. Everyone in the kitchen held their breath until, after an age, the helicopter moved away over the trees beyond the swimming pool at the rear of the house.

The collective expulsion of breaths was clearly audible.

Ohio — 8:30 p.m.

Katie Murcheson looked in her rear-view mirror to see if the car was still there, even though she knew it would be.

In her tiredness, she had already forgotten the details: the make of car, its color, and how far back it was, for those things had changed as the hours passed. The glance in the mirror reminded her: hanging about a quarter of a mile back was a blue Mercury. She tried to remember the sequence of vehicles, making a kind of game to help her stay awake.

The first couple of cars were easy. The first one had been an ordinary marked police car, somewhere in Pennsylvania. She had sworn as she had passed it, hidden on the side of the road to trap unwary speeders.

For perhaps half a minute, she had thought that her hurried prayer had been answered, that the God in whom she did not believe had kept the officer's eyes somehow from recognizing the distinctive white Porsche. She drove along the straight stretch of road at 57 miles per hour for nearly a mile, with her eyes flicking between the road ahead and the rear-view mirror.

She had almost believed that she had escaped when the police car pulled out and started following her.

For the next two or three minutes she looked desperately for a turning down which she could escape before the police car came too close. But there were no side roads. She considered putting more of the horsepower sitting under the hood to good use. Surely she could outrun the cop. But if she tried to escape, she would be giving him a reason to chase her. And if she did get away he would alert other cops to look out for her. No, it was better to try to brazen it out.

And there was still a chance, albeit a small one, that it was just a coincidence. Maybe she had passed the cop just as his shift was over; maybe he was just driving back to the PD. He hadn't turned on his lights or siren; surely that was a good sign. She slowed slightly — isn't that what people always do when a cop is behind them?

The police car came closer.

At last there was a junction. She turned left. Ten seconds behind her, the police car followed.

She began to sweat.

A couple of minutes later, she saw another junction. This time she didn't take it, and... Alleluia! the police car turned off. She exhaled, watching the mirror for some sign that the cop was going to return, but after five miles she relaxed and thanked her good fortune for her escape.

But after another mile or two, she began to wonder if she had been too hasty. A red sports car turned on to the road and began to follow. It was too far back for her to see if a cop was inside, but the car was certainly tenacious. She took two small side roads, and the red car followed her both times.

This went on for the better part of an hour. A decision slowly gelled in her mind, and she began to head for the westbound interstate some distance away to the north. Duke had told her to keep away from interstates, but now it seemed that her best chance of escaping her shadow was to join the interstate and try to lose the red sports car at the next major city.

It followed her on to the interstate. It dropped back a little, but every time she looked in her mirror she could see it half a dozen cars back.

Katie passed an exit, and was momentarily relieved to see the car signaling to leave the freeway. She watched as the sports car edged over and then left the interstate. For the next five miles, Katie was so relieved that she didn't notice her speed. Then she realized she was doing eighty, and lifted her foot from the accelerator.

Behind her, a nondescript pale yellow vehicle also slowed.

She swore.

As she approached the next exit, she signaled to turn off the interstate. The yellow car did the same, pulling over to the right lane. She entered the turn lane then, at the last moment, she swung back on to the freeway. Behind her, the car's indicator stopped flashing. The car followed her past the exit.

The yellow car followed her for a couple of hours. Then its place was taken by a meretricious blue sports car from whose mirror hung a pair of fuzzy dice. After that came a pale green sedan. Eventually its place was taken by the blue Mercury.

Jerking awake, she twisted the steering wheel violently to the right, just in time to avoid colliding with the median.

She breathed heavily as her heart thumped. That was close. She tried to figure out how long it had been since she had last slept, but the calculation was beyond her. All she knew was that she was dangerously tired. She needed to take a break, regardless of the fact that she was being followed.

Five minutes later, her eyes rested gratefully on a sign that promised food, rest and lodgings at exit 56. The next mile post was number 53. Only three more miles to go. She could last that long.

Replogle County Justice Center — 7 p.m.

"How're you holding up?" Painter asked the sheriff.

It was seven in the evening, and both of them had reached that stage of fatigue where they were functioning without thought. It was a dangerous state to be in, and they both knew it, but they could not yet afford to sleep. Perhaps in a few hours there would be time for a nap. But not just yet.

The sheriff's clothing was crumpled and a distinct aroma was beginning to accompany him. He had been awake since four, and the hours had taken their toll. His face was lined and sagging, and a stubble of beard was beginning to show. He had twice just stopped himself in time from snapping at Painter, telling himself that his short fuse was the result of tiredness, not any fault of his colleague from the FBI.

Armitage stretched out his hand for his umpteenth coffee of the day. By now its flavor was becoming positively repellent, but the caffeine kept him going. His hand was beginning to tremble. Painter was on his third can of *Jolt* in as many hours. He seemed more alert than the sheriff, but he looked just as bedraggled, and he had the unmistakably haggard air of a man in need of sleep.

The sheriff drained his mug before answering Painter's question. He pulled a face at the taste of the dregs.

"I'll make it, I guess. I keep thinking of Baker and Palmer, lying in the road. I'm going to get the bastards who walked away and left Palmer to die."

"I hope you're right." Painter seemed less certain. "How much longer do you think before we nail them?"

"Shouldn't be too long, I don't think. If we don't get them tonight then tomorrow. Don't you think they're in the house?"

Painter idly turned the can of cola around in his hands, looking at it without seeing it.

"I guess so. Yes," he said more certainly, "yes, I think they're there."

The intercom on the sheriff's desk buzzed. The sheriff pressed a button.

"Yes?"

"The SWAT team has arrived, Boss, and the stuff you wanted is in the conference room with them."

"OK. Have we found anyone yet who knows the McGuires and is willing to help? "

"Not yet, sir. We're still working on it."

"All right. Thanks, and keep trying. I'll be in the conference room in two minutes."

The sheriff seemed suddenly reinvigorated. He looked at Painter.

"Well, I guess we'd better get this show on the road."

The conference room was sealed, not just by the closed door, but also by an officer seated outside with orders to keep everyone else out. Inside, Armitage, Painter, both the Brewer brothers — Bill with his arm in a sling but otherwise apparently unharmed — and seven young men dressed in dark clothing were discussing strategy and tactics.

The conference table was covered with paper. At one end, Armitage and Brewer were studying half a dozen large aerial photographs of 10673 Valley Road and its surroundings. Next to the photographs were the plans of the house. Finally, at the other end of the table was a large-scale topographic map of the area.

There was no sign of Brewer's car on the photographs. But there were hints that even so the fugitives were at the house. Two cars were visible: both, as they quickly confirmed, belonged to the McGuires.

One, Alan McGuire's red Volkswagen Rabbit Cabriolet, was in the open, parked near the rear door of the house, in front of the closed door to the right-hand side of the garage. The other, more difficult to spot, was Mrs. McGuire's pale blue Toyota, which could be discerned in one photograph inside the garage itself, through the open doorway on the left-hand side. So both the McGuire vehicles were accounted for. Which left the sheriff and his colleagues wondering why the right-hand door of the garage was closed.

One logical explanation was that there was another car inside the garage, behind the closed door. But the McGuires owned only two vehicles. But perhaps the right-hand half of the garage was simply filled with junk.

A telephone on a table in the corner rang.

Armitage barked, "Someone get that."

Nate Painter picked up the phone. A brief conversation followed, then he extended the phone toward the sheriff.

"They've found someone who knows the McGuires well. Their pastor. Apparently the McGuires are active churchgoers."

Armitage grunted his thanks and took the phone.

"Sheriff Armitage here. Yeah, I understand.... OK.... All right. Well, see if you can persuade him to come here. If not, let me know and I'll talk to him directly. Tell him that we have reason to believe that the McGuires may be in some danger. Impress on him that all this is confidential; he's not to tell anyone. OK?"

Armitage handed the telephone back to Painter, who replaced it in its cradle.

"He should be here in half an hour or so, if he's willing to help," the sheriff said. "Then maybe we'll be able to get a better handle on things."

He returned his attention to the map and addressed the men gathered around the table.

"Anyone have any comments or ideas?"

"Yes sir, I have one," said Bill Brewer, who was examining a photograph closely. He turned the photograph so that Armitage could see it: it was looking almost straight down on Alan McGuire's Volkswagen and the empty concrete pad next to it, in front of the garage.

"You see that patch?" Brewer pointed to a dark smudge on the concrete.

Armitage examined the photograph carefully.

"Oil?" he hazarded.

"Sure looks like it. My car leaks oil, and that's just about where the engine would have been if the car had stood outside that garage for a while."

Armitage considered this for a few seconds. "How long to leave a patch that size?"

"Not long. It only leaks when the engine's warm. Jim and I have tried to fix it a bunch of times, but we've never had much luck. The leak always seems to come back after a few days. Anyway, once the engine's cooled it stops leaking. If my car stood on that pad while the engine cooled, that patch is exactly what I'd expect to see."

"Could be that one of the McGuires' cars leaks," objected the sheriff.

Painter interjected, "But if it did — and I grant you that leaking cars are pretty common — but if one of their cars leaked oil, then surely the patch would be larger and less clearly defined. After all, I'm sure they don't park in exactly the same position every time. This is just a single small patch. Like Bill says, it's exactly what we'd expect if the Buick had been parked there."

He sounded almost excited.

"And then it was maneuvered into the other side of the garage and the door closed behind it to hide it from view?" said Armitage.

"Yes. And Alan McGuire arrived home from work later, by which time there was no room for his car in the garage."

Armitage grinned.

"Nice. Yes, I like that. Anyone else any comments? Are we missing something obvious?"

He glanced around the room. No one said anything.

"Good," he continued. "I think we can be pretty sure we're not about to go hunting a wild goose. Right; let's get started."

Replogle — 7 p.m.

George Ellsworth picked at his food. His wife, worried, watched him from the other side of the table.

He had been moody ever since Wednesday evening. And, frankly, his talk about visions and direct commands from God scared her. Her husband was nothing if not a practical man. She'd never seen him like this before. She sent yet another prayer for wisdom heavenward.

She'd tried to talk to him about Wednesday. But it was impossible to get a clear answer. He kept saying that he knew he was supposed to be praying for David Williamson, but he didn't know *what* he was supposed to be praying. How was one supposed to pray for someone about whom one knew so little?

George had retreated to his study, where he spent hours poring over the Bible, especially the Psalms, looking for clear guidance. He found none. He told Mary he was beginning to think that maybe he was supposed to be doing more than just praying. Something more practical. But what?

Mary couldn't help him. All she could do was to pray that this trial would soon be over and their lives could return to normal.

The telephone rang. George looked up from his half-finished meal and focused vaguely on the instrument.

"I'll get it," said Mary. Unnecessarily, she added, "I'm finished eating."

She lifted the telephone. "Hello?"

"Good evening. Is the Reverend Doctor George Ellsworth available, please?"

The caller was male, and she did not recognize the voice. It couldn't be anyone who knew George; she couldn't remember the last time anyone had used his full title.

"Could I tell him who's calling, please?" She liked to protect him from salesmen.

"My name is Deputy Martin, and I'm with the Replogle County Sheriff's Department. I'd like to speak with him on a matter concerning a member of his congregation."

"Oh!" Her mind flew to thoughts of car wrecks and house fires. She wondered who had been the victim of some awful accident.

She held out the telephone. "It's someone from the sheriff's department, honey. I think there's been an accident of some kind."

Her husband took the phone. "This is George Ellsworth."

"Ah, Reverend Ellsworth. Good evening. Sorry to disturb you. I heard what your wife said, and I want to assure you there hasn't been an accident."

The minister responded with a wordless grunt that might have been relief, or might merely have meant that his thoughts were far away.

"My name is Deputy Martin, and I'm with the Replogle County Sheriff's Department. I'm calling because we need your help. Before I go any further, I need your assurance that this conversation will be confidential."

"I always reserve the right to share confidences with my wife. We're a sort of team, you see. But I will vouch for her. If I tell her whatever you tell me, you can be sure it'll go no further."

"That sounds fair enough. Now, I assume you're familiar with the story of the two fugitives who escaped a couple of days ago?"

George experienced a sudden surge of hope. Perhaps now, at last, he was going to be shown how he could help David Williamson.

"Yes; I've been following the news."

"Well, sir, we have reason to believe — we're not yet certain of this, mind — but we have reason to believe that they may have taken refuge in the home of a family that attends your church. If so, there's a good chance that they're holding the family hostage."

"I see. Which family?"

"The McGuires: Alan, Louise and Pamela. We understand they're active members of your congregation?"

"Yes, they are; very active."

The hope flared to excitement. Something was happening at last.

"Good. And we've been told that you know them well."

"As well as anyone, I expect. Yes."

"And you're intimately acquainted with their home?"

"Well, yes, I suppose so. I've been there many times. Usually at least once a week."

"Great! We were wondering, sir, if it would be possible for you to come to the justice center and help us with some details as we plan how to handle the situation."

"Oh, yes, I see. Well of course I'd be glad to help any way I can."

"Good. Thank you. Could you come right away?"

"Yes. I don't see why not." George glanced at his watch. "I should be there in about twenty minutes."

"Thank you, sir. We would very much appreciate that. Just give your name to the receptionist and we'll send someone to escort you in to talk to the sheriff and his team. Thank you again, sir."

"You're welcome."

George replaced the telephone. His wife was watching him speculatively.

He said, "They think Williamson and the other one may be holding the McGuires hostage. They didn't exactly say why they wanted me, but it sounds like they want me to help them understand the layout of the house. They must be planning to storm the building or something."

Mary's hand flew to her mouth and a frightened look came into her eyes.

"I have to go," he continued. "And you mustn't say anything to anyone about this. But you must pray that no one will be hurt. The two men are presumably still armed."

Mary nodded.

"All right then, I'll be off."

"Take care, George. Please be careful."

"Of course I will. I'm sure they just want me to help them with planning. They aren't going to want a civilian getting in the way when they go in."

Mary nodded. "I love you."

"I love you too."

They embraced; then George walked determinedly to the door.

Replogle — 9:00 p.m.

Mary Ellsworth turned the television on to watch the news. Beside the two anchors in the studio sat Todd Livingstone, the station's Replogle County reporter. The music had barely faded away when the principal anchor turned to Livingstone.

"Todd, you've been following the story over in Replogle County closely ever since it broke."

"I have."

"It seems that there's something in the background of one of the fugitives that makes him rather unusual, isn't that right?"

"Indeed it is, Bob."

Livingstone turned from the anchorman to face the camera that now zoomed in on him, edging the others from the screen.

"David Williamson, one of the two men who on Thursday escaped following the crash of the car in which he and another prisoner, Darren McLaughlin, were being transported to the state penitentiary in Ferguson, is indeed a most unusual man. While looking into the background of these two men who have evaded capture for the past two days, I discovered that the man we have been calling David Williamson should more properly be identified as *Professor* David Williamson."

Livingstone briefly recited some facts from David's former life; these were followed by a couple of snippets of interviews from people who had known him when he was a professor in Trenton. Then came the kicker: Livingstone described in detail the accident that had taken the lives of David's wife and children. Family portraits came on the screen; they faded away, replaced by police photographs of the fatal accident. Livingstone portrayed David as a gifted man who had cracked under the stresses of his life — a man, as Livingstone sententiously said, "Perhaps more to be pitied than censured."

Livingstone concluded: "This, then, was the man who held up a store clerk earlier this year with a weapon subsequently discovered to be unloaded. This is the man who is now on the run in Replogle County. It is right, of course, that the police have warned us that he is armed, and possibly dangerous. But along with the fear that each of us feels, and will continue to feel until Williamson and the other fugitive, Duke McLaughlin, are recaptured, surely it is right also that we spare a moment of pity for a man who was perhaps simply incapable of handling the difficulties and pain that life handed him."

Mary Ellsworth could hardly see the screen through her tears. She closed her eyes, and began to pray.

Southwestern Replogle County — 9:30 p.m.

The police car drew to a halt a dozen paces behind the unmarked car that was parked beside the road. Ahead of the parked car the road was blocked by a wooden barrier.

Two uniformed men got out of the police car and strolled towards the unmarked vehicle.

A uniformed officer got out of the car and greeted the two newcomers quietly.

"Hi. You Brewer and Whittington?"

It sounded like the title of a TV show.

"Yes," responded one of the men, "I'm Jim Brewer. Sam Whittington here is with the SWAT team."

The moon was at first quarter, and hung in the sky at the level of the treetops. Brewer's badge glinted silver in its light. Now that he knew what it said, the man who had spoken first could just make out Brewer's name on his shirt.

Whittington was much harder to see. He was dressed from head to toe in black, like a spy dropped behind enemy lines for a night mission: black sneakers, black socks, black pants, black sweater, black balaclava. The moon did not even light his face, for although the man was white he had blackened his face. Around his waist, almost impossible to see,

212

hung a black belt from which hung several small, vaguely rectangular objects.

Whittington nodded, but he might as well have not bothered, for the slight motion was almost invisible in the crepuscular dimness of the late evening.

The man from the unmarked car said, "The packet radio link warned us you were coming. Do you need any help?"

"No, thanks," replied Brewer. "I assume there hasn't been any activity at the house?"

"No, nothing."

"OK. How far to the house from here?"

"A couple of hundred yards. The driveway is about two hundred feet past that bend."

"All right. Just let me through the roadblock, that's all. I shouldn't be long, five minutes or so, I should think. Whittington might be a bit longer."

"Sure. Give me a hand with this thing, and we'll let you through."

They moved the roadblock. While they were doing this, Whittington disappeared silently into the darkness of the trees.

Brewer got into the police car. "You can send messages to the justice center, right?"

"Sure, over the computer link."

"Right. Please send a message to Sheriff Armitage. Just transmit the single word 'Alpha'."

"'Alpha'? That's all?"

"Yes. It's to tell him that the first phase is under way. Can you send it immediately?"

"It'll be there in about one minute."

"Right. Thanks."

Brewer drove the police car to the bend, then followed the road around to the right. Now he could see the McGuires' house ahead on the left. On the first floor, a couple of lights were on. He drove slowly on to the gravel of the driveway. He glanced at his watch. It had been two minutes and twenty five seconds since Whittington had vanished into the forest. Brewer lowered his window and listened intently. He heard only the loud calls of the katydids and tree frogs. He looked longingly at the radio underneath the dash. He wished he could use it, to know for sure whether the phone call had been made according to plan.

He counted slowly to fifteen under his breath, listening for the sound of a phone ringing inside the house. He glanced at his watch once more. He had to trust that everything was going according to the plan that Boss and Nate Painter had put together. It was difficult, though: a mistake might put the lives of the hostages at risk.

He got out of the car and looked around. The moon lit everything in a weak gray-silver light, creating a world of umbra and penumbra. He peered toward the forest behind the house, looking for Sam, but of course he saw nothing. Sam Whittington was invisible.

Scrunching on the gravel, he walked to the front door. There were no lights on at the front of the building, but some light leaked from rooms at the rear of the house as he passed a window. The kitchen and maybe the living room, he decided, remembering the plans on the table of the conference room.

He reached the front door and pressed the doorbell.

The McGuire House — 9:35 p.m.

Duke McLaughlin was in the kitchen standing next to the answering machine. The telephone was ringing. Williamson and the McGuires were in the living room, from which came the barely audible sound of a popular sit-com with the sound turned low. No one was watching the TV, but Duke wanted to be sure that if there were any sudden developments in their case, they would not miss the report.

In the living room, Alan McGuire was reading his Bible. Louise and Pam were playing a card game.

The atmosphere had been tense ever since the start of the nine o'clock news report, when the story of Williamson's past had been aired at length.

Williamson himself seemed to have withdrawn even further into himself. Duke was no longer certain that Williamson even understood exactly where he was and what he was doing here. The blank stare had returned with a vengeance. The pictures on the television had obviously reawakened old and painful memories, and somewhere inside himself, David Williamson was reliving events of years before.

Alan McGuire had begun to gaze at Williamson almost as soon as Livingstone had started his report, and Duke had seen that most dangerous of emotions, pity, written clearly on McGuire's face.

McGuire had said, "Oh, how awful for you," and started to rise from the sofa.

But Duke snapped the pistol from his belt and told McGuire to stay where he was.

"One word from you and you'll regret it," he threatened.

His hand trembled slightly with anger as he pointed the weapon at McGuire.

McGuire sank back in his chair, but for the rest of the broadcast, he kept glancing at Williamson. Williamson himself seemed not to have noticed any of this; his eyes were glazed over and his thoughts far away.

As the minutes passed, a semblance of normality returned, except that the look on David's face didn't change.

When the phone rang, Duke hurried into the kitchen to hear the answering machine. Maybe it was Katie, reporting on her progress.

On the fourth ring, the answering machine cut in. Louise's voice filled the kitchen, regretting that they couldn't answer the phone. Duke wished fervently for Katie's voice. The more he thought about the helicopter that had passed overhead this afternoon, the more sure he was that the police knew something that they hadn't told the press.

If it weren't for Katie, he would have already left the house, leaving David to fend for himself. But he had to talk to her, to arrange some place where they could meet.

Louise finished her message and the machine beeped. A voice came on the line.

The caller was female, but it was not Katie.

"Er, hello; good evening. I'm with the Replogle County Sheriff's Department. We were just calling to check whether any of you have seen any strangers in your neighborhood. I believe an officer visited your house this afternoon when some family members were unavailable. We called earlier, but we have no record that you called us back. We would appreciate it if you would give us a call when convenient, so we can cross you off our list. Thank you and, er, good evening."

The line clicked dead, and as it did so Duke heard the sound of a car turning off the road and on to the gravel of the driveway.

There was no sign from the living room that anyone there had heard the car. Duke ran to the doorway and poked his head inside the room. Williamson was gazing sightlessly at the floor. All three McGuires were seated on the sofa, their heads bowed close to one another. They were praying.

"We've got company," he said. "Stay quiet and no one will get hurt."

They looked up and Alan nodded.

Duke's voice seemed to have woken David from his reverie. Intelligence flickered into his eyes. He crossed to the television and turned the sound all the way down.

Duke ran into the hallway and bounded up the stairs. He swore, and came back down, and reached the living room just as the doorbell rang.

"It's the effing policeman. The one that was here this afternoon. He's come back. Can't they leave us alone for a minute? You," — he pointed at Alan — "get rid of him." Duke waved his gun. "And no monkey business. I'm effing fed up of you three and your prayers and your Bibles. You do what I say or your wife and daughter get it. Understand?"

"There's no need for the gun. I'll do as you say. Waving a gun will make no difference."

With terrible dignity, Alan raised himself from the sofa. He reached the front door as the bell rang for the second time. The fugitives hid in the living room and eavesdropped on the ensuing conversation.

"Ah, good evening, sir. My name is Officer Brewer. You are, er, Mr. Alan McGuire?"

"Good evening, officer. Yes, I'm Alan McGuire."

"I'm sorry for inconveniencing you at this time of the evening. I was here this afternoon and spoke to your wife."

"No inconvenience, officer. My wife told me about your visit. The men haven't been found?"

"No, sir. That's why I'm here. We're trying to talk to everyone in the county to make sure that no one has seen the fugitives. We think they're still in the county somewhere, probably not far away."

"I've been following things on TV of course, but I don't think we can be of much help."

"Your daughter, is she in? I'd like to speak to her too."

"Pam? Yes, she's here, but I'm afraid she can't come to the door right now. It is rather late, you know. But we've all talked about the situation, and I'm afraid she can't help you either."

"OK. I see. Well, one other thing before I leave. Do you have a weapon in the house? A gun or anything?"

"I'm sorry, officer; this is a house of God. We don't believe in protecting ourselves with weapons. God will protect us to the extent that we need protection."

"Ah, yes, of course. Well, I'm sorry to have troubled you. Good evening, sir, and thank you."

"You're welcome. And thank you for serving and protecting us."

"Oh... yes, well, er..., you're welcome. Good night, then."

Almost before Alan had closed the door, Duke sprang from his hiding place, waving his gun belligerently.

"I want your word of honor that you didn't give that policeman any sign that we're here."

"Mr. McLaughlin, I give you my word that I gave the officer no reason to believe you're here. Do you really think I would risk the lives of my wife and my daughter?"

With a bearing that was almost regal, Alan McGuire walked past the fugitive and regained his place on the sofa.

"Now, if you would allow us to finish our prayer before retiring? Or would you like to join us?"

With an impatient "Pah!" Duke turned and walked out of the room.

Outside, the police car trundled to the end of the driveway and drove away into the night.

Replogle County Justice Center — 10:30 p.m.

"Good evening, sir."

Sam Whittington tried to keep his news from his face, but everyone knew from the twinkle in his eyes that he had good news.

They were back in the conference room in the justice center. The McGuires' pastor had joined them. Most of the men clutched cans of cola. Whittington's face was still blackened, although he had removed his balaclava. Whittington addressed the others.

"It went exactly as we had planned. While Jim distracted them, I had plenty of opportunity to look through the windows at the rear of the house where the lights were on. McLaughlin and Williamson are both there. McLaughlin brandished a gun at the man of the house, and it was obvious that he was threatening the family. So the situation is as we'd assumed. It looks pretty easy. We can get the family out tonight without much difficulty, I think."

"Without loss of life?" the sheriff asked.

"I'm pretty sure. Yes."

"But you can't guarantee it?"

Whittington shook his head. "I'd never guarantee that, sheriff. There's always the chance of something going wrong; something no one could have predicted, no matter how carefully we plan."

"In that case, Officer Whittington, you and your men will remain hidden in the forest surrounding the building until we have managed to warn the family. It'll take longer, but I think it's safer. You understand the plan?"

"Yes, sir."

"Reverend Ellsworth?"

"I understand."

"Any questions? All right. In that case I will bid you all a good night and good luck. Officer Whittington, at the first sign that the men are leaving that house, I want to know about it, even if you have to break radio silence. Use the packet link if you can, otherwise use purple channel on the walkie-talkies. Under no circumstances are you to enter the house while the fugitives are inside until after the reverend has delivered his message to the McGuires. Is that understood?"

"Yes, sir."

"Good. Well, I guess that's all for now. Unless something happens, now we're just waiting for Ms. Murcheson. Tomorrow, I think, will see the end of this affair. Good night, everyone."

The McGuire House — 11:00 p.m.

Duke was on the edge of the chair waiting for the last news broadcast of the evening. Pam was asleep on the two chairs that had been pushed together, as they been the night before. Alan and Louise were holding

218

hands on the sofa, watching the TV. David had curled up on the floor near the doorway and was apparently asleep.

Not fifteen minutes earlier, a message had scrolled across the bottom of the screen: "News Flash: Fugitive spotted in Kansas City. Full details at 11."

Now it was eleven o'clock, the music faded, and the camera zoomed in on the face of the anchor of the late-night news report.

"Good evening," the anchor began. "This just in a few minutes ago from the Replogle County Justice Center. According to a press release from Replogle County sheriff Bradley Armitage, at approximately eight o'clock this evening a man tentatively identified as David Williamson, one of the two men who earlier this week escaped from custody in Replogle County and believed until this evening to be in hiding in that county, was seen in a fast food restaurant on the outskirts of Kansas City, Missouri.

"Accompanying him in a vehicle whose description has been circulated in the area was another man, believed to be the other fugitive, Darren McLaughlin, known as 'Duke'. As of eleven o'clock this evening, all officers in Replogle County are standing down. The roadblocks are being removed, and the search in the county has been officially brought to an end."

Duke let out a roar of laughter, waking Pam and David.

"What's the matter?" mumbled David from the doorway.

"Nothing," said Duke. "It's just that there really is a God after all."

NOWHERE TO RUN

D. R. Evans

SUNDAY

Southern Indiana — 12:20 a.m.

For several seconds after she awoke, Katie Murcheson did not know where she was. She was aware only that she was cramped into an unnatural position in a confined space. Then she remembered: she was in a stolen Porsche, parked at a service area somewhere in Indiana, on her way to her once and future lover in northwestern Arkansas. It was several more seconds before she also remembered that she was being followed.

She sat up and stretched, and adjusted her seat until it was upright. Her watch told her it was twenty past midnight.

With muscles that ached painfully, she unlocked the door and got out of the car. The spill from the massive overhead lights made it seem almost as bright as day.

She had to do something about the car that was following her. She remembered the blue car pulling off the interstate behind her, coming to a halt on the far side of the parking lot. She stood next to the Porsche and continued stretching, feeling life flow back into her muscles. As she stretched, she looked around.

The service area was busy, even at this time of night. Some distance away was a brightly lit building, in front of which was an enormous forecourt with forty or more gas pumps. Four of the pumps were in use, one by a small family sedan, the others by massive trucks. Dozens of vehicles were scattered around the lot, their colors washed into dark greens and grays by the unnatural light from the overhead lights.

At first she couldn't find the car that had been following her, but then she saw it a hundred yards away near the perimeter of the lot in a poorly lit corner. It was impossible to tell from this distance whether the car was occupied, but she was certain it was the same car.

Locking the Porsche, she walked toward the service station, keeping her eyes away from the distant blue car. As she was about to pass the corner of the building, she glanced at the car. The door was open and someone was getting out. She stopped and watched. A tall man locked the door and began to walk towards her. She hurried into the building.

Duke McLaughlin was dragged to wakefulness by the insistent ringing of the telephone near his head.

Groggily, he stretched out a hand as he cast an eye at the kitchen clock. Not long after midnight. He had been asleep only a few minutes. Who could be calling at this time of night? Katie? Or the police? No, he remembered. The police thought he was in Missouri. He smiled to himself.

He waited for the answering machine to kick in. In the doorway David Williamson fidgeted in his sleep. The ringing stopped and Louise McGuire's voice asked the caller to leave a message.

Duke snatched up the phone. He had recognized the voice as soon as he heard it.

"Katie? It's me. What's up? You aren't here already, are you?"

Katie sounded distracted. She poured out her story in long sentences, pausing only for snatches of breath. The longer she spoke, the deeper were the creases that etched Duke McLaughlin's face.

"You're sure about all of this?" he asked when she had finished. "It's not just your imagination? You're really being followed?"

He knew it was a stupid question. But it gave him time to think.

"No, Duke, I'm not imagining things. I can see the entrance to the service station from here and the man just walked in. He looked around, trying to find me, and as soon as he saw me at the phone he relaxed. Now he's just leaning against the wall, trying to look as if he's waiting for someone, but he keeps looking this way every few seconds. There, he just looked toward me, just for a moment. I'm sure he knows that I'm on to him. He's probably guessed that I'm talking about him. Maybe he even knows I'm talking to you."

"All right, all right. Let me think for a minute."

Duke racked his brains.

He said, "Hang on a minute; I need to check something."

He crossed to David and shook him awake. He asked David a question. David replied and Duke returned to the phone.

"All right, I think I've got it. It was on the news this evening that they think we were spotted in Kansas City this afternoon. You'll have to convince them that that's where we are. Now listen carefully. The first thing you must do, as soon as you finish this call, is to make some more calls. Have you got enough money?"

"What? Oh, er, yes, I guess so."

"Right; make calls to a few random numbers in Kansas City, three or four of them, and try to do it without the man who's watching you seeing what you're doing. Let the phone ring each time until it's answered. Don't say anything, just give it a few seconds, then put the phone down. They can trace the last call from a phone, but it'll take them forever to figure out the other calls. If you make several calls, by the time they figure out the number where you really reached me we'll be long gone. Until then, they'll think you talked to me in Kansas City. Got that?"

"Yes."

"All right. Now, here's what I want you to do...."

Kansas City — 6:00 a.m.

Katie Murcheson's heart was beating wildly. She was driving carefully at slightly less than the posted 45 mile per hour limit, her concentration on the sky-blue Dodge behind her instead of the road ahead. Residential neighborhoods lined the highway. Junctions every half mile or so led into the maze of residential side streets.

Once or twice, she pushed the accelerator pedal to the floor then immediately lifted it, getting a feel for the way the car accelerated. Each time, the blue car a couple of hundred yards behind her accelerated more slowly, then slowed down again.

She passed three likely turnings, each time rationalizing why they weren't suitable. She passed a fourth, with no excuse other than that she was frightened at what she was about to do. Another turning was signed half a mile ahead. She made up her mind. This time she would do it.

She almost didn't. The blue car chose the last half mile before the exit to close the gap between them. The car was no more than a hundred yards behind her when the turn lane began.

Katie tore her eyes from the mirror and tried to concentrate on what she was doing. Her eyes flickered between the road and the speedometer. She lifted her foot and her speed began to drop. 45... 44... 43....The turn lane widened on her right.

She was doing 41 when a triangle of painted stripes began to separate her from the turn lane. Her foot quivered in anticipation as it hovered above the accelerator. She drifted to the rightmost side of the rightmost lane, hugging the painted triangle.

The turn lane began to peel away to the right; the stripes in the painted triangle where cars were not supposed to venture increased in length. Ahead, an arrowhead of greenery was approaching; a tree near the point of the arrowhead marked the moment by which she must turn.

She hesitated, then, at the last possible moment, she swung the steering wheel hard to the right.

She didn't accelerate. Her foot moved over to the brake, where it hovered uncertainly in case she had misjudged. She bumped off the road and across a strip of grass. The tree slipped past, a couple of yards away. Her foot moved back to the accelerator and stamped down hard. For a fraction of a second the tires of the Porsche squealed and span without traction. Then the car shot forward.

The road was no more than a hundred yards long. Ahead was a T-junction. At the junction there were lights, turning from green to yellow. She swung through the junction, turning the wheel hard to the left, just as the lights turned red.

She drove two blocks and then turned into a nondescript residential street. She looked in the mirror. There was no sign of a blue car. She turned right, then left, then drove straight for some distance, until she came to a highway. She joined the highway and drove at the speed limit until she passed the city limit.

At the next opportunity, she headed south.

Replogle County Justice Center — 6:20 a.m.

The phone on the sheriff's desk rang. He grabbed it.

"Sheriff Armitage here."

"Good morning, sheriff. Captain Davidson here, calling from Kansas City. The tail just called in. Your subject just evaded him."

"She lost him on purpose?"

"Yes. He said there was no doubt."

"Thank you, captain. We appreciate your help."

The sheriff put the phone down and looked at Nate Painter, who was eyeing him quizzically.

"She lost the tail. She's on her own now," the sheriff said.

The men grinned at one another.

Northern Hill County — 10:45 a.m.

The white Porsche drew onto the forecourt of the small service station, and Katie Murcheson stepped out into the already-hot Arkansas midsummer morning.

The attendant hurried out to assist her.

"Fill it up, please. Unleaded. And do you have a phone? I need to call a number in Replogle County. Is that a local call from here?"

"Sure is, miss. It's the next county south of here. If you go inside the store there's a phone on the wall."

"Thank you very much."

"You're welcome."

The attendant watched appreciatively as Katie pushed open the door and went inside.

She almost misdialled the number in her nervousness. Before dialing the last digit, she forced herself to take three deep breaths.

The phone at the other end rang, then the answering machine began its tedious message.

When it finished, she said simply, "Duke, it's me."

He came on the line.

"Hi, babe. How's it going?"

"Oh, Duke. I made it. I lost them at the first try. You should have seen me. You'd've been proud."

"Well, babe, I wish I'd been there too. So, where are you now?"

"Some place called Periwinkle. There's a gas station and about three houses. It's in Hill county, maybe thirty five miles from Replogle. So what do you want me to do?"

"Head this way. According to the news reports last night, there shouldn't be any roadblocks. If you see anything suspicious, stop somewhere and call me. Otherwise, I'll see you soon, babe. Now, wait a moment...." There was a muffled sound, as of someone incompletely covering the microphone. She heard Duke call out: "Alan, get your ass in here. We need you." She could tell that Duke was rejuvenated. There was a new brightness in his voice. To her he said, "Be right with you, babe. Just getting directions for you."

To someone else he said, "Alan, you know a place called Periwinkle? In Hill county somewhere?"

"Periwinkle? Yes, I think so. It's north of Greenminster."

226

"Here. You talk to her. Her name's Katie, and you be real nice to her. When she gets here, I'm gone. You just give her directions so she knows how to get here. And no funny business, right? I'll be outta here inside of an hour. OK?"

"OK, sure. I understand. Miss?"

"Yes. Hi."

"Hello. Mr. McLaughlin wants me to give you directions to my house. OK?"

"Yeah, sure."

"Do you have something to write with?"

"Oh! Wait a minute."

She scrabbled in her handbag. The attendant ambled inside. He nodded to her, then retreated behind the counter and tried hard to keep his eyes off her.

"OK. I'm ready," she said.

"Mr. McLaughlin says you're in Periwinkle; is that right?"

"Yes."

"OK. Let me think now. Do you have a map of the district?"

"Hang on." She asked the attendant, "Do you have a map of the area you could sell me?"

He handed her one and she unfolded it on the floor. She bent down to examine it, and the attendant silently appreciated the view down what was once Duke's shirt.

"OK. I'm looking at a map now."

Alan McGuire explained how to reach his house from Periwinkle, then Duke came back on the line.

"The car full of gas?" he asked.

"Yes. I'm at a gas station."

"Great. Alan says you should be here in about about an hour. See you then, babe. Drive carefully."

"I will. See you soon."

She put the phone down and turned to smile her thanks at the attendant just in time to see him turn guiltily away to look out the window at the forecourt.

The McGuire House — 10:50 a.m.

Duke McLaughlin followed Alan McGuire into the living room. Everyone looked at them expectantly, but neither of them said anything. Duke beckoned to David to follow him into the kitchen, where they could talk without being overheard.

Duke said, "Well, David, I guess this is about it. My ride should be here in about an hour, then I'll be gone."

David didn't reply. He looked at the wall.

Duke said, "Come on, man. I'm not taking you with me, you know. What are you going to do? You can't just stay here. You can't control these people for very long by yourself. One of them will sneak out or make a call as soon you're asleep. You've got to get out of here. And don't forget it's Sunday. Somebody probably missed them at church."

David focussed on Duke.

"Don't worry about me," he said. "What are you going to do if they catch you?"

McLaughlin did not answer; he looked icily at David.

David said, "You're not going to let them take you, are you?"

Duke pulled his gun from the belt and looked at it. He shook his head.

He said, "No. Not again. If I get away, I get away. But I'm not going back inside."

"I'm sorry."

"Sorry? What for?"

"Sorry that you'd take a life so easily."

"You think too much, David. Take my advice: the whole thing is very simple; don't try to make it complicated. It's them or us now, that's all there is to it. I'm not planning on getting caught, but if they do catch me, I'm taking some of them with me. Anyway, they aren't going to catch me. They think we're in Kansas City."

David turned away and silently walked back to the living room.

Louise looked at him as he entered the room. There was a strange expression on his face, almost as if he were close to tears.

She asked, "What's happening? Duke's going, isn't he?"

David nodded. His eyes were fixed on the carpet.

"What about you? You going with him?"

David shook his head.

"How long are you staying? Is someone coming for you as well? What are you going to do?"

There was a long, heavy silence. David did not reply. After a while, he went back into the kitchen.

He said to Duke, "You can look after them until your ride gets here, can't you?"

"Yeah, why, where are you...?"

"Out. I need some air. I'll just be in the woods. I'll come back as soon as she gets here."

David walked outside.

It was the first time he had been outside for more than two days. The heat of the day struck him with a force that momentarily brought him to a halt. Then he walked slowly across the concrete pad where Alan's car was still parked. He looked at the car, knowing that he ought to be wondering if there was any point in stealing it. But his heart was not in it and he kept going, past the fenced-off swimming pool and into the trees.

The forest quickly hid the house from view. After a minute or so he was forced to stop when a creek barred his way. The creek was too wide to jump, so he simply sat down on a boulder and gazed at the dark, sluggish water.

The water drifted lazily past, patterned by fragments of twig and bark, tiny pieces of greenery, and insects skittering over the surface. A gentle ripple extended some distance in a wide "V" from a point near the opposite bank where a dead branch extended down into the creek.

Silence descended, and an empty tranquillity settled over David. A songbird began to sing in a nearby tree. He felt an odd, unexpected pang of regret that he was unable to identify the bird from its song. He knew nothing about birds.

There was a splash.

David turned just in time to see a flash of silver and brown a short distance upstream. A fish had jumped. He tried to see it, but could make out nothing in the muddy water. The circles from the splash widened, lifting the film of the creek's surface, then falling, rising, falling in waves of slowly decreasing amplitude.

David smiled to himself. Now *that* was something he knew about. He might, perhaps, even after all this time, be able to write the equations that described the way the ripples moved outward. He concentrated.

Yes, he was pretty sure he remembered how the math went. The thought comforted him.

A mosquito landed on his face. With a sharp slap he killed it. He wondered if the fish had caught a mosquito when it jumped.

Mosquitoes, he ruminated while he wiped the remains of the insect from his face, *why on Earth did God ever invent mosquitoes?*

The answer came just as suddenly as the question: *To provide food for fish.*

He tried to drag his mind away from the seductive tranquillity; tried instead to concentrate on his problems.

What was he going to do? Should he keep running? Or should he just give himself up as soon as Duke left?

He knew that he could never harm the McGuires. They had been good to him. They had never argued with him, never tried to talk him out of his chosen course. They could have tried to set him and Duke against one another, but apart from those few minutes when Duke had intended to rape Pam, the hostages had never tried to drive a wedge between the two fugitives. Even when he had killed their dog, they seemed to have forgiven him even before he had forgiven himself.

It was almost as if they understood what he was going through.

But what *was* he going through? Why was he so tormented?

He tried to think it through, but it was all too difficult. So much easier to let other people make the decisions; so much easier just to drift like the water in the creek; so much easier to let others take responsibility for everything; so much easier to sleep and let the world pass by.

In a sense he had been asleep for years now. He could pinpoint the exact moment when it had all begun. When life had become too difficult.

He forced himself to remember that appalling moment: that instant when he stood on the sidewalk near the school and knew that never again would he see his ebullient, steadfast wife, or his his smiling, fun-loving son, or his beautiful, vivacious daughter — all of them cherished beyond words. All gone. Forever.

His eyes moistened.

It was all so pointless. What was the point of life if the most precious things in it could be taken away at any moment?

What was the point of a God who cared so little that He could subject you to such dreadful torment? They said that God was love. But if this was His idea of love, David didn't want anything to do with it. Why couldn't God just be kind instead?

A wave of anger swept over him. He wanted to stand and scream his anger out loud. Tell God exactly what he thought of Him.

He got to his feet. The bird that had been singing stopped. There was a flash of red and brown as it took flight and disappeared into the trees.

He opened his mouth, but then he closed it again. What was the point? Shouting would do no good. Nothing would do any good. Not now, not then. Nothing would bring them back. Nothing. They lived only in his memory, and nowhere else.

He sat on the boulder once more.

"Why do You hurt us so?"

He spoke the words softly, pleading from his heart, aching to understand. In the quietness his voice seemed unnaturally loud.

No answer came, but he felt better just for having voiced the question, as if the lack of a response showed that God was just as powerless as anyone else in the face of tragedy.

He thought about the crash that had allowed Duke and him to escape. He knew now that he should have stayed behind and looked after Deputy Palmer, keeping him alive until help had come, regardless of what Duke had said. But instead he had taken the easy way out, just doing as he was told. After all, that was the way he lived now. That was the way he had lived all of the last five years.

But he could have saved the officer. At the very least he should have tried. He could have saved Charlie too. He should have taken his friend to a church, a hospital, *something*. If he'd been thinking, he could have found some way to help his friend. If only he'd been thinking. If only. God may not be kind, but that was no reason for him not to be.

His thoughts went back to the accident that had claimed his family. There were huge gaps in his memory. How long had he stayed in the house, alone, waiting for his family to return, knowing that they never would? He couldn't remember. Why had he eventually left the house? He couldn't remember what had spurred that decision either. He wondered what had become of the house. The bank must have repossessed it long ago. Presumably any money left over from the sale must be sitting in a bank account somewhere, accruing interest.

He brought himself up with a start. He hadn't given money a thought in years.

A distant sound reached his ears: the crunch of a heavy weight on gravel. He glanced down at the watch he had taken from Officer Baker and discovered that somehow nearly an hour had elapsed since he had left the house. The sound he had heard must be Katie arriving for Duke. He got up and headed for the house.

He arrived in time to see Duke greeting a pretty woman in her early thirties. On the concrete pad next to Alan's car was a white Porsche.

Duke spotted David. "Come on, man. Where've you been?"

Before David could reply, Duke turned to the woman and ushered her inside.

David joined them in the kitchen, where they were talking urgently. David observed with a long-forgotten pang that Katie was very attractive. The thought had barely crossed his mind before he realized that he hadn't thought about a woman in that way in years. First it was money, now it was a woman. What was happening to him?

Duke said, "OK, David. This is Katie. We're going now. From now on, you're on your own. If you'll take my advice, you'll pull yourself together and get out of here as soon as you can. It won't be long before the cops realize it wasn't us in Kansas City.

"And anyway the McGuires will figure out a way to contact the cops as soon as your back is turned. If I were you I'd take whatever money is in the house and just get out of here. Anyway" — he thrust out his hand — "I just wanted to say goodbye. And thanks for your help. It would've been a lot harder without you."

They shook hands. Then Duke turned to Katie. He pulled her to him and gave her a ferocious kiss on the mouth.

Releasing her, he said, "Come on, babe. We're outta here."

He cast one last glance around the kitchen, at David, and at the McGuires, who were standing in a group near the doorway. Then he opened the door.

Katie murmured something inaudible and followed Duke outside.

David watched them get into the Porsche. Duke was in the driver's seat. They kissed again. Then Duke took the keys from Katie and started the engine.

Duke reversed away from the garage, turned, and disappeared around the corner of the house. A few seconds later there was a squeal of tires from somewhere in front of the house.

He was gone.

David turned away from the window. The McGuires were still near the doorway. They were holding hands, and their heads were bent in silent prayer.

Filled with confusion, David looked out the window toward the forest, trying to figure out what to do next.

Southwestern Replogle County — 11:48 a.m.

"What are we going to do?"

"I don't know, babe," said Duke. The car raced around a bend and the McGuires' house dropped out of sight. "I guess I'll put a hundred miles between us and them, then find a nice big shopping mall with a parking lot full of cars and take our pick. Go another couple of hundred miles and do the same. That should make life difficult for anyone tailing us. Now, what about money?"

"I got about three hundred dollars in cash. I didn't take his credit cards."

"That's OK. He'd've stopped them by now anyway. Well, three hundred dollars should last us a while. Seems a pity to ditch a car like this, though. It'd be worth something if we could get it to a big city where I could fence the thing. Maybe I'll see how it goes. Seems a bit risky, though." He was talking to himself, weighing probabilities.

He drew up behind a Ford station wagon that was having obvious difficulties with a steep hill. Impatiently, he slowed down.

"Did you see any sign of the police anywhere? Roadblocks or anything?"

"No. There was no trouble at all after I dumped the tail in Kansas City."

Duke grinned. "That's my baby."

Katie looked at him. Ever since leaving Kansas City she had been wondering if it was all going to be worth it. Now she leaned across and gave Duke a peck on the cheek and squeezed his thigh. Yes, it *was* worth it, whatever happened next.

They were stuck behind the station wagon. The roads were too winding and narrow to risk overtaking. The speedometer wavered between 20 and 30. Duke swore under his breath. He kept his eyes on the mirrors, but there was no sign they were being followed.

He offered Katie a tight, conspiratorial smile. "Not long now. As soon as we reach a decent road, we'll pass this idiot and start putting some miles behind us."

A car came up quickly behind them, the driver obviously in a hurry. He braked hard and joined the line.

They reached the top of the hill and began to descend on the other side. Two more cars joined the convoy. Duke flashed his headlights impatiently, hoping the driver of the Ford would get the message and pull off the road to let them pass.

There were two young men in the car. They were relaxed, obviously in no hurry, chatting, and apparently oblivious to the lengthening line of cars wanting to get by.

The man in the passenger seat threw a cigarette butt out the window and leaned forward. It was a moment before Duke realized what he was doing. He was talking into a microphone.

"Shit!" Duke exclaimed.

There was a bend fifty yards ahead. Maybe there was room to get past before the turn. He floored the accelerator.

Southwestern Replogle County — 11:59 a.m.

The day was undeniably beautiful. The sky was cloudless and the air was still. A heavy, somnolent lethargy was everywhere. It was a perfect Sunday, but Craig Lang had no eyes for the beauty of the day. He drove slowly up the hill, putting off the moment when he would see Pam. To his left, and far below, was Lake Sylva, its sapphire surface unmarred, reflecting the bright gold of the sun. He thought about pulling off the road just to enjoy the view for a while: drink in the peace and quiet before he agreed to change his life forever. No, that would be cowardice. He'd made his decision, and he was going to stick with it. But he knew he was weak: the longer he put off meeting with Pam, the more likely he was to find a way to back out.

He had been wrong on Wednesday, and Pam had been right. She had to keep the baby. And now he realized that he had no choice but to live up to his responsibilities. It was time to stand up and be a man.

He would beg her forgiveness. They'd turn this into a positive somehow. They'd get married. That's what they'd been planning to do anyway. It would just be a bit sooner than they'd expected, that's all.

He had hoped that Pam would call him, but she hadn't. *But look at it from her point of view,* he said to himself. *She thinks I've deserted her. She's angry. Why would she want to talk to me?*

It would all be all right in a few minutes. He'd apologize for his behavior on Wednesday, and they'd put it behind them and move on.

He was glad she hadn't been at church. Although that was odd: he couldn't remember the last time the McGuires had missed church. Pastor Ellsworth hadn't been there either. Tom Murdoch had stood in for the pastor, presenting an obviously ill-prepared sermon. It was a strange day, to be sure.

The sunlight from the lake far below flickered through the trees. He was nearly at the top of the hill. Only a couple more after this one.

A car nosed around the bend at the top of the hill. Then came another car, overtaking crazily on the corner, on Craig's side of the road. It was white and low-slung: some kind of sports car.

There was no time to think.

Craig's foot stamped down on the brake.

There was nowhere to turn: both lanes were blocked by the oncoming cars. To the right the road was hemmed in by trees. To the right was a low guard-rail and then the long slope down to Lake Sylva.

The sports car tried to dodge back on to the right side of the road as it passed the slower car. It didn't make it. It slammed into Craig Lang's car and its momentum pushed both vehicles through the guard-rail as if it were paper.

There was an appalling crunch of metal on metal; and then the sound of metal slamming against rocks and trees as the two vehicles clinched and then separated, rolling over and over down the steep slope of the cliff.

The Ford that the Porsche had overtaken screeched to a halt, forcing the line to cars behind it to do likewise. Inside the Ford, two men watched in horror as the remains of the two cars, barely recognizable now, finally came to a halt only a few yards from the shoreline of the lake. A scarred trail extended from the break in the rail all the way down the hill.

The deputy on the passenger side depressed the button on his microphone.

"There's been an accident."

Southwestern Replogle County — 11:48 a.m.

From behind a tree, Sam Whittington watched Katie and Duke get into the car. They kissed and then McLaughlin started the car. Within moments they were gone.

Whittington swore.

He made his way through the trees to the point a hundred yards up the road where a car was on the verge with its hood up. A second, unoccupied, car was parked on the other side of the road. A man with a large wooden cross around his neck stood at the window of the first vehicle, talking to someone inside.

Whittington stepped out of the forest, and the man with the cross turned to look at him.

"'Morning, Reverend," the SWAT leader greeted Pastor Ellsworth.

Inside the car were two men, one in the driver's seat, the other in the rear with a notebook computer on his lap.

"The woman's arrived and picked up McLaughlin," Whittington said. "Williamson's still inside, so I guess the operation is still a go, although I'm sorry to leave that bastard McLaughlin to someone else. Transmit the word 'Bravo,' please."

He glanced at his watch and then turned to Ellsworth. "We're due to go in at noon. That gives you about ten minutes, Reverend."

"Thank you," the pastor said.

His throat was hoarse, and the words came out strangled. He tried again. "Thank you, officer."

"The message has gone," said the man with the notebook computer.

"Give me two minutes to get back in position, Reverend," said Whittington.

George Ellsworth crossed the road to his car. He put the key in the ignition and looked at his hand. It was shaking. He closed his eyes and offered a prayer that all would go well and no one would be hurt. He knew that the prayer was as much for himself as for the McGuires.

Then he turned the key, and the engine started. He pulled out on to the road and drove the short distance to the McGuires' house.

The SWAT team was in position. George Ellsworth knew that to be true, but he could not suppress the gnawing fear that filled the pit of his stomach.

He turned on to the McGuires' driveway. He could not help but give a long, slow look at the surrounding trees, desperately wishing for some sign that he was not alone. But he could see nothing. He had to take Whittington's word for it that the men were there, ready to move in accordance with the plan that had been so painstakingly worked out the evening before.

From behind a tree, Sam Whittington watched as the pastor got slowly out of his car and stretched.

Whittington lifted the microphone attached to the walkie-talkie that was clipped to his belt.

"Charlie," he said.

It was the first transmission on the walkie-talkies since they had moved into position just before midnight. The men hidden in the trees all heard the single word in their ear-pieces. There remained only the final phase of the operation, phase Delta, which would be launched by another single-word command transmitted exactly at noon. Whittington glanced at his watch. Six minutes to go. It should be plenty of time for the pastor to do his job.

Now that McLaughlin had gone, the whole thing should be a piece of cake. Although it really was a pity that others would have the pleasure of seeing McLaughlin's face when he realized that he had been caught.

David and the McGuires were in the kitchen. On the counter was the radio which had been making occasional strange beeping sounds all morning. A few minutes ago there had been a brief flurry of the incomprehensible electronic tones, but since then the machine had fallen silent once more.

David Williamson was standing near the radio, looking out the window, trying to pull himself together.

Alan was telling him that it wasn't too late for him to give himself up. But David knew he could still get away. It wasn't too late. The net had not been closed. He would have to head for a large city, somewhere where he wasn't known. Somewhere where he could hide among the rest of society's human detritus. He would become a hobo once again.

The radio spoke a single word.

"Charlie."

Charlie. The word reverberated around and around in his head, knifing through his thoughts.

Charlie.

Alan McGuire stopped in mid sentence, and looked quizzically at the expression on Williamson's face.

Charlie.

David had never had a friend like Charlie. If only he had not let Charlie down. If only he had been able to save him.

But he *could* have saved Charlie. He could have saved Charlie at any time when they were together. Charlie would not have died if they had had any money. If they had had money, David could have taken Charlie somewhere warm, bought him food and shelter and medical care. But David *did* have money. All he needed to do was to present himself at a bank, and they could have withdrawn enough money from his account in Trenton to live on for months, perhaps years.

All that wandering from town to town while Charlie's life slowly ebbed away: it had all been so unnecessary.

How stupid. How utterly stupid he had been.

I don't deserve to live, he thought. *It was all my fault. I let Charlie die when he could have lived. Charlie's dead, and it's all my fault.*

He began to cry — great, heaving sobs that dribbled down his cheeks and fell to the vinyl of the kitchen floor.

Why did I let Charlie die? And why did I walk away from the police car? He thought of Deputy Palmer. *Maybe he wouldn't have died if I'd stayed behind. Duke didn't need me. I should have let him escape without me. I should have stayed behind and looked after Palmer until an ambulance arrived.*

Now there were two deaths on his conscience. How could he have let them happen? How did he ever descend to this point?

And what would happen to him now if the police caught him? There would be another trial; he would be convicted of kidnapping and holding the whole McGuire family hostage. There was probably some charge they could level against him for leaving Palmer to die. And of course the escape... that would be more time in prison. He would spend the next two or three decades locked up. And all because he had stopped thinking.

What was he going to do? What could he do, except give himself up? Maybe he should find a way to end it all before they took him back into custody. There were plenty of ways to do that. He had a gun. Simple enough to use it on himself. And if there really was a God, maybe He would be merciful. Maybe David would see Derek and Danielle again. And Alice. Oh, how he missed Alice. How wonderful it would be to be with her again....

George Ellsworth halted in front of the door, breathed deeply, then pressed the doorbell. He left behind a wet smudge of sweat.

In the palm of his hand, he could feel the small square of paper on which was written the message: *The house will be stormed exactly at noon, stay out of the way; fall to the floor when it happens.* His sweat was in danger of turning the paper to mush. He tried to keep his hand away from the writing.

Inside, the sound of the doorbell cut through David's thoughts.

He looked blankly at the McGuires. He was no longer capable of making a decision. Let someone else tell him what to do. Let others bear the responsibility. It was too much for him.

"Would you get the door, Louise?" Alan said quietly.

Alan began speaking to David as Louise moved to answer the door.

"It's never too late to start over, David. You've had to bear too much on your own. Your shoulders weren't made to bear that much weight. Only one person can carry that kind of load. Why don't you let Him take it all for you? He promised that his burden was easy. He promised peace. That's what you really want, isn't it, David? Peace?"

David looked down through his tears and realized that he was holding his gun; his other hand was at his face, wiping away tears.

"I could have saved Charlie if only I'd been thinking."

His words were slurred and difficult to make out, and made no sense to Alan.

239

David continued, "I didn't mean to let him die. I wanted to help him. He trusted me and I let him down. I don't deserve to live."

Alan glanced towards the front door, and was astonished to see Pastor Ellsworth talking to his wife. The pastor was glancing nervously over Louise's shoulder. He was saying something in urgent, quiet tones, and she was nodding her head vigorously to show that she understood.

David looked at Alan.

"Why should I live when everyone I've loved has died?" he asked. "And I walked away from a policeman when I should have stayed to help. I never realized it before: I'm a bad person, and I don't deserve to live. I should just end it now."

Alan saw him look down at the gun in his hand, seeing in it the answer to all his problems.

"Would you do one thing for me, David?" Alan asked. His voice was quiet, and he felt calmer than he would have thought possible.

"Do something? What could I do for you? I'm a failure. You don't want to talk to me. There's nothing I can do for anyone."

His grip tightened on the gun. Another few seconds, and it would be too late.

"My pastor is at the door. We weren't at church this morning and he's probably worried about us. Would you mind if he came in? I'd like us all to pray with you, David. You're wrong about what you're saying. You're not a failure. At least, no more than we all are. It's obvious you're a very smart person. Didn't you say you have a Ph.D.?"

"That was a long time ago. I was a different person then."

"No, David, you weren't. Circumstances got the better of you, that's all. It could happen to anyone. But it's time to stop running now. Put it all behind you. That" — Alan pointed at the gun — "that's no way out either. It's time to let Someone else worry about you while you get on with the job you were put here for."

"Job? What job?"

"I don't know. But I do know that there is one. A job that belongs to you and to no one else. Something that no one else can do. Let me invite Pastor Ellsworth in, and perhaps together we can find out what it is."

David did not reply. He stood cradling the gun, looking at it.

Alan called quietly down the hallway: "Pastor Ellsworth, could you please join us for a moment? There's a man here who needs prayer."

George Ellsworth was taken aback. This wasn't part of the plan. He was supposed simply to warn the McGuires of the raid by the SWAT team, then leave as quickly as possible, to give the family time to prepare before the team stormed the house.

But how could he turn down a request to pray with a man who needed prayer so badly? Wednesday night came back to him: the voice in his head repeating, *Pray for him... pray for him.*

He had no choice. He found himself walking into the house, past Louise McGuire, and down the hallway toward the kitchen. He halted in the doorway. David Williamson was in the center of the room, looking at something in his hands. He looked up, and his eyes met the pastor's. David's eyes were red, and there were the marks of tears on his cheeks.

"I know you," David said. "You were in the jail."

"That's right," said Ellsworth. "And I've been praying for you ever since that evening."

"Praying for me?"

"Yes."

"Why? I'm nothing."

"Because God told me to. Do you mind?"

"Mind? No, I guess I don't mind."

David looked down at the gun in his hand. He suddenly seemed to realize for the first time what he had been contemplating, and he put the weapon on the kitchen counter and withdrew his hand sharply, as if the gun were suddenly hot. He stepped away from it.

"I remember your text, preacher," he said slowly. "'Vanity of vanities, all is vanity.' So what's the point of anything? Isn't it all meaningless in the end?"

"It's true that the works of man are vanity. We are nothing without purpose to our life. We are blown around by the circumstances that affect us like the chaff in the wind. The only way out is to acknowledge that there is One greater than we, One who gives our lives meaning just as He gives everything meaning."

"I wish I could believe that, pastor."

George Ellsworth opened his mouth and was as surprised as the rest of them at the confidence that filled his voice as he said, "Pray with us, David, and He will show Himself. Come; it's time to put all this behind you."

The McGuire House — Noon

The second hand crossed the "12" on the dial of Sam Whittington's watch. He pressed the button on the side of his microphone and uttered a single word.

"Delta."

The radio on the kitchen counter announced the word, but no one in the room paid it any attention. Four people were standing in a circle. In the center was a fifth on his knees. The hands of the people in the circle rested on the man inside the circle.

Alan McGuire was speaking when the back door splintered inward and a masked man burst into the room with a semi-automatic weapon in his hand. Behind him a second man carried a smoke bomb, ready to toss it at the first sign of trouble.

The intruders halted, dumbfounded. Not one of the people in the kitchen had even looked up.

Alan McGuire continued speaking as if nothing had happened. His voice was strong and certain.

"Just as the father in the story of the prodigal son left his house to meet his son when he returned, so we thank you, Father, that You have come to meet this, Your son, as he has made his decision to return to You."

Epilogue

Eleven years have now elapsed since the events recounted in this story. David Williamson served six years in prison. The District Attorney was frustrated in his efforts to bring him to trial for kidnapping because the McGuires refused to testify against him, saying that scripture was clear that no Christian should take another to court.

The D.A. tried to refute this by pointing out that the "religious conversion," as he termed it, had happened only *after* the crime of which Williamson was being accused. Alan McGuire responded by saying that scripture was equally clear that David Williamson was now a "new creation", so it was hardly fair to make him suffer unnecessarily for acts committed before his rebirth.

Even more frustratingly from the D.A.'s standpoint, he had reluctantly concluded that there was insufficient evidence to bring Williamson to trial on a charge of manslaughter in the deaths of the two police officers, Baker and Palmer. The evidence was too strong that their deaths had been due more to willful negligence in failing to wear seatbelts than to any action on the part of Williamson or the other man, McLaughlin, who had been killed while trying to evade capture.

So the D.A. had to settle for the reinstatement of the full sentence against Williamson and a charge of escaping while in custody, a charge to which Williamson entered no contest.

David Williamson used his six years productively, studying first for an undergraduate degree in theology and then for a Masters in Divinity. At the time of his release, he had completed by correspondence the coursework for a Ph.D. in theology and was ready to begin research on his chosen thesis topic: *The Action of Grace in a World of Law.*

Within a month of his release, he was called to pastor a small non-denominational church in southeastern Replogle County. The McGuires retained membership in George Ellsworth's church, but became (and remain to this day) frequent visitors at Pastor Williamson's church.

Pam McGuire married a believer from South Carolina whom she met at college; she is now Pamela Erickson. The wedding was held in David Williamson's church, with Pastors Ellsworth and Williamson officiating. The couple lives in Replogle and attends Pastor Williamson's church. Pam is pregnant with her third child, her husband's second.

Holy Communion is served once a month at the Sunday evening service at the Ericksons' church. The highlight of the service is at the end, when Pastor Williamson and Pamela Erickson stand together at the front of the church and sing *a capella* in close harmony the most famous hymn of all time:

> Amazing Grace, how sweet the sound
> That saved a wretch like me;
> I once was lost, but now am found,
> Was blind, but now I see.

Colophon

The main body of the text of this book was typeset with the pdfTEX digital typesetting system. The typefaces used are mostly from the Latin Modern family, set at 10·5/13.

The paper stock used for the body of the book and for the cover depends on the particular printer that created the book you are holding.

The VEDIT PLUS text editor was used to create the original text.

The cover was created with the Scribus desktop publishing system and the GIMP image manipulation program.

Computer processing for this edition of *Nowhere to Run* was performed on an Intel quad-core system running the Kubuntu 9.10 64-bit distribution of the GNU/Linux operating system.